Published by BSA Publishing 2017 who assert the right that no part of this publication may be reproduced, stored in a retrieval system or transmitted by any means without the prior permission of the publishers.

ISBN 978-1-9997640-0-5

Proof reading & editing by Zedolus

BOOKS IN THE DCS PALMER SERIES

BOOK 1.   FUTURE RICHES

BOOK 2.   THE FELT TIP MURDERS

BOOK 3.   A KILLER IS CALLING

BOOK 4.   POETIC JUSTICE

BOOK 5.   LOOT

BOOK 6.   I'M WITH THE BAND

All available as individual e-books paperbacks and double case paperbacks.

THE PALMER CASES BACKGROUND

Justin Palmer started off on the beat as a London policeman in the 1970s and is now Detective Chief Superintendent Palmer running the Metropolitan Police Force's Serial Murder Squad from New Scotland Yard.

Not one to pull punches, or give a hoot for political correctness if it hinders his inquiries, Palmer has gone as far as he will go in the Met and he knows it. Master of the one-line put-down and a slave to his sciatica, he can be as nasty or as nice as he likes.

The mid 1990s was a time of re-awakening for Palmer as the Information Technology revolution turned forensic science, communication and information gathering skills upside down. Realising the value of this revolution to crime solving, Palmer co-opted Detective Sergeant Gheeta Singh onto his team. DS Singh has a degree in IT and was given the go ahead to update Palmer's department with all the computer hard- and software she wanted, most of which she wrote herself and some of which are, shall we say, of a grey area when it comes to privacy laws, data protection and accessing certain databases.

Together with their small team of officers and one civilian computer clerk called Claire, nicknamed 'JCB' by the team because she keeps on digging, they take on the serial killers of the UK.

On the personal front Palmer has been married to his 'princess', or Mrs P. as she is known to everybody, for nearly thirty years. The romance blossomed after the young Detective Constable Palmer arrested most of her family, who were a bunch of South London petty criminals, in the 1960's. They have three children and eight grandchildren, a nice house in the London suburb of Dulwich, and a faithful 'springer' dog called Daisy.

Gheeta Singh lives alone in a fourth floor Barbican apartment, her parents having arrived on these shores as a refugee family fleeing from Idi Amin's Uganda. Since then her father and brothers have built up a very successful computer parts supply company, in which it was assumed Gheeta would take an active role on graduating from university. She had other ideas on this, as well as the arranged marriage that her mother and aunts still try to coerce her into. Gheeta has two loves, police work and technology, and thanks to Palmer she has her dream job.

The old copper's nose and gut feelings of Palmer, combined with the modern IT skills of DS Singh makes them an unlikely but successful team. All their cases involve multiple killings, twisting and turning through red herrings and hidden clues, and keeping the reader in suspense until the very end.

CASE 5.   LOOT

1945 MERKERS-KIESELBACH GERMANY

Spring 1945, outside the Merkers-Kieselbach salt mine in Germany. The USA 90th Division had pushed the German line back across the Werra River where it had broken and fled in disarray, even though Hitler had ordered that Merkers be held at all costs. The Allies had intelligence that the mine was a Nazi depository for looted art, and with the help of the British Royal Engineers Bomb Disposal Unit the sealed entrance had been breached with a land mine, trip wires made safe, and the thick steel doors forced open.

Colonel George Leyton RE turned to the US General behind him – a long way behind him.

'All clear General', he shouted. 'You want to go in, or shall we check inside for booby traps first?'

'After you Colonel,' shouted back the General. 'You take care now.'

Leyton nodded to his Sergeant and two sappers, and they gingerly moved forward into the gloom. Their torches swept the floor for tell-tale signs of buried mines and stretched wires across their path. After twenty yards of slow and painstakingly careful progress, the entrance tunnel widened into what their torch beams showed to be a very wide cavern indeed; at least sixty feet across, thirty feet high, and stretching far into the distant darkness beyond their torch beams.

'There's a large wall board on the right with switches on, sir.'

The first sapper behind Leyton pointed it out with his torch beam.

'Okay,' Leyton nodded. 'One switch at a time then, and slowly does it.'

As the switches were thrown, fluorescent lighting tubes splashed light down from their ceiling hangers into the cavern. The whole vast place was lit in a bright, white light that bounced off the white salt walls and roughly hewn roof.

'My God!'

Colonel Leyton stood transfixed by the view of hundreds of looted works of art stacked on pallets along the left-hand side of the cavern. But the big surprise was along the right-hand side, where pallet after pallet was stacked with gold ingots shining in the bright light.

'Is that what I think it is, sir?' his Sergeant asked as he started to move forward. Leyton held his arm.

'Steady Sergeant, slowly does it. Could be booby trapped.'

They inched their way to the first pallet. Leyton picked up an ingot, noting the eagle and swastika impressed into it. He looked along the seemingly never-ending street of gold ahead of them.

'I think we've found El Dorado, Sergeant. Back the Land Rover up to the door and tell the Yanks we've found some trip wires, and to stay well back until we give them the all clear.'

Chapter 1.   LONDON PRESENT DAY

'Busy isn't it, eh?

Detective Chief Superintendent Justin Palmer relaxed in the back of an unmarked Jaguar squad car as it made its way slowly along Knightsbridge towards Piccadilly. He put down the sheaf of documents he'd been glancing through and looked around the bustling area, the pavements brimming over with shoppers as the traffic nudged forward foot by foot.

Detective Sergeant Gheeta Singh nodded in agreement.

'Always is along here guv, especially this time of year – tourists.'

She glanced at the vast windows of Harrods, wondering why people were attracted to shops that charged the highest prices when you could buy the same goods much cheaper elsewhere; or better still, buy hassle free online with next day delivery. Must be the bag you get – a paper status symbol to take home and carry around your local neighbourhood with egoistic pride. You wouldn't throw a Harrods carrier bag in the trash bin like you would a Lidl bag, would you? She wondered if heads would turn if you walked around Harrods with a Lidl bag to put your shopping in? She smiled at the thought of the haughty shop assistants' reactions. Palmer broke into her thoughts.

'This was all an overgrown forest in the 1700s; there was a river crossing through it and a bridge. It was one of the main dirt roads out of London for the mail coaches. Amazing when you think of that and look at it now. A hundred a day thundered through here, and at night they travelled with armed guards on the top of the coaches 'cause of the highwaymen. Notorious place for them it was, and the gangs of robbers. They're still here of course – the robbers that is. Only now we call them solicitors and estate agents.'

He smiled to himself.

'Hard to imagine how it was back then.'

'Very hard to imagine, guv.'

Palmer laughed.

'Mrs P. would have liked it – all that horse manure for her rhubarb! The coaches would come through here then break off onto their various routes: Bath and the West Country, Gloucester and Wales. No Severn Bridge then, they had to go the long way around, through Gloucester and down to Wales. Some coaches went hundreds of miles up to the North. It was big business. No post offices in those days, you used the inns – left your post in the pub and picked up any incoming mail for you when the coach had been. You know, there was an inn up the road here.'

He pointed ahead.

'In Lincoln's Inn – it was called The Swan With Two Necks. The landlord had near on two thousand horses in the fields behind the pub. Big player he was; chap called Palmer too. It was the start of the transport system we have today.'

'You're a mine of information, guv.' Gheeta was genuinely impressed.

'Mrs P. says that. Only she says I'm a mine of *useless* information.'

He laughed to himself. The driver half turned and spoke over his shoulder.

'You want me to put the blues on, sir? Get through quicker if I did.'

'No, we're okay for time, thanks Harry. Anyway, it'll give me more time to read this lot.'

He patted the pile of documents.

'Now that *is* a mine of useless information.'

Chapter 2.

They were on their way to the massive excavation dug just behind Baker Street as part of the London Cross Rail programme. A body had been found that morning, inside the giant metal casing that was about to be filled with hundreds of tons of concrete and become a main sixty-foot diameter support strut. The body was inside a tough red plastic bag.

At the site the works foreman gave them each a hard hat and took them across to a viewing platform jutting out over the giant pit.

'Blimey! *That* is a big hole.'

Palmer was impressed as he and Singh stood at the top of the excavation looking down. The foreman laughed.

'Got to be; there's five underground rail tracks going through here, plus a maintenance tunnel alongside them.'

He pointed down to the metal casing jutting up a hundred feet from the floor.

'That's where we found the body, inside that casing. Found it just in time too; fourteen hundred tons of concrete were going into that later today. We had a load dropped in late last night, so the body must have been dumped after that. Stroke of luck the welders decided to do one last safety check on the rivets this morning and found it. It's very dark inside once you get eighty to ninety foot down, so you couldn't see a thing just peering in from the top. They go down on ropes with arc lights to check things. Gave them a shock I can tell you.'

'Is the body still there inside?'

Palmer didn't fancy a trip down a rope pulley.

'No, your Forensic chaps had it pulled out and put in our cold store.'

'That was handy. What have you got a *cold* store for?'

'Chemicals, fuel and oil mainly. We use a lot of cooling fluid on the tunnel drill heads. These drill heads are not your normal Black and Decker DIY type; they're six hundred feet across and bite into solid rock, so you can imagine they get very hot and need a lot of cooling. That's the cold store.'

He pointed down to a Portakabin below them.

'Are our Forensics people still in there?'

'Hang on, I'll find out.'

The foreman made a call on his radio.

'No, the body's been taken away and your chap is on his way up here now.'

Palmer raised his eyebrows questioningly to Sergeant Singh, who consulted her open laptop on which she'd been making notes.

'Reg Frome, sir. He's the one who called us in.'

Reg Frome was overall head of the Yard's Forensic labs. He and Palmer went back a long way, having joined the Met. at the same time and completed their training at Hendon together. Frome had opted to move into the Forensics side, while Palmer had his eye on the CID as a career. Both had wildly exceeded their own expectations in achieving their current high positions.

A two-person steel lift clattered up from below and came to a jarring halt against the side edge of the platform. Reg Frome pushed aside the metal lattice door, squeezed himself from between two piles of cement bags, and stepped out. He had the appearance of the Doc Brown character from the *Back to the Future* films; a wild shock of unkempt grey hair, and a suit that any decent charity shop might politely refuse to take. He brushed cement dust from his clothes.

'Not the most comfortable lift I've ever been in.'

Palmer shook his hand.

'How are you, Reg? I hear you called us in on this one.'

'Hello Justin, I'm fine. Good morning Sergeant,' he said, nodding to Gheeta.

'Hello Mr Frome,' Gheeta smiled. 'Good to see you again.'

Palmer was getting impatient.

'So what have you got then, Reg? I'm getting a bit queasy up here; never did have a head for heights. God knows how these chaps manage it.'

'You get used to it,' the foreman explained through a sympathetic smile. Palmer had forgotten all about him.

'I think we've taken up enough of your time, young man. No doubt you're up against a time frame on this sort of job, so we'll not keep you any longer. Many thanks for your help.'

He shook the foreman's hand.

'Come on Reg, you can travel back with us and explain things on the way.'

His quick exit was to keep any information that Reg might let slip out away from the public domain. For all he knew, the foreman might have links to the murder; he might be getting a back-hander to let a major crime gang dump their victims in the cement inthe dead of night. The rumour that four bodies are buried somewhere inside the main concrete supports of Spaghetti Junction on the M6 is still a pretty strong one.

They made their way back to the squad car, having swapped back the hard hats for their usual headwear. The driver wasn't too delighted to see Reg Frome and his cement powder-coated trousers slide onto his clean back seat with Palmer; but everybody loved Reg, so he let it pass and eased the Jaguar out into the traffic for the return journey.

'It's the plastic bag, Justin,' explained Reg after he settled in. 'It's a special type that councils use for putting asbestos roof sheets into when they're sent for disposal. They are tough and impervious; you can't buy them at the local DIY store.'

Palmer had had experience of Reg Frome's explanations before. He usually went twice round the block the long way before giving the answer.

'So what's so interesting about this type of plastic bag?'

'It's the second one to turn up in the last two months with a body inside it. The other one was washed up on a Sussex beach.'

Chapter 3.

Back at the Yard Palmer entered his office on the third floor, flicked his trilby at the old hat stand in frisbee-throwing manner, missed it, picked it up off the floor and placed it on the nearest hook, hanging his trade mark Prince of Wales check jacket next to it. He checked his messages for anything important – important usually meaning a list of shopping to get on his way home from the Co-op for Mrs P. No messages this time, so he crossed the corridor into his Team Room.

Having just finished the Saturday's Child case, the write-on-wipe-off case progress boards on the walls were clear, the tables and chairs neatly stacked, and the only occupants Detective Sergeant Singh and Claire the technical operator who was hard at work, tapping away at her keyboard in front of a bank of computer screens as Gheeta directed her.

'Anything come through yet?' Palmer asked. He was waiting for the details of the first body in the bag to come through from Sussex CID. The bag had been washed up on a Brighton beach, much to the annoyance of the local Tourist Board who had only just gotten their Blue Flag ranking from the Keep Britain Tidy people for clean beaches and water. So murdered bodies floating around in bags was not what they wanted at all.

'Not yet, guv. But Reg Frome sent some pictures.'

Gheeta handed Palmer a sheaf of ten printouts of the pictures from the file Frome had sent. Palmer pulled a chair from a stack and sat looking through them.

The victim had been strangled, judging by the red welt around his neck; middle-aged, unclothed, overweight and white. The red bag was large, six-foot by four-foot, and two of them had been used; one pulled over the head and down, to meet another one pulled over the feet and up. Tape had secured the bags together, and some tape remnants remained. He read Frome's report, that went into great detail about the bag and little detail about the victim, except to confirm that death was due to strangulation by a thin rope, which was probably a three-strand polyester type; Frome concluded this by the minute strands left embedded in the victim's skin.

'The Sussex file is through now, sir,' Gheeta called across the room as Claire set the printer clicking away. Palmer put down the pictures and crossed over to take a printout off the tray and read it. The other two did likewise, and the three of them read in silence.

The Sussex victim was one Charles Plant a registered bullion dealer, aged fifty-five; single, and lived above his rented shop in The Lanes, Brighton; no previous convictions, but of interest to the Art and Antiques Crime Unit. It didn't say *why* he was of interest to them; in fact it didn't say much at all. No signs of a break in at his premises, and the landlord had taken a month's notice from Mr Plant just a fortnight before his demise.

'Now why would he want to do that then, eh?' Palmer mused.

'Do what, guv?'

'Give a month's notice on his shop and flat just before he got whacked? Check and see if he gave a forwarding address to the landlord. See if he paid for a mail re-direction at the Post Office, and if so where to.'

'And if he didn't?'

Gheeta sensed Palmer was onto something.

'Well… if not then it points to him about to do a disappearing act and not wanting anybody to catch up with him, which will beg the question: why? Maybe he was trying to avoid somebody, and unfortunately for him they found him. Give George Gregg a call at the Art and Antiques Crime Unit and see why this Charles Plant was 'a person of interest 'to them – their answer could put us on the right road. Be interesting to find out what our body at the Cross Rail pit was involved in. Hopefully there will be a connection between the two.'

'Has to be guv, hasn't there? They were both in the same type of bag.'

'And that's another line of enquiry – names and addresses of every household or individual who's ordered those bags from every council in the country over the last couple of months.'

Both Gheeta and Claire stopped what they were doing and turned their incredulous looks slowly to face Palmer.

'Okay, only kidding. But it might be worth sending a couple of the team to Brighton and taking a peek at their list.'

'I'll organise it,' Gheeta said, making a note.

'And while they are there, tell them to have a snoop around the local shops and pubs near Plant's old premises. Somebody may have got an inkling of what he had in mind.'

Chapter 4

The next day information came through that body number two from the Cross Rail excavation had turned out to be one John Fenn, a forty-six year-old freelance auctioneer; married, no children, no previous. Death was caused by the same MO as Charles Plant in Sussex, strangulation.

'So, we have a link.'

Palmer was pleased. It was the next day in the office and the victim detail file had arrived.

'Bit of a tenuous one, but both our victims were in the antiques game, eh?'

Gheeta threw him a questioning look.

'Antiques game? Plant was a bullion dealer, not an antiques dealer.'

'And most bullion these days comes from melted-down antique silverware, and old gold chains and coins; mostly from hard-up pensioners. You see the adverts everywhere – sell us your gold, best prices paid.'

Gheeta nodded.

'Right, I see. Well, they *were* in the antiques game, guv; not any more though.'

Palmer stroked his chin thoughtfully.

'Be interesting to know if they knew each other. Might be worth having a visit to see Mr Fenn's widow. See if we can get to see her tomorrow.'

Gheeta nodded.

'Local uniformed chaps have been in and broken the news to her this morning. She's got a WPC with her for today.'

A loud knocking at the office door was followed by the large figure of George Gregg opening it and entering, a manila card folder under his arm. Gregg had never been one to order the regular burger when 'extra large' was available, and it showed; Palmer likened his physique to the same shape as a bowling pin. His big round face broke into a smile as he saw Palmer.

'How the devil are you, Justin? I thought they'd have retired you by now! Still hanging on, eh?'

'Cheeky sod,' Palmer said as they stood and shook hands. 'You're older than me George, and still living the good life by the look of you.'

He patted Gregg's large paunch.

'Hope you've got a double plot booked in the cemetery.'

'And how are you, Sergeant?' Gregg asked, turning to Gheeta. 'You look lovely, dear. Still having to put up with this old fart every day?'

'I manage.'

'Well,' he said, taking the chair in front of Palmer's desk. 'Charlie Plant finally pushed somebody too far, did he? I'm not surprised.'

He opened the folder on his knees as Palmer sat back at his desk.

'Our report said he was a person 'of interest' to you, George.'

'He was, yes. We've had our eye on him for some time – one of those people that you know is involved in something but can't pin it on them. Mostly receiving stolen goods – bits of antique silver mainly, which he moved on or melted down before we could get enough evidence to get a warrant issued. He'd achieved a high ranking in the *legal* bullion business; well respected, but just a bloody good con man really. As most of the top dealers in that business are – but don't quote me on that.'

He laughed.

'Anyway, Mr Plant was getting a bit out of his comfort zone lately. We know he was moving on some high quantities of gold, around the quarter million price range each time.'

'Pounds?'

Palmer's interest level shot up the scale.

'Yes, we suspect he was getting dodgy ingots from somewhere; can't see enough family heirloom chains and rings coming his way to melt down to make the weights he was selling. We think he was getting the ingots on the black market and cutting them to sell into the jewellery trade.

'Cutting them?'

'You get a one kilo ingot which is worth about twenty-five thousand quid, and cut it or melt it down and recast it into several hundred gram ingots at a couple of thousand quid each. Then it's easy to sell them at a discount off the London Gold Exchange spot price to jewellers – for cash, of course. Probably get rid of fifty at a time in the Birmingham jewellery quarter alone; loads of little factories up there making stuff for the Asian market, with no questions asked if the price is cheap enough.

'He couldn't have done that on his own though, could he?' Palmer said, trying to make two and two equal four. 'He must have had a few contacts? Somebody must have been selling him the ingots for a start.'

'Of course he had contacts, one of them being your other corpse, John Fenn.'

He pulled another sheet from the folder.

'Hang on, George…'

Palmer was lost.

'How do you know about John Fenn? We only got his name through this morning.'

'Another 'person of interest' to us, Justin, so I get copied into anything on him that goes on the system. I got the forensic and the victim detail reports this morning, same as you.'

'So, what was Fenn up to then?'

'The old game of auction ringing.'

'Ringing?'

'It's a very simple scam. Let's assume something nice comes up for sale at the auction and a few dealers want it, so they get together before the sale and only one of them bids, which means they aren't pushing the price up by bidding against each other; and then, if they win it, they have a little auction amongst themselves afterwards and split the difference.'

'Split the difference?'

'Yes. For example, say there are four of them interested in buying it and one of them buys it for ten grand at the auction. They get together afterwards and start bidding at ten grand, and one of them buys it at, say, twenty grand. That's ten grand on top of the real price paid; so they split that – four of them – so they get two and a half grand each, which means the end buyer gets it for seventeen and a half, and saved himself two and a half grand. Plus his mates all get two and half grand each, so everybody's happy.'

'Except the person who put it into the auction; he's been done out of ten thousand pounds.'

'Yes, but he'll never know, will he?'

'Does this go on a lot?'

'Oh yes, mainly in the out-of-town sales as there are so many of them nowadays. That's where John Fenn operated; as a valuer and auctioneer he'd get some nice items for valuation and suggest to the seller that one of his country sales would be just the right place to get top price for them. If the seller agreed, then Fenn tipped off his bent colleagues and they went into action.'

'And his cut?'

'Usual seller's commission, buyer's commission; and instead of the ring splitting four ways it would split five ways to include him'

Palmer leaned his chair back on its back legs against the wall, where the top slotted into the dent he had made over the years by repetition of this action. Perkins, the Yard's maintenance man, had long ago given up smoothing over the dent, having decided he was fighting a losing battle with Palmer's habit.

'Amazing. So Plant and Fenn were working together then?'

'Don't know, Justin – could well be. Finding that out is your job, mate. Here, I've got a few mug shots for you,' he said, pulling them from the folder. 'These people are both Fenn and Plant's known associates – people they've been seen around with a lot, attended sales with, things like that.

Most are 'people of interest' to us. Maybe a few more will turn up in plastic bags and cut my workload down a bit.'

He smiled and passed the photos across to Palmer.

'And increase my workload,' Palmer said, as he glanced at a few of the photos. 'These could be very handy George, thank you. So, it could be one of these little 'rings' went wrong then, or somebody didn't get what they thought they'd get.'

Gregg shrugged.

'Have to have been something big to end in two murders, Justin. Something very big.'

'Hmm… we'll run these faces past Mrs Fenn, see if she recognises any of them.'

Chapter 5

Sylvia Fenn, the widow, looked young for the wife of John Fenn the mid-fifties auctioneer; Gheeta put her age at about thirty-two. Slim and attractive, she obviously took care with her appearance and greeted them in an expensive Ted Baker blouse and dress, that ran par with the Mulberry handbag left casually, maybe purposely, on the worktop in the Fenn's kitchen. She sat at the table while Palmer showed her the pictures one by one; it wasn't yielding any faces she recognised.

He came to the last one.

'No. Sorry, don't know him either.'

Gheeta wasn't sure whether this was the truth, or just the expected reaction from a recent widow whose husband had been tied in with some criminal actions. Fear usually triumphed over honesty; if somebody or some gang could murder your husband, then why not you? Silence could be the best option.

Palmer stroked his chin, rose from the table and wandered over to look out of the window onto the small, but immaculate garden.

'Who's the gardener Mrs Fenn, you or your late husband?'

'Me.'

'My wife's the gardener in our house too. It's a lot of work. You've obviously got green fingers, it looks lovely.'

Gheeta smiled to herself. Palmer was taking the 'shared interest' route to break down the wall that Sylvia Fenn seemed to have put up between them.

'Thank you.'

'Did you notice anything strange about Sidney's behaviour lately, any changes to his regular routine?'

'No, everything was good. In fact he was having his best time ever financially. Lots of top end fine art coming in for his sales.'

'I have to tell you, Mrs Fenn, that he *was* on the Art Crime Unit's list of people to keep an eye on. But that was probably because he'd moved into an area where a few, shall we say, suspicious characters operate, namely the bullion market. But I expect he was just seen with them in the course of his legitimate business, eh?'

Palmer was laying paths for Sylvia Fenn to take as a way out of her apparent lack of knowledge of her husband's dodgy dealings, which Palmer, like Gheeta, felt sure was not true. She knew more than she was letting on.

Mrs Fenn took a deep breath.

'Well… There were two men he dealt with over the last couple of years that I told him I didn't feel very comfortable with; but it was his business and he said they were kosher.'

She shrugged.

'Kosher,' thought Gheeta. So, underneath the designer West End clothes lurked an East End girl, eh?

'Any names attached to these men?'

Palmer feigned disinterest by still peering out at the garden, but inside his copper's heart skipped a beat in anticipation as he awaited the hoped-for answer.

'Yes, one was a Mr Finlay, I never knew his first name. Sid always referred to him as just Finlay. Could have been his first name, I suppose. I only met him twice. To be honest I didn't like him at all. Young flash type.'

The name didn't register with Palmer.

'You said there were a *couple* you didn't feel comfortable with. Who was the other one?'

'I don't know his name, he was always with the Finlay chap. But I never was introduced, and he rarely spoke. Heavily built, older than Finlay; around the forty-five to fifty mark I would have thought.

Charles Plant, thought Palmer. He noticed Gheeta taking notes.

'The Finlay man, were there any peculiar things about him? Broken nose, three eyes?'

He turned and smiled at Mrs Fenn. She smiled back. Gheeta smiled at her too, but she knew this light attitude from

Palmer was just to relax the woman and make her memory sharper.

'Nothing really, but he was always very smartly dressed and his shoes positively gleamed. I always notice a man's shoes. It gives away his character my mum used to say.'

Palmer was glad his black brogues were clean and polished. Good old Mrs P., even after forty-five years of marriage she would always stand in front of him before he left for the Yard each day and straighten his tie, check his shoes, and put his trilby to the right angle. He smiled at Mrs Fenn.

'I'm glad mine are clean then. What colour hair did Finlay have?'

'Jet black, very distinguished. I think it was dyed. Oh!' she said, seeming to recall something else. 'And a pencil moustache – I always thought he looked like that chap in *Gone With The Wind*, but a bit younger.'

'Clarke Gable?' Gheeta suggested. Palmer was impressed.

'Yes, that's him; very suave. Except his speech wasn't, that was basic East End.'

'Bangladeshi?'

It was Palmer's little joke. Gheeta smiled in appreciation.

'No, no. English, Cockney like.'

His joke was lost on Sylvia Fenn.

'Oh, right.'

Palmer picked up his trilby from the back of a Windsor chair where he'd parked it on entering.

'Right then, well, thank you for your time Mrs Fenn. I think we've got a few bits to get to work on, so we'll leave you in peace. You know where to contact us if you need to.'

'I hope you catch them Mr Palmer, I really do. How can you do such things to another human?'

'Don't get up we can see ourselves out. And I'm sure we will catch them, we always do in the end.'

They bade their farewells and left. In the car on the way back to the Yard, Palmer was unconvinced.

'She didn't seem very upset at her husband's death, did she?'

'You noticed that too eh, guv? I thought it, but people are very resilient at those times. Some can hold in the grief in public, and let it all out in private.'

'True, but I think we ought to put Plant and Fenn into your comparison programmes. I reckon Plant was the older chap; with this Finlay character it would tie in. And see if we can't find a connection between the two of them, Plant and Fenn, other than just the Art Crime department's suspicions. Need something rock solid. Have Claire get hold of Fenn's yearly business account statements from Companies House and give them the once over. Let's hope Gregg comes up with an ID on this Finlay character, that would help.'

Chapter 6

George Gregg couldn't come up with anything on the Finlay character; Art Crime didn't have any Finlay on their list of persons of interest. Sussex CID had been busy and trawled the local council files for people who had ordered asbestos refuse bags in the three months prior to Charles Plant's murder and checked them against known felons in the area. No match, nothing.

'That's a shame,' sighed Palmer as he read the negative result in the Team Room as it came off the printer.

Gheeta was on one PC pulling up Plant and Fenn's family trees. Claire was checking the CCTV footage from various premises around the Cross Rail excavation for the evening and night before Fenn's body had been found.

'This is a bit strange, sir.'

She looked over at Palmer who turned his attention to her.

'What is?'

'The cement tanker. They moved it.'

'What cement tanker?'

'The one delivering a load late on the night before the body was found,' Claire explained.

Palmer stood behind her, as did Gheeta.

'Right, so what's strange about it?'

'Well, look.'

Claire played the CCTV footage on her screen.

'See, the cement tanker comes into the place... and parks up next to the big hole. One man gets out and releases the pipe from the back and dangles it over into the hole. He goes to the back of the vehicle and is about to release the cement through the pipe, when the driver leans from the cab window and stops him. The driver is waving his arm and pointing towards us – us being the CCTV camera. They exchange shouts. The pipe is put back into its clips and the tanker is re-positioned, see? Repositioned so that the back of it is obscured from the CCTV camera's view. Then the driver joins the other man at the back and, we presume, they unload the cement into the hole.'

Claire turned to Palmer.

'Why change the tanker's position?'

'Probably so the camera couldn't see what was happening at the back of it,' said Palmer.

'Like a body in a red plastic bag being tipped in the hole,' added Gheeta.

'Yes, I'd lay money on it. Scroll back to the tanker sideways on, Claire.'

She did so and froze the screen.

'What's the company name on the side of it?' asked Palmer, peering closely at the screen. 'I can't make it out.'

Gheeta strained her eyes at the dim image.

'It looks like City Concrete. Hang on and I'll Google it.'

She tapped the keyboard of her computer and a few seconds later had a match.

'They're listed: City Concrete and Demolition, for all your major structural support systems and area clearance. UK Government and Local Authority Contractors. Looks like a big concern, guv.'

She pointed to a picture of a large yard with twenty or so tankers and a similar number of hoppers.

'Based at Finsbury Park.'

Palmer stood and stretched.

'Right, I think we might pop along and get a statement from the driver and his mate tomorrow, eh? Should be interesting. Well noticed, Claire'

Chapter 7

City Concrete's offices were two Portakabins welded together. The door had RECEPTION stencilled in large letters across it, and opened into a surprisingly plush and tidy area, considering what it was housed in.

A middle-aged smart lady with strikingly deep red-coloured hair sat behind a long counter working on a computer. She stopped, turned, and gave Palmer a smile as he walked in. The smile left her face for a brief moment when Sergeant Singh in her uniform followed him.

'Can I help you?' she said, regaining her smile.

Palmer returned the smile and held his ID card towards her.

'Chief Superintendent Palmer to see Mr Finlay.'

It was a gamble that had paid off in the past. This time it didn't.

'Mr Finlay?' Red Hair shook her head. 'We don't have a Mr Finlay working here – '

She referred to his ID.

'Chief Superintendent.'

Palmer gave her one of his reassuring smiles.

'I must have got the name wrong. We are looking for the driver and his mate who delivered concrete in one of your company tankers to the Baker Street Cross Rail site three days ago at eleven at night.'

Red Hair was out of her comfort zone.

'I think I'd better get Mr Robson to see you. Please take a seat.'

She pointed to a round table with a half-circle sofa behind it.

'I'll give him a call.'

'And Mr Robson is…?' Palmer asked as he and Gheeta took a seat.

'Mr Robson is the owner.'

Red Hair pressed a button and spoke into a microphone. The site loudspeakers outside could be heard relaying her words.

'Would Mr Robson please come to Reception, thank you.'

She turned back to them.

'Tea or coffee?'

'No I'm fine, thank you.'

Gheeta shook her head.

Red Hair sat back in her seat, looking at the door expectantly.

'He shouldn't be long. He's somewhere on the site; he'd have said if he was going out anywhere.'

Palmer looked at the various building trade magazines strewn on the table in front of them. Being a person who was not DIY motivated in any way, and who needed expert help to even get a flat pack furniture item out of its box, he decided to sit back and just wait for Mr Robson, rather than pretend some false interest in a magazine that might as well be written in Chinese and upside down.

He didn't have to wait long. Mr Robson came into the Portakabin dressed in a dark blue one-piece builder's overall, wellington boots and goggles, which he removed. He was middle sixties, with greying hair and clean-shaven. Palmer looked at him. Robson looked at Palmer. Recognition bloomed on both faces.

'Mr Palmer!'

'Harry Robson.'

Palmer stood and took the outstretched hand and shook it.

'I thought you'd be retired on a big fat police pension by now.'

'And I thought you'd be banged up on a life sentence, or in an unmarked grave in the middle of a forest somewhere.'

They both laughed.

'No, not me Mr Palmer; you must be thinking of a different Harry Robson. I'm a legit business man now. Any small misdemeanours in my past are long, long gone.'

Palmer turned to Sergeant Singh.

'This is Detective Sergeant Singh, my second in command.'

He addressed Gheeta, who nodded to Robson.

'Way back in the bad old days Sergeant, when I was a young detective, this gentleman – and I use the word loosely – was the scourge of our lives. He had fingers in all the wrong pies and was running with the Richardson brothers' little empire in South London.'

Robson hung his head in false shame.

'I blame my parents; they should have kept me away from such people.'

He smiled as he said it.

'Harry's parents ran an unregulated bookies and a group of so called massage parlours, which we won't go into now.'

Robson put his arm round Palmer's shoulders.

'This copper got me put down for seven years.'

'If *all* the charges had stuck Harry you'd still be inside now, and you know it.'

He extricated himself from Robson's friendly arm.

'I'll just check my wallet and wristwatch are still there.'

'Well, well, well…'

Robson shook his head in a resigned way.

'I shouldn't say it's good to see you Mr Palmer… but I will. How's the Princess – still together are you? I'll bet you are.'

Princess was Palmer's name for Mrs P. 'Princess' had been the daughter of a well-known family of small-time career criminals, and their romance had blossomed strictly due to the number of times that young Detective Palmer had knocked on her door with warrants for the arrest of her father, one of her siblings, or to search the place for stolen property. Sadly she was the only one left now, as all her three brothers had been much older than her and departed to the unknown – amazingly, as Palmer had often remarked, of natural causes.

'Yes, we are still together Harry. But we haven't come here to chew over old times.'

'I didn't think you had, Mr Palmer; I've never known a copper make a social call. Do I need a brief? '

'Not unless you've been up to something that you shouldn't have.'

He threw a questioning look at Robson, who pursed his lips in a thoughtful way.

'No, not me; all strictly legit.'

'Good.'

Palmer sat back down, as did Robson on a handy chair. He turned to Red Hair, who was sitting open-mouthed at the revelations she had just heard about her boss.

'Don't worry Cherry, it was all a very long time ago. And it won't go any further than these four walls, will it.'

It was a statement; an order.

'No, no,' Cherry said, turning back to her screen to continue whatever it was she was doing. 'No, of course not.'

Gheeta thought Cherry might be a nickname, because of her hair colour. Palmer continued in serious mode.

'Harry, your company – this company – made a delivery of cement to the Cross Rail excavation off Baker Street at eleven p.m. on Monday.'

Gheeta pulled a printout from the CCTV footage, showing the tanker sideways on at the site, and passed it to Robson. Palmer gave him a second and continued.

'That is your tanker, isn't it?'

'Yes, it's one of ours. What have they done, delivered short and sold some off on the side? I'll kill the buggers if they have. That contract is one of our top ones.'

'No, nothing like that. But we'd like to take statements from the driver and his mate.'

'Why, have they been nicking stuff from the site? All our people are CRB tested.'

Palmer smiled.

'Really? How come you got a job here then?'

Robson saw the funny side of that.

'I know the boss.'

'Being serious Harry, there was a body found on the Cross Rail site the next day and we just want to ask if they saw anything out of the usual in or around the site when they were delivering.'

'A body?'

'Yes, on top of the cement they poured in.'

'Must have been after they'd left then. Some poor chap jump in? Suicide?'

'Possibly. I didn't say it was a man, Harry.'

Robson smiled at Palmer.

'Same old Palmer, same old tricks.'

He turned to Cherry.

'Cherry love, have a look and see who was doing the night shift on Monday and took out the Cross Rail delivery.'

He turned back to Palmer.

'They'll probably not be in 'til around seven tonight; our night shifts go Monday to Friday. You'll have to come back later or go round to their homes.'

Cherry shouted across: 'Mooney and Hilton, they're on all week.'

Gheeta made a note in her book.

'First names?'

She smiled across to Cherry, who returned her gaze to the PC screen.

'Patrick Mooney and Mark Hilton'

'Thank you. Do you have their employment record on file?'

'Employment record?'

'Details of their shifts, days and hours worked and where they delivered to?'

'Well, yes.'

'May we have a copy?'

Cherry looked at Robson. He shrugged.

'Take a bit of time to print it off.'

Gheeta stood and crossed to behind the counter and stood beside Cherry.

'Is it on a spreadsheet?'

Cherry nodded yes.

'Good, that's easy. Would you bring that file up and open it?'

Cherry did so. Gheeta took a USB she'd quietly taken from her shoulder bag and pushed it into the side port on the

PC. A menu box came up, and quick as lightning Gheeta leant over Cherry and using the mouse brought the cursor to 'download' and hit 'go'.

'It shouldn't take a minute.'

She smiled at Cherry who looked at Robson, who shrugged.

'We've nothing to hide, feel free. Mind you, you probably should have had a warrant to do that.'

He smiled at Palmer,

'But for old time's sake I'll let it pass.'

The download finished and Gheeta removed the USB and pocketed it.

'That's it all done, thank you.'

'Right then.'

Palmer rose and put on his trilby.

'Harry, I'd appreciate it if you kept this quiet – just between us for the present. Probably nothing to it, but better that Mooney and Hilton weren't told until we take a statement. People tend to fret and think they saw things they didn't if they get too much thinking time.'

'Fine, I've no problem with that Mr Palmer.'

They shook hands.

'One day when we both retire I'll let you buy me a pint, and we'll have a laugh at the old times, eh?'

'I'll hold you to that, Harry. As long as I'm sitting with my back against the wall and can see the door.'

They both laughed as Palmer and Gheeta made for the door, which suddenly opened sharply inwards as they reached it, causing Palmer to hurriedly retreat backwards into Gheeta who steadied him.

'Oops, beg your pardon,' said the smart suited gent who entered. 'I didn't know there was anybody in here. Are you okay?'

Palmer nodded and gave a reassuring smile.

'Yes, I'm fine.'

Robson laughed.

'You wouldn't have met this lad before, Mr Palmer. The missus always kept him away from the… you know, the family business. Detective Chief Superintendent Palmer, meet my nephew, Finlay Robson.'

Chapter 8

'Well, well, well. That was an opportune time to be at City Concrete, eh?'

They were in the plain squad car sitting outside City Concrete.

'I think we now know the identity of Mrs Fenn's Finlay bloke. We've got quite a little pattern beginning to form.'

Palmer rubbed his thigh and winced.

'Ruddy fool coming through that door like a whirlwind nearly had me over. Set my sciatica off.'

Gheeta turned to face him from the front passenger seat.

'Did you notice a neat pile of red plastic sacks outside that cabin, sir?'

'Were there really? No, I missed them. Well, that ties in nicely as well, doesn't it?'

'How about filling me in on this Robson chap, guv? You obviously knew him of old.'

'Harry Robson,' Palmer said, his mood darkening. 'Yes, we all knew Harry Robson – not a very nice chap. I first got to know about him in the 70's, when he was a part of the notorious Richardson gang, south London's equivalent of north London's Krays; a nasty, violent lot with their fingers in every illegal pie going. Robson was an enforcer with them – collected the rent arrears and protection money. Anybody got out of line, the Richardsons had Harry Robson pay them a visit.'

'You make it sound like the Mafia.'

'It wasn't dissimilar. The gang really rose into prominence when the Krays tried to go south of the Thames, and the Richardsons weren't having any of it; a bit like the Corleone family in Sicily when the big boys from the mainland tried to move onto their island. They saw them off.'

'Corleone? I thought that family was fictional in the *Godfather* films, guv.'

Palmer laughed.

'They weren't fiction – the *Godfather* films were based on the *real* Corleone mafia family Sergeant, and they were real enough.'

'I never knew that.'

'Anyway, Harry Robson's violent reputation was known well enough in London's gangland that when the Richardsons told the Krays to sling their hook, they did. Robson had a reputation akin to that of Jack 'The Hat' McVitie, who was a notorious Kray enforcer. If those two went to war it would have had only one winner, and the Krays weren't sure it would be them. So they bottled out and stayed north of the water; Robson rose through the ranks, and when drugs became the big earner he was into it in a big way. Anybody stepping onto his turf met a brick wall – him and his new best mate, Kenneth Noye.'

'I've heard of him.'

'He's still inside, doing a life stretch for a 1996 murder; and I bet if you check his visitor list you'll find our man Harry Robson on it. Both of them were thought to be implicated in the Brink's-Mat gold bullion theft in '83 along with John Palmer – no relation to me, I hasten to add – who had a smelting works in the grounds of his mansion outside Bath where they reckon most of the Brink's-Mat gold bars were melted down. Cheeky blighter even had two guard dogs, one called Brinks and the other called Mat.'

Gheeta laughed.

'Palmer's dead, I read about that not so long ago. They thought he'd died of natural causes, until a post mortem uncovered bullet holes in his chest that the original doctor thought were just scars from a recent heart bypass operation. Hope he's not my doctor.'

'Yes, Palmer used his Brinks money to set up a massive time share scam in the Tenerife area; but he obviously trod on some big toes, and bang bang! Funny thing is, he's dead and so are seven other villains that were involved in the Brinks-Mat hoist. They reckon there's a curse on that gold, but I think the truth is that Noye's and Palmer's shares of the gold are still around buried somewhere; ten million quid's worth in 1983 is worth a great deal more now, so well worth looking for. But no doubt Noye has his contacts, even inside; and if he still does have that gold, which we suppose he has, then fencing a little at a time would pay for anybody who's getting a bit too near it to be… shall we say disappeared.'

'In an asbestos plastic bag?'

Palmer shook his head.

'No, going after the Brinks gold is well out of Plant and Fenn's league. No, last I heard a couple of the young East End Romanian drug gangs were interested. If they've any sense they'll stay well clear.'

'So how does Harry Robson fit in with Plant and Fenn's murders then?'

'I don't know yet Sergeant, but I'll bet my pension he's in here somewhere. He always denied he had anything to do with the Brinks job, but this concrete business looks to be worth quite a bit and that takes money to set up; and Harry Robson never earned a legal pound in all the years I knew him. But what he has to do with Fenn and Plant we have yet to find out. He's a crafty bastard and his dealings will be well covered up. He's a nasty one, too; when I put him away he swore in court he'd get even, and you didn't take those threats lightly in those days. When he came out I had six weeks of 24-hour armed protection at home, just in case.'

He rubbed his thigh again.

'I've got to get this sciatica sorted one day. Harry Robson is a very hard and very nasty piece of work Sergeant, and I bet he's up to his ears in this gold caper somewhere along the line. But he's also very clever as I said, and covers all the tracks.'

'Do we need to have a good look round that site, having already seen the red bags? I bet we'd find a few interesting things if we got a search warrant.'

'I bet we would too, but I don't want to get Robson thinking that we are onto anything. Just want him to think it's a straightforward interview of two of his employees who may have witnessed a crime. Keep it low level and see what happens.'

'So what do we do about Finlay, guv?'

'I never even knew Robson had a nephew. George Robson was an older brother who had a bookies in the Walworth Road. Didn't know he had a son. Far as we knew at the time he was straight; probably laundered some of brother Harry's ill gotten gains through the betting shop, but nothing was ever pinned on him. No, I think Finlay is the chap to major on now. See what Claire can turn up on him.'

'Not bring him in for questioning? Mrs Fenn did name him.'

'Maybe later, but let him run for the time being and see what we can find out. No doubt Harry will have told him who we are, so he'll keep his head down for a while. If he is connected to the two murders he's going to distance himself from Mooney and Hilton as far as he can if they are in it with him.'

He thought for a few moments.

'Tell you what we can do – get a photographer out to quietly take a picture of Mr Finlay Robson so we can run it past Mrs Fenn. If we can get a positive from her then we can reel him in anytime we like. I reckon the bloke with Finlay when he visited Fenn's house was Plant. It's got to be. So why didn't she pick him out from the photos, eh? There is definitely something funny going on there. In the meantime, I think we'll pay Mooney and Hilton a visit at their homes; hopefully before Robson tips them off, but I expect he's on the blower to them right now.'

Sergeant Singh plugged the USB into her laptop and pulled up the City Concrete staff records from it. Mooney was the nearest in Hillingdon, just off the Western Avenue. The driver put the post code into the sat nav and twenty minutes later they stood outside the door to a first floor maisonette in a quiet suburban street.

There was no answer to the bell or knocker, or Palmer's fist thumping the door. The pensioner from the ground floor part of the maisonette poked his head out and told them Mooney had left about fifteen minutes earlier on his 'damn noisy motorbike', the one that woke him and his wife up every morning at six am when Mooney came home from his night shifts.

They did get a response at Hilton's council house in Acton, though not the one they wanted as his mother answered the door; obviously it was her council house that he shared. No, he wasn't in; he'd had a phone call about an hour ago and had an urgent job to go to. City Concrete? He didn't say.

'Funny that. Both of them work nights and both are suddenly going out during the day.'

Palmer settled back into the squad car.

'As you thought guv, somebody warned them a visit was in the offing.'

'Yes indeed. Harry or Finlay though? I'd like to know which one.'

Chapter 9

Harry Robson's kindly smile left his face in a hurry when Palmer and Singh were safely off the premises.

'Take an early lunch, Cherry dear. I have a few things to sort out with Finlay.'

The false smile he threw at Cherry said 'don't argue, just go'. Cherry had been asked to take 'early lunches', 'long coffee breaks', 'half days' and similar requests from Mr Robson before, usually when people she didn't know in the concrete business came in out of the blue without an appointment. She obeyed straight away, and taking her coat and handbag she was gone. Only once in the past had she protested, when asked to take a break five minutes after finishing her lunch hour when a pair of young Rastafarians had arrived without an appointment, and obviously not to discuss building work; but the strength and language of Mr Robson's rebuke for arguing and not just doing as she was told had left her near to tears. She did need her job, and it was well paid – very well paid. As Robson had told her a few weeks into the employment: 'For this money you see nothing, you hear nothing, and you say nothing.' So she did just that.

As the door closed behind her, Robson pushed Finlay down into a chair and thrust his face close to Finlay's.

'Are you fucking stupid or what?'

Finlay didn't know what Robson was on about.

'What, what's happened? What are you on about?'

'That was Chief Superintendent Justin Palmer of the Serial Murder Squad and his sergeant. That's what's happened.'

Finlay smiled.

'She can arrest me anytime. Good looker for a copper.'

'Listen, you stupid arsehole. If she's on Palmer's squad she's not there for her looks – she's there because she's top notch at what she does. And what she does is put dickheads like you inside.'

Finlay was getting the picture and getting worried.

'What's happened then?'

Robson took a deep breath.

'That pair of tossers Mooney and Hilton who disposed of Mr Fenn for us put on a lovely CCTV display as they did it. Only a pair of fucking morons would tip the body in *after* the bloody cement and not before it! Lucky they weren't actually recorded with it, or we'd have had the whole fucking armed murder squad down on us like a ton of bricks and we'd both be in cells and the whole business would be fucked! What the fuck were you thinking of giving the job to Mooney and Hilton? We use outside people for that sort of work don't we, professionals – you know that. Not fucking amateurs. And I still don't know why you had to whack Fenn in the first place. He was okay; did a good job, shifted plenty of the stuff for us through his sales.'

'I told you before, he wanted a bigger cut – said he'd grass if he wasn't equal partner on the cash, plus his commission. Greedy bastard, I wasn't going to give him equal shares, no way. Don't worry, I'll get another auctioneer – plenty of bent ones about. Anyway, the boys did alright on the Brighton job.'

Robson lowered his voice to a harsh whisper.

'They did what?'

'They did okay with the Brighton job, didn't they? Got rid of Plant okay. I told you he was skimming a few grand off the top.'

'Tell me you're kidding me. Tell me you didn't have them do that job too!'

Robson held his hands out as though pleading for alms.

'Jesus, I gave you a number to ring for that! A pro!'

'They did it, no problems.'

Finlay seemed quite at ease until Robson kicked him hard in the shin.

'Ouch! What's the fucking matter with you? Calm down.'

'You get on the phone to them two dicks and get them out of the picture. And do it now, 'cause Palmer won't charged on each sale, in his case 18 per cent – wasn't growing, which it should have been to correspond with the growing sales.'

Gheeta offered the answer before Palmer asked for one.

'So he's selling a load of stuff for no commission. Not a way to run a successful business.'

'Unless he's on a cut from those sales in some other form, like a cash backhander afterwards,' Palmer suggested. 'Have we got his bank statements? They'd make interesting reading.'

'Need a warrant from above for that, guv. How's your relationship with Bateman?'

Gheeta raised her eyebrows, knowing there was no need to ask. Assistant Commissioner Bateman was not on Palmer's favourite people list; quite the opposite. A product of the university, then into the police force at management level, Bateman had now reached the heady atmosphere of the top floor of the Yard as Assistant Commissioner; folically challenged by hereditary DNA, and always challenged on anything he could, whenever possible, by Palmer, who hadn't time for any of the top floor 'suits' as he called them.

In Palmer's book, you didn't have the right to be called a policeman or policewoman if you hadn't done the three years on the beat and seen from the front line what was involved – and none of the top floor had, no matter how many degrees in various 'ologies' they had that came with them from their universities. Palmer had more respect for the latest cadet to come out of Hendon. In Assistant Commissioner Bateman's book, you weren't a good officer if you didn't stick to the rules, fill in all the reports in triplicate, keep your records and expenses up to date daily and get permission for just about everything while keeping him in the loop at all times; so Palmer was his nemesis. He'd offered the Chief Superintendent early retirement more than once, but he wouldn't go. Bateman wouldn't promote Sergeant Singh to take over the Serial Murder Squad if Palmer did go; he'd replace him with one of his 'yes sir- no sir' officers, or indeed, as was his favourite scenario in the current context of government budget cuts, close the Squad and let local CID units do the work in unison. He dearly wanted Sergeant Singh and her technical expertise to transfer to the Cyber Crime Unit, and had on more than one occasion had heated arguments with Palmer when he had tried to prise her away from him, a move that neither Palmer nor Singh wanted.

Being cooped up in his top floor turret all day, Bateman didn't realise that none of the local CID units liked him or respected him, and most of their officers shared Palmer's negative view of him. The very idea of different station CID units working 'together' was a total non-starter; their patch was their patch and that was it, budget cuts or not.

Palmer sat and thought for a while on the Fenn bank statement issue. Then he smiled broadly at Gheeta, reached for an internal phone on its wall hanger and punched in some numbers. Reg Frome answered at the other end of the line.

'Reg, it's Justin… Good, and you? Good… Look, I need a favour mate. We seem to be making progress on this asbestos bag case with a few names in the frame now, but I really need to get a look at a chap's bank statements and cheque stubs to follow the money trail – and you know what that means, a bloody warrant. And you know what that means… yes, Bateman. And if he gets a request from me, he'll try everything in the book to slow it down, and want copies of everything and daily meetings to brief him and all that crap. So I thought that if you could get one of your forensic accountant pals to do the warrant request through their AC, it would keep Bateman out of the loop and we'd be able to press on quicker with the case. Could you do that, or am I asking the impossible? Thanks Reg, I'll get Claire to get the details ready and phone them through. Thanks again Reg, I owe you one.'

He hung the phone back on the wall.

'Sorted.'

Gheeta looked at Claire.

'I always say it's not what you know, but who you know.'

Palmer laughed.

'That certainly helps. Right then.'

He crossed to the far wall, to which was screwed a large white Formica 'write on – wipe off' board, twelve foot by four foo,t on which the team plotted the case as it progressed, adding names and situations. Palmer spoke as he wrote.

'Plant, dead. Fenn, dead. Asbestos bags. Robson and Finlay employ Mooney and Hilton.'

He drew lines between each with arrow heads.

' Finlay knows Fenn. Mrs Fenn knows Finlay. Money starts at Fenn… and goes where? Don't know yet – and where does it come from? Plant? Don't know yet. Why are Plant and Fenn killed? Knew too much? Want too much? Hmm...'

He sat down on a nearby chair and surveyed his work.

'Right, we need Mrs Fenn to ID Finlay, then we can work on him. It has to be the Finlay that her late husband brought home a couple of times 'cause her description fits, doesn't it: jet black hair, pencil moustache. So we know there's a tie up there.'

He took a deep breath and blew it out.

'Okay, we've got two officers at Brighton poking around, haven't we? Have a word with personnel and get another three of our usual chaps into the team and have them tail Finlay. Let's get a profile going on him – who is he really, what's his game, who does he do business with, all that sort of stuff. He's a bit of an unknown quantity at the moment. And get a plainclothes photographer to get a few pictures of him that we can show Mrs Fenn.'

'Talking about Brighton sir,' Claire interrupted. 'We just got the first report in from the team down there. Seems Plant was a secretive type; no known friends, and the neighbours hardly knew he was there. His shop was hardly ever open. Could have had a lady friend about the same age whom he was seen around with a few times, but nothing known about her, not a local. The shop opened very occasionally, and no social life known; but he had a small smelter in a large shed behind the property and spent a lot of time in it. And that's it. No paperwork in the premises, shop's empty, as is the flat above. Our chaps say it looks like a good cleaning job's been done on it.'

Palmer thought for a moment.

'Hmm, but who did the cleaning? Plant, before he did a disappearing act? Maybe he didn't want any trace to be left that could lead to him? Or was it the people or person who killed him cleaning up afterwards, which would point to a professional job? No shop CCTV in place I assume? Jewellers usually have that at least.'

'No, nothing listed here.'

'That's a pity. If I recall the Brinks Mat job they could trace the gold by analyzing it chemically. Better get our lads to take a few scrapings off the inside of the smelter crucible and some sweepings from the shed floor with a soft brush – I don't want a bin bag full of stuff, just a small amount. Get it sent to Reg for analysis and we will see what he can come up with.'

'You think all this could be linked in some way to laundering stolen gold, don't you sir.'

'Not a hundred percent Sergeant, no; but with Robson's possible, if not probable, involvement, it's a distinct possibility.'

'Brinks Mat gold?'

'Could be – but up to now any of the villains involved in that job who have put their head above the parapet have met with an early death.'

'Eighty percent,' Claire said incredulously.

'What is eighty percent?' Palmer asked.

She pointed to her PC screen.

'On Wikipedia it says that in the decade after the Brinks Mat robbery, they estimated that over eighty percent of all gold jewellery sold in the UK was made from the gold stolen in that one robbery.'

She looked at her engagement ring.

'I could be wearing some,' she laughed. 'Could I be charged with receiving stolen property?'

'Not unless you've a bar or two of it under the bed.'

Palmer smiled and crossed to the progress board and wrote 'gold' under Plant's name.

'Follow the money, and now follow the gold.'

Chapter 11

Mrs Fenn didn't look much like a grieving widow when Gheeta called the next afternoon, with a clear picture of Finlay Robson that the 'snapper' had taken that morning and sent down the Wi Fi to the team room computer. Copies had duly been printed off for the team members and the progress board.

Gheeta thought Mrs Fenn again looked and acted quite bouncy and happy for a recently bereaved wife. But then Gheeta didn't know what sort of relationship the Fenns may have had; perhaps love hadn't been the major ingredient.

'Yes, that's him. That's definitely him.'

Mrs Fenn was sure that the photo was of the Mr Finlay her husband had brought home a couple of times.

'Who is he?'

'We are still working on that, Mrs Fenn. He may have nothing to do with the murder and just be a genuine business acquaintance of your late husband, but if we get any further information we'll let you know. Have you any idea what sort of business your husband may have had with the gentleman?'

'No, we didn't talk much about business. Sidney used to say he talked business all day and didn't want the same all evening, so I can't help you there. He was probably a vendor, I know he had a few good vendors who put in a fair amount of quality items every sale. He said that you need that in the auction business – can't rely on what comes through the door.'

What came through the door at Sylvia Fenn's house was Finlay Robson; but he came through the rear kitchen door, and not until darkness had fallen. They embraced in the kitchen.

'Has Palmer been back yet?'

Sylvia Fenn nodded.

'No, but his sergeant has and with your photo – quite a good one too, and recent.'

'Shit! He must have put a snapper onto me. What did she say?'

'Questions mainly – did I know you? *No.* Did I recognise the picture? *No...* That was about it.'

'Uncle Harry's getting a bit panicky. He knows Palmer from way back and reckons he's good, so Mooney and Hilton are out of the picture.'

'They're what?'

'Gone, like your old man. Gone and never to return. Don't ask. They really cocked up with your old man's body; they might just as well have left it on the steps of the local nick.'

'I'm having to play the grieving widow. I had a bloody WPC here for a day trying to get me to contact victim support. So, what do we do now?'

'We sit tight. Let Palmer make the next move, and when he does it will give us some idea of what he knows – or what he thinks he knows. If only your old man and Plant hadn't got greedy, eh?'

'What about the Leytons? We need to keep the money rolling, or they'll start getting worried.'

'They'll be alright. They can't really do anything, can they? One thing Leyton doesn't want is Mr Plod asking questions about his gold.'

Chapter 12

'You have got to be kidding me, Reg.'

Palmer could hardly believe it.

'Absolutely no question about it, Justin.'

Palmer looked open-mouthed at Gheeta and shook his head in amazement as Reg Frome continued.

'The scraping samples your lads got from Plant's crucible and the dustings from the floor have been analysed to one hundred percent certainty: Nazi gold, from the Merker mine in Germany.'

Gheeta laughed nervously.

'Why does the word 'Nazi' still make me shudder?'

Frome nodded.

'Me too. That gold we tested, however small, could have come from… well, I don't really want to think about it.'

Palmer sat in his chair and pushed it back into the wall groove, swinging his feet onto the desk.

'This does put a different slant on the case doesn't it, eh? I was pretty sure we were on the track of some Brinks Mat stuff coming up for air – not Nazi gold. What's this Merker mine got to do with it?'

'I'll explain.'

Frome took a spare chair and sat down.

'When the Nazis looted all the private gold and jewellery and stuff as they marched across Europe, it was sent to the Merker's salt mine near Buchenwald POW camp in Germany – together with the bullion they had taken from the country's banks – and all heaped together and melted down into ingots; one hundred and fifty million dollars worth of the stuff at 1945 prices. In melting it down and mixing it all together, a chemical footprint was made of the gold; that means the different types of gold and purity were combined in the smelter and produced a distinctive, recognisable type – bit like a unique DNA in humans. We have samples of the Merkers gold bars from the US Federal Reserve, as that was where it was officially moved to. But, as in most times of war, a few bars disappeared on the journey without being noticed.

Let's face it, there were no accountants counting it up, no paper trail – just soldiers heaping it onto lorries by the ton. A lot of American soldiers came home from war very, very rich, I can tell you.'

He laughed.

'Nothing ever proved and nobody ever charged, but… could you resist it?'

He glanced from Gheeta to Palmer. Neither flinched.

'You like to think you would,' Palmer said. 'But after six years of being shot at in muddy fields you might feel you deserved some little bonus, eh?'

Gheeta shot him a surprised glance.

'Not that I personally of course would have even contemplated such a deed,' added Palmer, looking like butter wouldn't melt in his mouth.

'Of course not, sir. I didn't think for one moment that you would have.'

'I bloody would have,' Frome said more bluntly. 'Anyway, that's it. Your man Plant was melting down Nazi gold.'

'You're sure it wasn't Brinks Mat?'

'Absolutely sure – Brinks has a totally different footprint. We see quite a lot of Brinks, but very little Nazi. In the USA it's the opposite – lots of Nazi and hardly any Brinks.'

Palmer shifted his feet off the desk, brought the chair back to ground level and stood up.

'You live and learn, eh? Thanks Reg, and thanks for the use of your accountant chap for the bank statements warrant. I have a meeting with him later. Well, well, well, Harry Robson is becoming a real Goldfinger, isn't he? First Brinks and now the Nazi gold – this is getting to be a very unusual case.'

'And a very interesting one for me, Justin. Keep me in the loop.'

He stood and nearly knocked over Assistant Commissioner Bateman, who was coming in as he went to leave. Bateman gave him a perfunctory nod.

'Morning, Frome.'

Frome gave one back and left quickly.

'Mr Bateman, always a pleasure when the gods from on high descend to visit us lower mortals, sir. To what do we owe the pleasure?'

Palmer affected his false smile. Bateman ignored him and turned to Gheeta.

'Would you give us a few minutes please, Sergeant?'

'Of course, sir.'

Gheeta gathered her files and left for the team room. Bateman took over the chair vacated by Frome.

'Sit down, Palmer. You know why I'm here.'

'I do, sir?' said Palmer innocently, taking his seat.

'Yes, you do. Why was a request for bank warrants on your current case sent through Forensics and not you?'

'Well, I thought that as Forensics would be studying the statements it would quicken up the process sir, and keep the case moving forward.'

Although Palmer didn't like Bateman, he always made a point of using 'Sir' when addressing him so no charge of insubordination could be levelled at him.

'Seemed the quickest way to proceed, sir.'

Bateman exhaled a long '*I'm fed up with you*' type breath.

'No Palmer, you just didn't want to call my attention to how this case was going on, did you. I have had no daily reports from you on the case at all, absolutely no information or updates. As usual you think you don't have to follow the rules and do the paperwork that every other team does quite easily. I think we both know that neither of us is on the other's Christmas card list Palmer, but this continual ignoring of basic reports and updates will end today. I have made a note on your record of the fact that you have been warned before about ignoring case procedures, and if it happens again it will bring on a disciplinary hearing. Do you understand?'

'Did you glance through my record when you made the note, sir?'

'I don't need to Palmer, I know your record.'

Chapter 16

That evening Gheeta sat at her dressing table in the bedroom of her Barbican apartment, deep in thought. She had arranged all her gold jewellery on the dressing table in front of her, glinting as the dying rays from the sinking sun lit it through the panoramic window. She stood and slowly walked through into her living room and stood looking down onto the Thames five storeys below, flowing slowly past as the tide began to turn; the fading sunlight hitting the bow waves from the passing boats flashed and glinted up at her.

She didn't think she could wear any of that gold again; not now, not after what she knew about where it might, just might, have come from. How would she feel? She didn't feel good now, just thinking that some part, however small, of her bracelets, necklaces and rings, could be from the body of a POW, their ashes sifted for gold in some awful camp. Christ, what a conundrum for her Asian race –a race that loves its gold so much, profiting from the awful crimes perpetrated on another race by a vicious, awful regime. She wondered if her parents and relatives who had given her these Christmas and birthday presents had ever thought along those lines. But then almost everybody likes gold, not just Asians; and the Royal Mint used tons of it every year on commemorative coins to part gullible collectors from their money. Did they question its pedigree? Even Palmer hadtwo gold teeth. Did he ever think that some part of them could be from the gold teeth of Holocaust victims? She inhaled deeply. The matter of conscience was a hard one to answer.

Her computer pinged and broke her chain of thought. Aunty Raani from America was on Skype.

'Hello aunty, 'Gheeta said, settling in front of the screen and turning her webcam on. 'How are you?'

'Gheeta, I am very well thank you and so are your uncle and cousins. I have a favour to ask you.'

Gheeta knew what was coming.

'Who is he this time, aunty?'

It was a long, ongoing quest by her mother and her aunts to find a suitable husband for Gheeta; her father would never consent to an arranged marriage, and knew that Gheeta could well handle the overtures the older ladies of the family made about her single person status. Gheeta was very much her own woman and liked the independence she could afford as a police officer, combined with the healthy annual dividend payment from her shares in the family IT business. An electronic business started by her father as an asylum immigrant fleeing Idi Amin's brutal Uganda regime in the 1970's, the business was now internationally respected, supplying computer and mobile phone parts to major suppliers and government organisations worldwide.

Aunty Raani dismissed Gheeta's bored response with a wave of her hand.

'He is the son of a very old friend of your uncle. They have a very good business in manufacturing jewellery here in New York, and he is coming over to England to find a suitable shop premises in London – the better part of London, of course. I have said you may be able to assist him. He is very handsome too.'

'There are lots of very handsome young men in London already, aunty. Maybe I am seeing one of them already.'

Aunty Raani's face lit up.

'You are? Who is he? Who is his family? What do they do?'

'Whooah! I said 'maybe' – and in any case I really don't have time to be a London guide. We are very busy at work.'

'Chasing criminals.'

Aunty Raani shook her head in disappointment.

'That is not a job of work for a young lady, Gheeta Singh; not at all.'

Gheeta was feeling tired.

'Okay, Aunty – give him my number and tell him to ring me when he's here, and I'll see what I can do. Now I really do have to go. Give my love to the family. Good night…or good morning, or whatever it is in New York.'

She clicked off the connection before Aunty Raani could tread the usual conversation course of 'your mother would like to have grandchildren'; the fact that Gheeta's brothers already had five 'grandchildren' for her mother to spoil seemed to be of no consequence.

In her current state of mind, Gheeta could think of nothing worse than showing an Asian jeweller around London.

Chapter 17

'I thought it was 'toad-in-the-hole' tonight?'

Palmer stood in his kitchen as Mrs P. pulled a dish from the microwave and unveiled a supermarket 'meal-for-one'. She put it on the kitchen table and took a knife and fork from the drawer and handed them to him.

'It was going to be, but Benji went into hospital this morning and what with taking his laundry to the cleaners, tidying up his kitchen and then taking some clean clothes into him this afternoon, I haven't had time to cook anything.'

Benji, real name Benjamin, was Palmer's next-door neighbour; a retired advertising executive, early sixties going on twenty-one, with pony tail, spray tan, designer clothes, and as far as Palmer could ascertain by the way he spoke, waved his hands about and walked in tiny steps like Poirot, of dubious sexuality – although of course Palmer wouldn't think to broach that subject to Mrs P. who, together with most of her lady friends, thought Benji a wonderful man. Benji had obviously taken a large pension with his retirement as he took numerous expensive holidays, had a new car every year, spent a fortune on anything he took a fancy to, and was a great favourite with Mrs P., her gardening club, and the local WI. In fact, Palmer was quite jealous of him and the attention he got from the women of the area – attention that used to fall on Palmer quite a lot before Benji arrived on the scene.

'Has he had an accident then?'

He showed false concern as he sat at the table and looked at the Sainsbury's offering in front of him.

'What's this?'

Mrs P. was busying herself putting on her coat.

'He's having a new hip. It's chicken korma.'

'What's wrong with his old hip?'

He refrained from eating the mustard-coloured mess in the dish, mentally earmarking it for Daisy the dog's bowl as soon as Mrs P. left.

'Osteoporosis, it's very common. The joints wear out.'

'His shouldn't, he doesn't do anything to wear them out. Can't wear them out by sitting in the garden sipping wine all day or mincing down the shops in your flip flops.'

'Don't start.'

Mrs P. was fully aware of Palmer's opinion of Benji, and she gave him a cold stare as she buttoned her coat.

'Where are you going?'

'Hospital – I said I'd pop in to see how he is. Three of us from the Gardening Club are going along; cheer him up a little, take some flowers in. Mrs Haskin is driving.'

She glanced at the kitchen clock.

'They'll be here any minute.'

'You saw him this afternoon when you took his clothes in! He'll be just the same, just a few hours older.'

'He had the operation this afternoon. I didn't see him then as he was in recovery. It's very quick these days; in one day and out two days later.'

'Did he go private?'

'No, NHS. He's in Kings College.'

'The cheeky bugger – all the money he's got and he goes NHS. That means the tax payer is funding his new hip; me.'

'I would expect he's paid more tax in his working life than you and most other taxpayers. The nurse on the ward was saying the cost for his new hip is twenty-three thousand pounds.'

'Blimey… What's he having, a gold one?'

'I don't know what they're made of.'

A car horn sounded outside.

'That's them.'

She patted Daisy the dog and gave Palmer a perfunctory kiss on the cheek.

'Right, I'm off. I'll try not to wake you if you're in bed when I get back. And eat that korma before it gets cold.'

And she was gone. Palmer put the meal on the floor by the dog. Daisy sniffed it and turned and walked off into the lounge. Palmer laughed.

'Yes, I agree.'

He popped outside the back door and emptied it into the compost bucket, before taking a lump of mature cheddar from the fridge and opening the bread bin.

Chapter 18

Mrs P. half opened her sleepy eyes and checked the luminous dial of the bedside alarm clock. Two twenty AM.

'What are you doing?

She peered over the duvet to where Palmer was peeping through the bedroom curtains into the night.

'Nothing, Princess. I thought I heard a car pull up. Just making sure it wasn't for me. Something might have happened in the case I'm working on that needed my presence.'

Mrs P. pulled the duvet back snugly around her.

'They would have rung you.'

Palmer made his way back to the bed.

'Anyway, there's nothing there so go back to sleep.'

He *had* heard a car quietly pull up and the engine cut out, and the thought of Harry Robson turning up with a firebomb or similar had got him quickly out of bed and to the window. Across the road, away from the street lamp, a car was parked. Palmer saw it just as the sidelights went out. He could make out two occupants, a driver and a passenger in the front. Then he made out the number plate. It was a squad car from Brixton CID pool.

He made his way back to bed, smiling to himself. So, Bateman was concerned enough about his welfare to get surveillance mounted on him at night, eh? Perhaps the Assistant Commissioner wasn't such an arsehole after all.

Assistant Commissioner Bateman was sound asleep in his bed, content in the knowledge that he'd covered his 'duty of care' to his employees charter by having the South Thames Region make a few patrol stops during the night outside Palmer's house.

Part of him would have liked Robson to blow the irritating old sod to kingdom come. If that *did* happen, now at least he'd covered his own back.

The pale moonlight couldn't penetrate the thick rambling buddleia against the side wall of the Palmer front garden; so the officers in the squad car pulling away to answer another call didn't notice the dark hooded figure crouched hidden within it. When it was sure they were well away from the area, the figure slowly and quietly came out of the undergrowth and keeping in the shadows of the wall and house, made its way to the porch.

Once inside the porch it knelt by the front door and listened for a minute. All was quiet within. Taking a plastic washing up liquid squirter from its pocket, the figure flipped open the cap and began quietly squirting the liquid through the letter box. A smell of petrol wafted back.

Curled up in her comfy bed at the bottom of the Palmer residence stairs, Daisy the Springer raised her head and paid attention as the letter box opened and the tube appeared. This wasn't normal. Normal was the letter box to open early on Sunday morning and the master's papers to be pushed through. No, this was not at all normal; especially when a horrid-smelling liquid trickled from the tube. She got out of her basket, stretched her back legs and padded quickly upstairs to the master's bedroom.

Nudging open the door, she went to Palmer's side of the bed and putting her front paws up onto it, licked his face.

Palmer was quickly awake, alert and out of bed in a trice. Something had scared Daisy downstairs, and she was telling him so. His first thought was Harry Robson. He came onto the landing and smelt the petrol; his heart beat like a drum as he grabbed the baseball bat he kept behind the bathroom door, switched on the lights and hurried downstairs to face the would-be arsonist.

'Shit!'

The figure in the porch saw the lights come on and put the box of matches it was about to ignite and toss through the letter box back in its pocket. It backed quickly out of the porch as Palmer reached the hallway and switched on the porch and front garden floodlights.

Keeping close to the wall, the figure was out of the garden and running silently in soft trainers along Palmer's road and then down two unlit side streets, and it was gone into the night.

Chapter 19

'I can't understand Mrs P. taking it so calmly, guv. I'd be out of there and booked into a hotel by now. Christ! What if the bastard had set it alight?'

'Well he didn't, did he? And in any case, the amount squirted through wouldn't have made a very big fire. Would have been able to put it out easily, which is why I wonder what the idea really was. Trying to scare me off the case, or somebody trying to get Robson fitted up? His threats against me in the past are very well known in certain circles; somebody could have latched onto them to settle their own score with me. I've made quite a few enemies in my time.'

'Forensics get anything?'

'Yes, interesting that. Whoever it was wore size six trainers.'

'Size six? Then it's going to be a youngster, guv. Some kid you banged up looking for revenge?'

'I haven't *banged up,* as you put it, any youngsters lately – and Harry Robson couldn't get his feet into a size six.'

'Going to be a female then?'

'Could well be.'

'Have you been upsetting any ladies lately then, guv? Spurned any romantic overtures?'

Gheeta put her finger to her lips.

'You can tell me. My lips are sealed.'

They both laughed.

'Mind you,' Gheeta continued seriously. 'Robson could have paid somebody to do it?'

Palmer nodded.

'He would have done exactly that if it was him. He always was a two-step villain.'

'Two step?'

'An old trick: you always put two steps between you and the crime. If Harry Robson had wanted my house torched, he'd have told one of his mates to sort it out, and his mate would have got some other toe rag to do it. Then if the toe rag got caught he'd have no idea who originally ordered the score, leaving Harry in the clear.'

They were in a Sussex Constabulary panda car heading for The Manor House, Hove to see Mr Stanley Leyton MP. Having been awake most of the night as Forensics did all they could in his hall and porch, Palmer had taken the opportunity to sleep all the way down on the train from Victoria Station to Brighton. Sergeant Singh left him to it and went over the case history documents in her shoulder bag and used the train Wi-Fi to read up on Brinks Mat.

'I think they'd know that wild horses wouldn't drag you off a case, guv. Let alone scare tactics.'

She looked out of the side window as they came into Hove.

'Nice houses around here, aren't they? Bet they cost a bomb.'

'Inherited wealth, Sergeant – the scourge of Britain. Do you know that under one percent of the population own seventy percent of the land in Britain? And it's the same families that owned it in the nineteenth century. I bet this Leyton family have been here for generations; one of their ancestors probably fought on the winning side in some historic battle and was rewarded with the house and land.'

Gheeta had never really been able to label Palmer as Left Wing or Far Right. His political observations had varied from *'blow up the House of Lords and all the hereditary bastards inside with it'* to *'stop all the benefit payments and then the lazy gits would have to find a job.'* Palmer didn't sit on the fence on any subject and said what he thought, which is why Mrs P. always took him aside before one of her WI or Gardening Club social evenings at the Palmers' and gave him strict orders on what not to talk about – and it was always politics, the unions and the judiciary; absolute no go areas. Or better still, say nothing about anything and just smile nicely and pour the drinks.

The panda car turned off the road and up a two hundred-yard pebble drive to The Manor House, pulling up outside a large stone porch that jutted out from the three-storey seventeenth century building. Large ground floor windows reflected the midday sun and the whole place was surrounded by beds of rhododendrons in full flower; wisteria coated the front walls, hiding the parlous state of the mortar and crumbling stone beneath.

The driver stepped out and opened Gheeta's door.

'I've been told to wait for you, Sergeant. No rush, I'll be here.'

Gheeta looked at Palmer over the car's roof. He had heard the driver.

'That's fine, hopefully we won't be too long. Have a quiet nose around the outside if you would.'

He gave the driver a knowing nod. Meanwhile the large oak-panelled front door inside the stone porch had opened, and Mrs Stanley Leyton emerged to greet them. Obviously wealthy, she was a woman of sixty years plus in 'county' clothes that suited her admirably, pleated thick wool two-piece and sensible shoes. Her light brown hair was shoulder length, feather cut and highlighted just to the right amount, and the outstretched hand of welcome had enough gold in its rings to start a jewellers shop.

'How do you do? I'm Margaret Leyton, Stanley's wife.'

She shook Palmer and Singh's hands as Palmer introduced himself and his Sergeant.

'I hope you had a pleasant journey. Do come in.'

She led them into a large open hall, the half-panelled walls hung with large painted portraits of what Palmer took to be the family ancestors. Most were draped in the traditional cloaks of ermine and velvet of the titled few; ermine sounded so much better than stoat, which was the animal that originally wore the skin. Gheeta noted the peeling ceiling and poor condition of the oak wall panels. Perhaps the family's wealth wasn't as robust as Mrs Leyton's outfit suggested.

They were greeted in a large, dimly-lit lounge by Stanley Leyton MP, a rather portly gentleman, round-faced and follicularly challenged, which is what the PC brigade called bald men these days; his attempt to cover the bald head with an ill fitting and awful wig really didn't work, and actually called attention to it. Tweed jacket and cavalry twill trousers completed the 'country' look.

Introductions over, Palmer and Gheeta were offered a large old sofa that had seen better days, while the Leyton's sat on a pair of equally distressed leather-button arm chairs. Gheeta noted that the carpet was nigh on threadbare in parts. In fact, the overall poor state of the place was bewildering her a little; after all, MPs got a very good salary and lots of expenses. But it didn't look like this MP spent any of it on his ancestral pile.

Drinks were offered and refused. Gheeta took her laptop from her shoulder bag and opened it on her knee, ready to make notes.

'Well,' Stanley Leyton said with an inquisitive smile. 'Your Sergeant was a bit evasive on the phone, Detective Superintendent; but I imagine this must be about something quite serious to bring you all the way down here. Either that or you've heard how good the local fish and chips are, eh?'

He laughed at his own little joke. Mrs Leyton's expression showed she was not at all amused.

'I am sure Mr Palmer has not come all the way here for the fish and chips, Stanley.'

She gave a condescending nod and smile to Palmer.

'No ma'am, we haven't.' *Why had he used the royal 'ma'am'? She wasn't aristocracy. Must be the surroundings.* 'We are investigating a double murder.'

That shook them. Both the Leytons were obviously not prepared for that bombshell. They looked quickly at each other, Stanley Leyton turning so fast towards his wife that his wig nearly slipped off and he had to adjust it. Mrs Leyton was the first to react.

'I hope you are kidding us, Mr Palmer?'

'I am afraid I'm not.'

'What can we possibly have to do with a murder, let alone a double one?'

Stanley Leyton was quite white. Palmer smiled.

'Don't worry, sir. We are not accusing *you* of committing murders.'

Stanley Leyton visibly relaxed into the armchair.

'Thank God for that.'

He took a handkerchief from his sleeve and wiped his shiny brow. Gheeta knew what was coming; she'd seen Palmer do his *relax them and then hit them* scenario many times.

'But we know your father's looted Nazi gold is the reason for the murders.'

He fixed Stanley Leyton with a look of hard steel. Stanley Leyton didn't actually physically squirm in the chair, but inside his mind was crashing around his brain like a ball bearing being shaken in a box, looking for a non-existent exit. Palmer waited.

Mrs Leyton was first to react again. This time she stood up, crossed to an old oak refectory table by the massive window that looked out onto a lawn that seemed to stretch for miles, and poured herself a large glass of something from a decanter. She took a long drink before turning back to face Palmer.

'Bloody fool, I told him it was stupid. As usual he didn't listen to me.'

She fixed her husband with a glare that could kill.

'You stupid know-it-all, fool! You and your pal Plant, and his mate Fenn.'

She sat back in her arm chair.

'I told you, didn't I? I said they were a bunch of spivs.'

Stanley Leyton had regained a little of his composure.

'Do I need a lawyer, Inspector?'

'Chief Superintendent,' Palmer corrected him. It had taken him a long time to achieve his rank, and he was very proud of it.

Margaret Leyton was scathing.

'Ha! A lawyer – and how do you think you can pay for one, Stanley?'

She turned to Palmer.

'Mr Palmer, would you please tell us what has happened, and how involved we are?'

'Of course. But first, please tell me the story of you, the gold, Plant and Fenn.'

Gheeta quietly pressed the record button on her laptop. She had positioned it on her knee so the camera was pointing at the Leytons. Margaret Leyton took the lead.

'Mr Palmer, as you can see it doesn't take a genius to notice that despite the outside appearance of this house it is, to put it mildly, falling to bits. Unfortunately, it is my husband's family seat and we have tried over the years to remedy the problems; but the dry rot, damp rot, rotten roof and a host of structural defects – caused by it being built on old ancient sand dunes and having no proper foundations – has meant we were pouring all our money down an ever-widening hole.

'We've re-mortgaged it and have bank loans up to our ears on the damn place, but it has finally beaten us. We can't sell as the negative equity against the money owed is several hundred thousand pounds, and we can't put it into the safe hands of English Heritage or a similar organisation because it is not of any great historical interest. There are thousands of old rotting manor houses in the UK, and this is just one of them; and even if they were to be interested they would only take it debt free, which is impossible.'

'Up the damn creek without a paddle,' said Stanley Leyton.

'Be quiet Stanley.'

Margaret Leyton continued.

'We had a few old oil paintings – nothing of any great value but they were insured for about forty thousand. We'd known Charles Plant for several years, having used his services to sell various pieces of my jewellery over the years; he would find the best specialist sale room for them and handle the whole episode. That small income and Stanley's salary as an MP kept us afloat day to day, but didn't mend the big leaks. So, when Plant suggested selling the paintings we happily agreed. It would mean a few more years' grace, and just like Mister Micawber, we hoped 'something would come along'.'

She sighed heavily.

'And that something was Stanley's father's gold bars, which you obviously know about. God, I wish we'd never found them. Shortly after Stanley's father passed away ten years ago we had a letter from the bank saying that there was a safe deposit box in his father's name, and as executor and prime beneficiary of his father's will – only beneficiary in fact – it was now Stanley's property. No need to tell you what was inside. We thought all our Christmases had come at once; all our financial problems would be solved. And then we noticed the Eagle and Swastika on the bars.

'We should have handed the box in to the War Reparations Committee; we should have done anything but what we actually did do. We stupidly asked Plant for his advice – our big mistake. He said we'd get nothing by handing the bars in, and that he had contacts who could sell them quietly and nobody would know.'

'How many bars?' Palmer wanted to know.

'Two hundred and fifty.'

'Two hundred and fifty?' Palmer said, taken aback. 'That's a lot of gold.'

'Yes it was, and at that time, according to Plant, about six million pounds' worth. We could see an end to our financial problems and a new life.'

She paused and shook her head slowly.

'But life's not like that. It's never easy. Things don't just fall from Heaven without the Devil waiting to make the catch. Plant brought the Devil in, a chap called Fenn – they came to see us. Fenn was an auctioneer who assured us he had buyers for the gold who would ask no questions, pay by cash, and then he could launder the money through his auctions somehow and pay us out legitimately, with no questions being asked. We should have stopped then; alarm bells were ringing in our heads, but debt collectors were ringing at the door. The letters from the banks and debt collection agencies were coming thick and fast, and we grabbed what we thought was a financial lifeline.'

She paused and took a deep breath of resignation. Her shoulders had slumped, and the haughty lady who had met them at the porch was looking somewhat deflated now, as the realisation of total defeat overwhelmed her.

'Apart from Plant and Fenn, was there anybody else involved?'

Palmer knew there must have been. George Gregg had said that Plant and Fenn were small-time, and this amount of six million was definitely big-time.

'Yes, that was when it all went wrong. We had an uninvited visit from two men about six months ago. At first, I thought they were from the police or some government agency and we'd been found out, but it soon became apparent they were quite the opposite – a very nasty pair of thugs, and they knew all about our little scheme. They knew Plant and Fenn; they said they were working with them in moving the gold, and they wanted half the proceeds or they'd tell the authorities and the press. Stanley's career would be over, the gold would be impounded, and that would be it; we'd be bankrupt and basically *persona non gratis* everywhere.

'I lied and told them we were nearly at the end of the gold bars anyway, but they had already been told by Plant how many we had and that only eight had been sold off. I lied and said Plant had got it wrong, and that we'd told him twenty-five bars, not two hundred and fifty, he must have misheard. They got very rough – pushed me about a bit, gave Stanley a black eye and made lots of threats; and when I still insisted that we'd only got a few bars they rang Charles Plant and he spoke to me and advised that we handed the lot over. There was about two hundred bars left, and he assured me it would be okay and we'd get our half of the money. I trusted Charles, so we did just that.

'They went but left us in no doubt as to what they could do to the house with a can of petrol and a match if we ever mentioned them to anybody. Funny really, we'd already thought about setting the place on fire; but it's not insured anymore, couldn't afford it, so that wouldn't be a way out. So, we had to say yes to a fifty-fifty split and gave them the bars for Fenn to sell. They said they would take their half from him as it sold through the auctions, and he'd bring us our half. They knew the whole set up.'

'Have they been back since?'

'No.'

He turned to Gheeta.

'Sergeant, show Mrs Leyton the mug shots of Fenn, Plant, Robson and Finlay.'

He turned back to Mrs Leyton.

'Tell me any of these people my Sergeant shows you that you recognise.'

Sergeant Singh stepped across to Mrs Leyton with her laptop and pulled up a picture of Plant.

'Yes, that's Plant.'

A picture of Fenn.

'Yes, that's the auction chap Fenn.'

A picture of Robson.

'He's one of the two that came here.'

A picture of Finlay.

'He's the other one that came here – a very threatening pair. I hope they are the ones who have been murdered.'

Gheeta went back to her seat as Palmer rubbed his left thigh, which was beginning to ache from being positioned too long in the lopsided armchair whose cushion stuffing had given up the ghost decades ago.

'No, they are both alive and kicking. It's Plant and Fenn who have been murdered.'

He rose and with a slight hobble made his way to look out of the window as the shock sank in with the Leytons.

'Oh my God.'

Stanley Leyton was shaking.

'Are we in danger Inspect- Chief Superintendent?'

'I would think so sir, yes. The murders are linked to the gold, and you are too. Word spreads fast in the criminal underworld, and if some other gang gets the idea that there could be more gold where that lot came from, you might well get a visit… or two.'

Gheeta thought Margaret Leyton was looking rattled for the first time.

'Mr Palmer, what should we do?'

Palmer turned and faced them.

'Do you have somewhere you can go and stay?'

'My mother's house in Dorset. She doesn't like Stanley much – she's staunch Labour, but needs must.'

'Okay,' Palmer nodded. 'I'd get yourselves packed and off to mother's as soon as you can. I will have a twenty-four hour guard put on this house; I don't think there will be any attempt to get to you or the house, as the criminals know we are investigating and will probably lay low. But you never know.'

'Do we take the rest of the gold with us?' Stanley Leyton asked.

Palmer was surprised.

'What 'rest of the gold'? You said Robson and Finlay took it.'

'We had ten other bars hidden in the garage.'

Palmer thought for a moment. The images of concentration camp POWs flashed through his mind.

'It is stolen gold, sir. However, my interest in this case is one of murder, not theft. But our case report, which we have to send up to our superiors each day-'

He gave Sergeant Singh a sideways look.

'-will have to mention it as the catalyst for the murders, and also that much of the original hoard is still intact. What the powers that be do with our report, and who they pass it onto is up to them.'

He paused for effect.

'What *you* do with the gold you have is up to you. Not my place to offer advice.'

Gheeta smiled inwardly. *That was a nice way out guv*, she thought. If Palmer had seized the gold as evidence she really didn't want to be travelling back on today's equivalent of the Brighton Belle clutching two hundred thousand quid's worth of gold bars. And the paperwork at the office tomorrow would be horrendous.

Margaret Leyton had made a decision.

'It will go into the bank tomorrow, and I will contact the Ministry of Defence War Office and make them aware of my deceased father-in-law's war looting.'

In the car on the way back to the station, DS Singh had to ask the question.

'That was a wig on his head wasn't it, guv?'

Palmer smiled.

'Wasn't the best fitting syrup I've ever seen.'

'Syrup?'

'Cockney rhyming slang: *syrup of fig…* wig. You should know Cockney rhyming slang, living where you do.'

'The Barbican?'

'Yes, if you come down out of your tower and mix with the locals round the back streets you'd hear a different language altogether.'

'Yes, I've heard some of that different language drifting up to my 'tower' late on a Saturday night when the pubs turn out.'

Chapter 20

'Right then,' Palmer said as he swung his feet up onto his desk, tipped his chair against the wall in his usual manner and looked across the office to Gheeta, who was finishing off yesterday's daily report of their visit to the Leytons ready for delivery to Bateman. 'Robson's waiting in the interview room downstairs with his brief. I think I'm going to play it like a fishing trip – not let him know just how much we know; make it seem like we are in the dark and searching for leads. But I'm going to throw in a bit of bait that will get him really worried.'

'You don't like him much guv, do you?' Gheeta said as she continued to tap out the report.

Palmer swung his feet down and the chair banged onto the floor. He stood up.

'Would you like a bastard who threatened to murder your young family and burn down your house? And all said in front of a judge and jury. I know it was nearly twenty years ago, but Harry Robson was a very nasty piece of work then; and leopards don't change their stripes.'

'Spots.'

'What?'

'Leopards have spots not stripes, guv.'

'Wouldn't really matter if one was chasing you, would it?'

'No, guv.'

'And he still is a nasty piece of work, make no mistake about it. So let's give him something to worry about and keep him occupied in saving his own skin. Come on – showtime!'

They made their way down to the interview rooms on the lower ground floor.

In room two Harry Robson was sweating a little; he always used to in the old days when he was pulled in 'for questioning'. He wasn't scared or worried, just nervous. But he sweated a little and had to mop his brow with a tissue that Palmer offered him across the interview room table.

'A bit hot in here for you is it, Harry?' Palmer enquired with a false smile.

They'd had Robson pulled in early in the morning and kept him in a cell, until Palmer thought he'd be starting to get worried about just how much he knew.

'No, I'm fine Mr Palmer. It's always a pleasure to be held in a cell for hours and then stuck in a small room with yourself and others.'

He returned the smile with sarcastic overtones. The *others* he had referred to were Gheeta, a uniformed officer at the door, and Robson's solicitor, Grenville Wildenstein. Wildenstein was getting uncomfortable as his large, overfed body was not suited to the wooden Home Office-issue office chair that had been made in the era before obesity due to over indulgence of fast food was the norm.

Wildenstein had been Robson's solicitor from way back, and he was also solicitor to most of the middle ranking range of criminals in the London area. Being of good old Jewish stock, he'd soon worked it out as a young solicitor that you avoided the low end of criminal fraternity as they would be on legal aid, and you also avoided the big guns – the 'diamond geezers' as they were known –because you'd take a pasting and get told to whistle for your money if you didn't get them off scot free, no matter what the severity of the crime or the size of the stack of evidence against them. Subsequently, the middle area of villain – like Harry Robson – had been Grenville Wildenstein's food ticket all his legal life.

'What is my client charged with, Chief Superintendent?'

'I don't know yet, Mr Wildenstein, depends on how this interview goes. Been to Hove lately, Harry?'

'Can't say I have, no.'

'Paid a visit to a Mr Stanley Leyton and his wife maybe?'

'Doesn't ring a bell.'

'Well, you rang theirs. You rang their bell at the Manor House, Hove – you and your nephew, young Finlay.'

Silence.

'They both identified you and Finlay from our mugshots. Funny you can't recall it, because their CCTV can recall the pair of you in glorious colour.'

Gheeta remained looking at Robson. What was Palmer on about? There was no CCTV at the Manor House. Wildenstein leaned close to Robson and whispered. Palmer's little lie had woken him up.

'No comment.'

Robson took his solicitor's advice.

'I didn't think there would be. Okay Harry, let's put you and your legal friend in the picture, shall we? First of all, we have two murders, Mr Plant and Mr Fenn. With Mr Fenn your company would seem to be involved.'

'How?'

Robson was aggressive.

'Just 'cause we delivered concrete to the site where his body was found doesn't necessary *involve* us.'

'But that body and the other one were both inside plastic sacks your company uses. Specialist plastic sacks.'

'Every demolition company uses asbestos sacks. It's the law.'

Palmer waited for five seconds before landing his first blow.

'Harry, I didn't say what type of sacks they were. How do you know they were asbestos sacks?'

Robson was hit. Wildenstein was into his ear again.

'No comment.'

Palmer took his time.

'Okay, let's proceed then. Both the victims were involved in a scam to launder money through fake auctions run by Mr Fenn. Have you had anything to do with those auctions, Harry?'

'No comment.'

'Well, once again that's quite remarkable. The auctioneer's wife remembers both you and your nephew Finlay visiting her house with Mr Fenn, her deceased husband. Do you recall visiting a Mrs Fenn? Luckily for us she picked both of you out from mug shots.'

'No comment.'

'The money that was being laundered through the auctions came from the sale of stolen gold ingots.'

Wildenstein sat up a bit at this. He'd obviously not been briefed about the gold by his client. Palmer carried on.

'Plant was a bullion dealer and was able to cut or melt down the original kilo-size ingots into a more manageable size. These were then sold on for cash at a greatly reduced price to the current legal spot fix – sold for cash only, and on a no questions basis no doubt, and the cash laundered through Fenn's auction house Country Auctions to your company'

'Never heard of it.'

Palmer nodded to Gheeta, who pulled a foolscap printout from her folder and passed it across the table. Palmer took a deep breath.

'Harry, all this 'no comment' and 'never heard of' stuff is just making this take a lot longer than is necessary. If I hadn't got proof of what I am saying I wouldn't have brought you in.'

He pointed to the paper.

'That's a copy of City Concrete's bank account – your company – showing three very large payments from County Auctions. You're bang to rights on money laundering Harry, minimum eight years.'

He sat back in his chair.

'But I'm the Murder Squad, I'm not really interest in money laundering. I want the killer or killers of those two chaps Plant and Fenn; so let's get to the hub of this little charade, shall we? The merchandise, the gold, Mr and Mrs Leyton's gold. Gold they shouldn't have had that Leyton's father nicked and passed down to them. Gold that their old friend Plant told them he could convert into cash for them, 'no questions asked' – how did you come to get involved, eh?'

'Don't know anything about this.'

Robson put the account printout down.

'First I've seen of it. Finlay does the accounts.'

'Does he now? How very convenient. We will be having a chat with Finlay very soon. But just how do you fit in, Harry?'

'I don't. Not seen any of this before,' he said, jabbing a finger at the printout.

Now Palmer was going to keep his cards close to his chest, and not let Robson know just how much he knew.

'Brinks Mat.'

Robson visibly stiffened.

'Eh?'

This was Palmer's ace. If he could get Robson to think that he thought it was Brinks Mat gold he was laundering, Robson would be a very, very worried man; because if it got out and about in the criminal fraternity that Robson was moving Brinks Mat gold, some very big hitters would want to know where he had got it from; big hitters that had already seen seven of the original BM team and hangers on die in mysterious circumstances when mouths had opened and hidden gold surfaced. Palmer wanted Robson to panic.

'Brinks Mat gold. Remember that little escapade, Harry? You were part of that team.'

'I wasn't. That was never proved.'

'No, it wasn't – and no doubt you have a lot to thank Mr Wildenstein here for in that case.'

Wildenstein spoke up.

'This is an irrelevant surmise and I must protest. My client was acquitted on that case.'

'Yes, he was – and may I remind you and him that the law of double jeopardy doesn't exist anymore in UK law?'

Robson looked a little worried now.

'I believe that the gold from the Leyton's was Brinks Mat gold,' Palmer continued. 'We don't know how they got it, except that it was hidden by Stanley Leyton's father. We know there's an awful lot of the BM haul out there unaccounted for, so perhaps the father was something to do with BM – a minder perhaps –looking after the gold for somebody else? He might even have been the elusive Mr Big who masterminded the whole caper; and maybe you knew that Harry, and as soon as Fenn brought you into the deal you probably recalled the name Leyton.'

Robson was getting very fidgety, as Palmer knew he would; the ruse was working. He continued.

'You knew it was out there, but didn't know where any of it was – and then 'hey presto', it was served up to you on a plate.'

He passed Robson another tissue as beads of sweat began to run down his brow.

'I've not had anything to do with Brinks Mat, Mr Palmer. Nothing, I swear it – nothing!'

'Okay. Well here's what I'm going to do, Harry. I'm still making a lot of enquiries about the Leytons; I'm still after your two chaps Hilton and Mooney who did a disappearing act immediately after we'd visited your premises, and I'm still not convinced that you aren't up to your eyes in this. I'm going to bail you on twenty thousand pounds security in the care of Mr Wildenstein – that is, if he's agreeable. If not, then you stay here and I'll keep getting an extension on keeping you here; and that will be easy, seeing as it's you with your criminal record, and it's a double murder that we are investigating. Oh, and then there's the little matter of petrol being squirted through my letter box two nights ago, and we all know your threats against me in the past don't we, Harry? Mr Wildenstein, will you stand bail?'

Wildenstein didn't really have much choice, the way Robson looked at him.

'Yes. Yes of course.'

'Good – oh, and I'll also do my best to keep a lid on the fact that I'm looking into you Harry for laundering Brinks Mat gold. I'll do my best, but these rumours do have a way of getting out and spreading quickly, don't they? So, you might expect a few visits from past acquaintances, might you not? I'll want you back here in four days. Duty officer will do the paperwork. Cheerio, Harry.'

Palmer rose and went to leave. Stopping at the door, he turned back.

'And do take care.'

'You bastard.'

Robson made a futile lunge at Palmer, but the officer was too quick and had him bent forward over the desk, his arm up his back in a second.

'You bastard, Palmer! You're hanging me out to dry, you bastard!'

'I am, aren't I?' was Palmer's parting remark.

Chapter 21

'I didn't notice CCTV cameras at the Leyton's place, guv.'

Gheeta and Palmer were in the lift going up to his floor.

'They must have been well concealed.'

He gave her a knowing smile.

'Well Sergeant, it's called evening the score. You see, he sat there and lied his head off, so I thought that telling one back was quite in order.'

'You didn't mention the ten bars of gold he and Finlay got from the Leytons.'

'No, don't want to frighten him or Finlay into getting rid of it quick. Those bars are solid evidence if we can find them in their possession. They can't do anything with them, can they? No auction to put it through, and they now know we are aware of it and looking. So, the only answer for them is to keep it. Lot of money – over three hundred thousand pounds, and it's going to be sitting somewhere and preying on their minds.'

Gheeta could see a bigger problem for Robson.

'I think the only thing preying on Robson's mind once he's bailed and on the outside is the thought that every gang in London will think he's unearthed some of the Brinks Mat gold. There will be a few people looking to have a word with him – people who will take a lot of calming down if I understood your description of them correctly, guv.'

'You did.'

Chapter 22

Sylvia Fenn closed the back door against a stormy night of lashing rain and turned to Finlay. He was sat at her kitchen table, his raincoat dripping onto the floor, and looking at her as he wiped the drips from his face.

'They had him in for an interview.'

'Who had who in for an interview?'

'Palmer, you stupid cow! Palmer had Harry in. He rang me, he's out on bail – they're trying to pin the murders on him. They traced the money from your old man to us.'

'Us?'

'City Concrete, it shows in the accounts and on the bank statements.'

'Well that was bloody stupid, wasn't it? I told you to do it all in cash.'

She sat down opposite him.

'Well, I suppose on the other hand it's alright really. If they had *him* in then they think he's involved and not you. And don't call me a stupid cow.'

'He'll try and swing it on me though, won't he – I know he will. He's been inside for a good stretch, and he said he'd never go back. He'll make up some story and try and pin the whole thing on me. We have to think of our next move.'

'We could run. There's two hundred thousand in cash upstairs and the gold bars in your office safe. It's enough to set us up somewhere well away from here.'

'No, if we run it's pretty obvious we're involved. Harry's shitting himself – he reckons Palmer's spreading a tale that he's fencing Brinks Gold.'

'So?'

Finlay smiled.

'If that were true then there's a few very heavy, well-connected people who'd be pulling his finger nails out to get their hands on it; and they'd want to know where it came from in case there was more. You don't piss about with Brink's Mat unless you've a death wish.'

'What are you going to do then?'

'Not much choice really. Harry's going to try and fit me up – so I've got to stop him.'

'Why wouldn't he do a runner? Seems the logical thing to do.'

Finlay sat bolt upright.

'Oh fuck! I didn't think of that.'

He got to his feet, fumbled his mobile phone from his inside pocket and tapped the keys. A few seconds later he tapped in a password and then scrolled down the screen.

'The bastard!'

He made for the door. Sylvia Fenn was startled.

'What's the matter? Where are you going now?'

'The office – the bastard's emptied the company bank account. He is doing a runner, I should have thought of that; and he won't run without the gold, will he?'

He slammed the door behind him. Sylvia Fenn stood deep in thought for a while, and then tapped in a number on her own mobile.

Chapter 23

Harry Robson turned the office safe combination lock clockwise and anti-clockwise as he said the code numbers under his breath; six turns, and then he heard the distinctive click inside. Swinging open the heavy door, his eyes fell on the stacked gold bars shining in the office fluorescent light, and his mouth stretched into a wide smile. The smile quickly disintegrated into panic as the office door opened behind him. He quickly pushed the safe door to hide the contents, turned, and recognising the figure he relaxed.

'What are you doing here?'

'I was passing and saw the light on.'

Robson nodded.

'I remembered I had a bit of important paperwork to catch up on.'

He turned back to the safe to fully close it. The monkey wrench that hit the back of his head was delivered with such force that had Harry Robson really had a death wish, it was now granted. He slumped forward, banging his empty face onto the safe as he slid to the floor. Another mighty blow was administered by the assailant, just to make sure. A third was about to be aimed when the sound of a car pulling up on the wet gravel and mud outside halted the raised arm. The figure quickly moved away and stooped behind the reception counter out of sight as footsteps approached the cabin. The office door was flung open.

Finlay took a step inside.

'I thought I might find you here – going to leave me and...'

His words tailed off as he saw the body sprawled in front of the safe, the safe door slightly ajar.

'Jesus, they didn't hang about did they?'

His thoughts were for the gold, not his uncle as he moved to the safe and bent to pull the lifeless body away from the front of it. He opened the safe door and saw the gold intact. His quick mind was telling him, screaming at him, that if Harry was dead and the gold still there… then whoever killed Harry was probably still there too…

The thought registered at the same time as the monkey wrench did its fatal work again, and he fell across his uncle's body.

Chapter 24

'I can't believe this.'

Palmer stood under his umbrella and shook his head in disbelief as he stood outside the City Concrete office and watched the fire brigade dousing down the smouldering remains of Harry Robson, sat behind the wheel of his burnt-out car, and the similarly smouldering remains of Finlay Robson, in the same position in his burnt-out car. It was two in the morning. He'd been called out as soon as the local force had checked the car numbers to their owners and found both owners were on a 'persons of interest' file which Palmer – or rather Gheeta –had posted on the Met Intranet.

'Did you actually put out that rumour about them and Brinks Mat, guv? If you did, it didn't half get a quick response.'

Gheeta had been trying to keep the Fire Brigade lads from trampling all over the crime scene, and with the help of two uniform officers from the local station had managed to put a crime scene 'no entry' tape around the area and the reception portacabin, in the hope that Forensics would have something left to work on. She'd only just gone to bed when Palmer had phoned to tell her what had happened. He'd told her not to bother attending as there was little they could do at the scene, but there was no way she wasn't going to go and get a first-hand look at it.

The duty pathologist had made a quick visit. Judging by his evening dress, frilly shirt and bow tie he'd been at some formal dinner when his mobile had ruined his evening. Nothing he could do at the scene except pronounce the pair dead and arrange for the bodies to be taken to the mortuary freezer for a post mortem later in the day.

Now that the scene had been taped off, SOCA could come in the morning and take their time. The duty Forensics officer had made sure Gheeta's tape extended far enough around the scene to preserve any foot or tyre prints for the morning; although that would be a painstaking job after numerous size eleven firemen's boots had all but destroyed it. But you never knew.

Chapter 25

Later that morning, after a short four-hour fitful sleep at home, Palmer yawned loudly and stretched his arms above his head.

'Don't start that guv, or you'll have me at it too.'

Gheeta stood in front of the progress chart in the team room and watched as Claire added the latest details of the case. Claire put the top on the felt tip.

'Finlay dead, Harry Robson dead, as well as Plant and Fenn dead; so all the main players have gone to meet their maker now.'

Palmer sat down and rubbed his eyes.

'I'm getting too tired now to think straight. What are we missing? Who else is in this little game, eh? Where's our fifth man?'

'Fifth man?'

Claire took the top back off her felt tip and drew a head and shoulders outline on the chart with a question mark above it.

'Sounds like a Le Carré novel.'

'Well,' Palmer said, rubbing his chin thoughtfully. 'If Robson and Finlay killed Plant and Fenn, who killed Robson and Finlay? There's nobody else in the frame, is there?'

'The Leytons?' Gheeta said, clutching at straws. 'She was a bit of a feisty lady.'

'No, too much to lose. Did we check whether they'd handed the rest of the gold in?'

Claire nodded.

'Yes, I checked with the War Office. Leyton rang the Defence Ministry and had a word with one of his pals there. They will be having a visit from a couple of high ranking officers tomorrow.'

'Won't make the papers, I'll bet on that,' Palmer said with a smile.

'Won't it?' Claire said. 'Why because he's an MP?'

'No, the Ministry couldn't care less about that. But what they do care about is for the past seventy years the

British Army has never been tainted with any war looting accusations – not one; while America and Russia have museums full of the stuff and legal actions going on all the time as the families of the rightful owners try to get it back.'

'Elgin Marbles comes to mind.'

Palmer laughed.

'Yes but that wasn't war loot, Claire. That was just plain theft.'

Reg Frome came into the room carrying a printout.

'Good afternoon, all.'

They all mumbled greetings as he sat at a desk and put on his glasses.

'I have the initial Forensics report on last night's little fracas.'

'Aha!' Palmer said, leaning forward. 'Loads of fingerprints from a known villain, I hope?'

Frome scoffed.

'Would be nice Justin, but no. The killer used paraffin to set the fire, and the can was in the fire too so no use to us for prints. There were tyre prints of the two cars but no others, so the killer was on foot. Footprints – what was left of them after the fire brigade hoses had just about washed the place clean – were of the two victims and one other. And you'll love this – size six trainer, same as at your place the other night, Justin. A perfect match.'

Palmer clapped his hands.

'Our fifth man.'

'More likely to be a lady,' Frome corrected him. 'Size six is not a man's size, Justin – child or lady. Know any children with a grudge against you?'

'Only the grandkids – I was supposed to take them to Alton Towers last half term, but the Poetic Justice case took longer than I thought and put paid to that little adventure. Grandad was not very popular, to say the least.'

Frome laughed.

'Hardly a big enough grudge to burn your house down. Anyway, to continue…'

He looked down at his printout.

'Both men were dead before they were incinerated; heavy blows to the back of the head from the same weapon, probably a steel bar or similar. Harry Robson's blood was found on the front of the safe, and a few minute splashes on the safe's inner door edge which was closed and locked. So that would indicate he was killed when the safe door was open, and then it was closed. Nothing in the safe except office papers, but – and you'll like this too – traces of gold on the shelf inside that indicates one or more bars were slid off that shelf. Both the victims' mobile phones are being analysed, but they are unregistered pay-as-you-go types, and basically lumps of tangled metal and silicon from the heat so not much hope; although if we can get a number out of them we can trace the calls. So, fingers crossed on that. And so far, that's it.'

He removed his glasses and placed them in his pocket.

'The receptionist lady turned up for work when we were there. She got a shock, I can tell you. Anyway, we took her fingerprints so we can discard them from the ones we've lifted off the safe and door. And that's about it so far.'

'Well done, Reg. At least that gives us one lead to pursue,' Palmer said sarcastically. 'Somebody wearing size six shoes.'

'Good luck with that,' Frome laughed as he rose to leave. 'Cuts the possibles down to about forty million people I should guess. I'll email our reports for your file, Justin. I'm sure you'll want to add them to your daily report sheets for Bateman.'

He shot Palmer a big smile, and Palmer returned it.
'Piss off.'

They all laughed as Frome left.

'This is a real teaser, isn't it?' Palmer said, rubbing his tired eyes again. 'Two bodies in sacks, two witnesses disappear, two suspects get whacked; so that's four bodies and no names in the frame. I think we'd better have a word with that receptionist – Cherry or whatever her name is. I can't believe she doesn't know a bit more than meets the eye.'

Claire tapped her keyboard.

'Real name Angela Rathbone. I'll print off her address.'

'We'd better check her shoe size too while we are at it,' Gheeta said with a knowing nod. 'And Mrs Fenn's, and Mrs Leytons.'

Palmer leaned back in his chair, stifling another yawn.

'This case is turning into a bloody Cinderella pantomime, checking shoe sizes…'

'You'd make a lovely Buttons, guv – curly wig and tights.'

Claire and Gheeta giggled.

'Oh yes? Well, guess what parts you two would have then, eh?'

He had the last laugh.

Chapter 26

'A very nice lady, very respectable tenant, never any problems – I wish they were all like her. I hope nothing has happened to her? Is she alright?'

Angela Rathbone's landlord seemed genuinely worried as he led Palmer, Gheeta and a uniformed officer to the second floor flat he rented out to her. Being of a portly size he was puffing with the exertion of two flights of stairs as he fumbled for the keys while mopping his brow.

'Yes sir, as far as we know nothing out of the ordinary has happened to her.'

Palmer gave him a relaxing smile. He didn't like landlords.

'We just need to take a statement from her. Trivial matter really – four murders.'

'What?' the landlord said, turning visibly white. 'Oh My God.'

They stopped outside the flat's door.

'This is it,' he said, offering Palmer the key. 'You can open it. Oh God, what if there's a body inside?'

Palmer shrugged.

'Or two or three.'

Gheeta smiled to herself as the landlord turned very pale. She was very aware of Palmer's dislike for the 'establishment' types, which in his mind included private landlords. He half opened the door and called out to anybody inside.

'Hello, anybody home? Hello? This is the police… anybody here?'

No reply, so he pushed the door fully open and looked inside.

'You sure this is her flat?'

He turned to the landlord, who had retreated a few yards away down the landing in expectation of something very nasty being found in his property.

'Yes, yes of course I am.'

He ventured forward timidly and stepped inside.

'What the…?'

The flat was empty except for the landlord's furniture; no sign that it had ever been occupied by a tenant other than a few old newspapers on a sofa and crockery in the kitchen sink.

'When did you last see Miss Rathbone, sir?'

The landlord was confused.

'Just last week. She gave me her rent for the month.'

'Not since then?'

'No, no I don't think so. But I tend to only see the tenants when something needs doing – repairs and things like that. We all keep ourselves to ourselves.'

Gheeta was snooping round the cupboards.

'How did she pay the rent, sir – by cheque?'

'No, cash; always cash. All above board. She had a rent book.'

He sat down in one of his deep, well-battered armchairs.

'Is Miss Rathbone suspected of being a murderer, Inspector? I can't believe that.'

'Chief Superintendent,' Palmer corrected him. 'And we don't know yet, sir. The investigation is at an early stage. Unfortunately, I'll have to have our forensic people give the flat a good once-over, so you won't be able to rent it out until you get the okay from us.'

'Rent it out?'

He gave Palmer a doleful glance and shook his head.

'I'll be lucky… I only hope Miss Rathbone isn't involved in these murders. If she is, and it gets out that a murderer lived here, it will never rent. Look at that chap in Gloucester, they had to knock his council house down and pave it over. No one would take it – not even the homeless.'

'West, Fred West. He was a serial killer too.'

Palmer wasn't helping to calm the landlord's fears.

'But the lady may have a perfectly good answer to our enquiries when we find her sir, so let's wait and see, not jump to conclusions. We will need to take a statement from you, I'm afraid. Just the usual questions: how long was she

here, anything unusual about her, any regular visitors –
nothing to worry about. My Sergeant will arrange a time to
suit you.'

'Can do it now if you like sir, and get it over with?'

Gheeta wanted to get any information while it was
fresh in the landlord's mind. He shrugged.

'Nothing to tell you really. Lovely lady, must have
been here for about two years by now; I can check, no trouble
at all. Her boyfriend was a damn nuisance, though – revving
his motorbike up in the early hours when he left.'

Palmer and Gheeta exchanged glances.

'Don't remember his name do you, sir?' Gheeta
asked, hoping against hope.

'No, we were never introduced.'

Gheeta took her iPad from her shoulder bag and
tapped on the photo app, then scrolled down to a prison mug
shot of Mooney. She showed it to the landlord.

'Is this him?'

'Yes, yes I think so; he looks familiar. Noisy sod. It
was always dark when he left, and he would put a helmet on
as soon as he got onto the bike; but I did catch a glimpse of
his face a few times. If that's not him, it's somebody very
similar.'

Chapter 27

Mooney's motorbike was still outside his door, a large wheel clamp secured it; the curtains in his upstairs maisonette were closed. It was a long shot that he and Angela Rathbone would be there; but now, armed with the knowledge that they were 'an item', Palmer thought it was one that had to be played. They'd come from her empty flat more in hope than expectation.

'Odds on he won't be in and the place is bare, eh?' Palmer said, pressing the bell for the third time.

The front door of the downstairs part of the maisonette opened, and the pensioner they'd met on their last visit stood with it half open. The sight of a uniformed officer with Palmer and Sergeant Singh this time sent warning signals to his brain that this was a bit more serious than the last call.

'Haven't seen him for a couple of weeks,' he said. 'Or heard that bloody bike coming and going at all hours. What's he done?'

Gheeta gave him a nice smile.

'Has anybody else been round looking for him, sir?'

'Not that I know of; been nice and quiet. What's he done?'

'We don't know that he's done anything. We just want to ask him a few questions.'

'What about?'

Palmer had had enough.

'Nothing for you to worry about sir, and nothing that concerns you; so just go back inside if you wouldn't mind, and let us get on with our job.'

'I can stand here if I want to, it's my doorway. Anyway, makes a change to see a copper round here; you can't be bothered to come out when I ring in about the little bastards kicking their ball against my wall can you, eh?'

Palmer had really had enough. He turned to the uniformed officer.

'Officer, take this person and put him in the back of the car. Read him his rights and charge him with obstructing the police in their line of duty. He can spend a night in the cells.'

The pensioner's door closed very quickly as he sensibly retreated inside and gave a V sign to Palmer through the frosted glass door panel.

'Another one for the fan club, sir.'

Gheeta and the officer smiled. Palmer shook his head in disbelief; sometimes nosy neighbours were a bonus in an investigation, but not this time.

'Right then, let's have a look inside.'

Shielding his actions with his body, he deftly selected a key from a dozen on a ring from his pocket and on the second attempt the door opened.

'Oh look, he left the door unlocked. What a stroke of luck.'

Gheeta and the uniformed officer exchanged glances.

'That was a real stroke of luck, sir.'

Inside, an immediate staircase led up to Mooney's flat, which was the absolute opposite to Angela Rathbone's. It was a mess; clothes strewn over the furniture, crockery in the sink, half empty take-away food trays on the table with grey green mould taking hold, and an unmade bed in the bedroom.

'It looks like he left in a hurry, sir. Halfway through his meal.'

Gheeta pointed to the food trays.

'Yes, and I bet we know when that quick exit was. Harry Robson gave him the tip that we were on our way when we left City Concrete the first time we went there; for some reason, Harry just didn't want us to talk to Mooney or Hilton. I wonder why?'

'Perhaps they knew too much.'

'You bet they did. And if Harry Robson thought they might save themselves and do a deal with us, he would get them out of the way. Fast.'

'That sounds ominous.'

'Yes, I told you he was a nasty man. No signs of a struggle or anything like that here though, so I think Mooney got out quickly under his own steam.'

He opened the wardrobe in the bedroom.

'And it looks like Angela Rathbone spent a lot of time here too.'

Gheeta walked over and saw the wardrobe's hangers; empty except for a pair of men's jeans, various female tops, skirts and a lady's full length coat. She hoisted up the bottom of the coat from the floor; three pairs of ladies shoes and a pair of trainers came into view.

'Three guesses what size they'll be, sir.'

'Six?'

She used the tail of a nightdress to pick up the trainers and look.

'Correct.'

Palmer turned to the officer.

'If you wouldn't mind hanging on here until we get a SOCO team over I'd appreciate it.'

'No problem. sir. I'll radio in right away.'

Chapter 28

Patrick Mooney took a spoonful of sweet and sour chicken from his plate.

'I was in the middle of eating one of these when Finlay rang and told me to get out quick 'cause the fuzz were on their way. Rest of it is probably still there on my table.'

He looked around the Chinese restaurant table at his fellow eaters and raised his wine glass.

'To us.'

Mark Hilton and Angela Rathbone raised their glasses in unison.

'To us.'

'And what about me?'

Dennis Parks – otherwise known as the 'magician', who had been to the men's room – joined them and took his seat. Mooney raised his glass again.

'To Dennis, without whom we probably wouldn't be here.'

'To Dennis.'

Angela Rathbone raised her glass and whispered: 'To Harry and Finlay, may they rot in Hell.'

They all drank to that. Hilton sat back in his chair.

'So, what's the plan now then?'

Parks spoke quietly to keep the conversation within the table; the restaurant was busy, and walls have ears.

'Well, we sit tight for a bit – let it all cool down. You can stay at the Airfield for a while; it's not the most comfortable place I know, but at least you've separate rooms, a shower room and a kitchen at the back of the hangar.'

Hilton laughed.

'That's better than a cell, eh?'

Dennis agreed.

'Yes, we don't want any of that again, do we?'

Angela wanted to know something.

'Patrick said you knew each other from Wandsworth, Dennis?'

Dennis nodded.

'We were neighbours, adjacent cells.'

They all laughed.

'When Finlay turned up at the Airfield, with Mark and Patrick as the two *parcels* I was supposed to fly out over the ocean with and come back without, I couldn't believe it.'

Mooney nodded.

'Nor could I when I saw it was you. I knew what your trade was, from our conversations while resting at Her Majesty's Pleasure.'

'Trade?'

'He's a magician,' Mooney explained.

Angela was none the wiser.

'A magician?'

'I make things disappear,' Dennis explained. 'People mostly.'

Angela covered her mouth.

'Oh my God.'

'So when we got shot of Finlay, Patrick filled me in on what was happening.'

'As soon as we got to the airfield and Dennis came out I recognised him,' Mooney explained. 'And knowing his trade, I understood what Harry and Finlay had planned for me and Mark. I signalled Dennis to be quiet, not to give away that he'd recognised me. We weren't going to be flown to Spain or somewhere safe to hide like Finlay had told us on the journey down; we were going to be killed and pushed out of a plane somewhere over the ocean.'

'With twenty kilo weights tied to their feet,' added Dennis.

Angela was taken aback.

'I thought that kind of thing only happened in films?'

Dennis laughed.

'Oh, no… How do you think people like Robson get to where they are in the criminal pecking order? They don't politely ask others: '*move over and let me have your business*'. Anyway, as we were saying, we keep our heads down for a little while, and then we'll book separate trips to wherever you decide you want to go. Book a genuine holiday flying out of Bristol or Birmingham – one of those cheap Thompson or Monarch package things. Once there, you disappear; or I can pull in a few favours and get something set up for you in Spain. I've got a few mates out there.'

'And the, err... *chocolate bars*?'

Angela could see that that whatever plan they chose it would cost.

'Well...'

Dennis sat back and became serious.

'There's two hundred and thirty-two of them *chocolate bars*, so I reckon the odd thirty-two would cover the... shall we call it, resettlement costs; the rest you can do with as you like once you get sorted. Current spot price is thirty-two grand a kilo, so you'll have about six and a half million – more than enough to buy a bar or something in Spain and stash the rest away. It's very cheap out there at the moment. Good time to do it.'

'And you? What will you do?'

'Nothing, absolutely nothing – just carry on as I am. Launder the gold slowly and put it in an ISA, eh?'

They all laughed, and then Dennis grew serious again.

'What about this Fenn woman, I thought she was involved?'

Angela sighed.

'Sylvia? Yes, she was. I feel a bit bad about her.'

'Why?'

'Well, it was her husband who first told Finlay about the gold. He'd been asked by a mate of his who was a dodgy bullion dealer in Brighton – he was the one cutting and selling the bars to help launder the money, as he was an auctioneer and could put it through as legit sales bit by bit. He'd been doing the same scam for Finlay Robson on other stolen items and told him – stupid thing to do, really. Anyway, to cut a long story short, Finlay and Harry Robson got themselves involved and leaned on the owners of the gold – some rich couple in Brighton – and upped the ante, wanting more of it fenced quickly rather than dripping it out slowly like Fenn had been doing. Then Fenn and the bullion dealer wanted a bigger cut, saying it was a bigger risk; and with Finlay and Robson knowing where it was originating from, they were… shall we say, 'expendable'.'

Dennis nodded slowly.

'Harry Robson never did like sharing. Mind you, the tight bastard never gave me that job. He got a couple of bloody amateurs to do it, so I'm told.'

He looked from Mooney to Hilton with raised eyebrows, and they all laughed. Hilton nodded ruefully.

'Perhaps he should have given you the job; we made a pig's ear of it, which started off all the police interest.'

Angela continued her story.

'Anyway, as I was saying, Sylvia Fenn was having an affair with Finlay; Fenn had taken Finlay to their house a couple of times, and things happened. I only knew what was going on between them because she came into the office a few times to meet him there, when her husband was away up country doing one of his auctions. We got on quite well, and it was obvious what was happening between them. And she knew all about the gold; Finlay must have told her, or perhaps her husband. She was quite open about it, and her relationship with Finlay. She was fed up with scrabbling to make ends meet with her husband and wanted a better life.

'She didn't seem at all upset when her husband was killed. It dawned on me later that she probably knew it was going to happen; she might even have planned it with Finlay. Let's face it, a future with a criminal who's got a few hundred thousand quid in gold is better than one with an auctioneer who's scrabbling to make ends meet. She knew I was with Patrick, so when he and Mark disappeared Finlay must have dropped a hint. She rang me, told me she suspected Robson and Finlay were involved in Patrick and Mark's disappearance; said she knew they were definitely behind her husband and the bullion dealer Plant's deaths, and that she was just biding her time. I couldn't tell her that Patrick and Mark were okay, that Patrick had phoned me and filled me in on the whole story, so I went along with her by pretending to be upset. She said knew where Finlay kept a couple of hundred thousand grand, and she was going to get it when he was arrested. She was sure that copper Palmer was onto them, and if they went down she'd be sitting pretty with the money.'

'Which we assume she's now got?' Dennis asked.

'Yes, which is why I'm not feeling too bad about ditching her.'

'Ditching her?'

'Well, sort of. Finlay must have told her the gold bars were in the office safe; she told me they were there, and we had a plan to get to them at the first sign of trouble, split them and Finlay's cash and run. I knew the combination for the safe; I'd watched them open it enough times but I didn't have a key, so I got Finlay's off his key ring in his jacket pocket when he was occupied up the yard for a morning, made an excuse about running out of coffee, and went and got a copy made. We were going to plan to take the bars on a Friday evening, so we'd have all weekend to get away. Anyhow, Robson being taken in for questioning changed all that.'

'How?'

Dennis was following the story intently.

'She rang me that evening; said Robson had been arrested and Finlay was going bananas. He was sure that Robson would lose his bottle, that he'd get bail and take the gold from the safe and scarper while he still could. So Finlay was going to get to the safe first, and seeing that I had the key, I should go and get the gold before either of them did, take it back to her place, split it and we'd disappear. Easy, eh?'

'Sounds like it. What happened?'

'Well, I got there as fast as I could, but the light in the office was on. I thought Finlay was already there, but I was so angry about what they'd tried to do to Patrick that I picked up a heavy wrench outside and strode in bold as brass with it behind my back; and there was Robson, kneeling at the safe with the door open. He said something, I said something; he turned to close the safe door and I hit him, hard. He went down, and I think I hit him again. I was so angry. I was going to put the gold into bags when I heard a car pull up outside; so I hid behind the counter and Finlay came rushing in like a bull in a china shop. He saw Robson on the floor and the safe door partly open and said something like 'they got to you first.' Then he knelt to pull Robson away from the safe so he could open it, and I rushed out and hit him too. I didn't check whether they were dead as it didn't matter; yhey were both laying still, and all I could think about was to get the gold into bags and into my car, which I did. It seemed to take an age, it was so heavy – I didn't realise how heavy. I had to use four bags, and even then I could hardly lift them. Then, when it was all done and in my car, I was starting to think straight again. I pulled Robson and Finlay out and dragged them into their cars, doused them with paraffin and set them alight. I've never been so scared in my life.'

'Very professional job though.'

She gave a small laugh.

'Not really, just that every time you hear about a crime on telly they say the getaway car was found 'burnt out'. No clues.'

Dennis was worried.

'And the wrench?'

'I threw it into Finlay's car.'

Mooney took hold of one of her hands reassuringly.

'You're shaking. It's okay, it's over now.'

'Then I drove to your place and stayed the night. I couldn't sleep. I went to work in the morning as normal and feigned shock when I got there and saw the police all over the yard and in the office. The burnt-out cars were there, with blue and white tape all round the place. The bodies had been removed, thank God. They took a brief statement and said I could go home and they'd be in touch, and would I like Victims Support or a WPC to stay with me – ironic, eh? I said I was okay and went back, threw a few things into the car and drove here.'

'You're a very brave lady.'

Dennis was impressed.

'I'll get your motor put through a crusher soon as I can. Life goes on just as normal; you two lads will be a couple of helpers I've taken on temporarily over a busy period, and

Angela will be an agency secretary I've hired, so wander around and look busy now and again. It's easier to do that than try to keep out of sight, 'cause somebody is bound to see you and start to ask questions. So, I'll just put it about to the other people on the airfield that business is good and I need a hand.'

He raised his glass again.

'Here's to us.'

'To us.'

Angela's mobile rang. Mooney stayed her hand as she went to answer it.

'Don't. Don't answer it. Probably the police wanting to know where you are, so they can interview you. Let it ring; we don't want them tracing the call.'

Dennis nodded in agreement.

'Turn it off and give it to me later, and I'll make sure it goes through the crusher with your car.'

Chapter 29

Across the road from the Chinese restaurant, a figure stood deep in the shadows of a shop doorway and watched as the four diners looked at Angela's mobile. The figure looked down at the lit screen of the mobile phone in its hand as it rang out Angela's number. It rang off after twelve rings. No answer.

Sylvia Fenn put it back into her coat pocket, pulled the coat hood further over her face and slipped unnoticed from the doorway, making her way along the road to her parked car. She was tired and needed to find a hotel. It had been a long day.

Having rung Angela the evening before to warn her Finlay was on his way to the office because he was sure Harry Robson would go there, take the gold and run, she had waited for an update back from her; Angela had said she would go to the office and see what was happening, get the gold if she could, and ring back later. But no call came. Sylvia had a sleepless night wondering whether Angela was alright. Perhaps she should get away now, take Finlay's hidden money and run. Why hadn't Angela rung? She wasn't answering her mobile either. Had Robson or Finlay found her at the office and realised she knew all about the gold, and decided to silence her too?

In the morning the TV news was full of the double murder at a cement works, with pictures of the burnt-out cars and naming Harry and Finlay Robson as the victims of a violent robbery gone wrong. Camera shots of the inside of the office showed an open and empty safe. No mention of Angela – she must have got the gold. Still no answer from her mobile, so Sylvia decided to drive to Mooney's place, as she knew Angela stayed there with her boyfriend and not at her flat. No need to worry about taking Finlay's money as he wouldn't be coming back for it, so she left it hidden.

As she drove to Mooney's all sorts of scenarios flashed through her mind. Had Angela seen the carnage and run? Surely she couldn't have killed the Robsons? But if not her, then who had? Was there another person in the game, maybe a gang? People like Robson and Finlay must have made enemies in their circle of associates over the years; it seemed very professional, with the cars and bodies being burnt afterwards.

As she got near Mooney's she was amazed to see Angela hurriedly putting armfuls of clothes into the boot of her car parked outside. She pulled up the hood of her coat, drove past and parked further up the street and watched. Two more armfuls of clothes, and then Angela locked the front door of the flat and drove off, straight past Sylvia who ducked as she did so. Was the gold in the boot with the clothes? She was angry now. When Finlay had hinted that Mooney and Hilton had been killed, she'd told Angela.

They had made a plan together; she'd worked it all out and they'd agreed to it. She'd even put herself at risk squirting petrol through Palmer's letter box; she'd come up with that after Finlay had told her about Robson's previous run in with Palmer, and the threats he'd made against him in court. He'd have to be chief suspect for the petrol attack, and if the police pulled him in on remand they'd just have Finlay to worry about, and he wouldn't be much of an opponent. They would take the gold from the safe and Finlay's money and go. But giving Harry Robson bail, and Finlay getting very uptight about his uncle maybe doing a runner with the gold, had changed that plan.

She followed Angela's car south of the Thames and towards the M4. Angela pulled in for petrol just before the M4 at Hammersmith, and Sylvia thought she'd better fill up too, just in case a long journey was ahead. She slid her motor to the pumps at the back of the petrol station. It was busy, and Angela was three lanes away and in front of her. When Angela went in and queued at the counter to pay, Sylvia used her card at the pump and was all paid and back in the driving seat when Angela returned. Up onto the M4 they went, Sylvia keeping a good distance behind.

So intent was she on keeping Angela in sight, she completely missed the green Jaguar a few cars behind her that had followed the pair of them from Mooney's flat. Just past Bristol they turned on to the M5 north, and then off on the A40 towards Gloucester, before finally Angela turned off along a side road and into the Staverton Airfield. Sylvia pulled into a small layby in the verge and watched as Angela's car skirted the main buildings and pulled up outside a double hangar at the back of the field. The large sign across the hangar told her it was the South Western Air Taxi Company. She couldn't really tell who they were, but three men came out; one hugged Angela, and they took the bags from the car's boot and all went inside.

Four hours later, as evening was drawing in and Sylvia Fenn was getting rather tired of watching executive jets and helicopters landing and taking off, they all came back out. They got into a large 4x4 and came out of the airfield gates straight past Sylvia, who hit the floor as they did so.

She followed them at a discreet distance into Gloucester and pulled up and parked fifty yards behind them, on a street that seemed to be a row of ethnic restaurants. Sylvia was very hungry, and the smells assailing her senses made it worse; but she pulled up her coat hood and found a dark shop doorway opposite the restaurant the four had chosen to eat in. She recognised Mooney and Hilton with Angela, but not the third man. So, Mooney and Hilton weren't killed after all. She wondered whether Angela knew that all along. Had Angela taken her for a ride? Used her to get to know Finlay's next moves?

She watched, pondering her own next move. They all looked to be in a good mood, laughing and jolly. The anger welled up inside her. Let's give them something to think about then. She dialled Angela's number, using the 'no caller information' button just as they all raised their glasses for a toast. Sylvia watched as their laughter turned to silent concern and their glasses slowly returned to the table as Angela held up the ringing phone.

Chapter 30

'That's really amazing. How do they do that?'

In the office, Claire was looking at her computer screen where a listing of telephone numbers was scrolling down.

'How do they do what?'

Palmer stood with Sergeant Singh, their backs to Claire as they updated the progress chart, putting 'deceased' under Robson and Finlay's pictures.

'How the hell do Forensics manage to retrieve the phone numbers of the calls Robson and Finlay made from a pair of melted mobiles?'

'They don't.'

Gheeta turned and went to look over Claire's shoulder at the screen.

'They retrieve the mobile number and then get the call record from the mobile company it's contracted to. Anything interesting?'

'Well, both made plenty of calls to each other and the office. The only other number that stands out is a Gloucester code.'

Palmer joined them.

'Gloucester?'

'Yes, all on the same day, which was the day you visited their office: one call from Robson and three from Finlay, all to the same Gloucester number.'

'Can we trace who it is?'

'No, it's a mobile number.'

'Could ring it, guv?'

Gheeta picked up her mobile and held it in her hand questioningly. Palmer gave her the go ahead with a nod of his head. She tapped in the number from the screen, and it was answered at the other end. Gheeta raised her eyebrows to Palmer before talking into the phone.

'Oh, I am sorry – I've dialled a wrong number. Sorry to trouble you.'

She clicked off the phone.

'Well?' Palmer said impatiently.

'South Western Air Taxis.'

'South Western Air Taxis?'

'Yes.'

Claire was on it and had already put the name into Google.

'Internal and European Air Taxi service for business and urgent deliveries. Flies out of Staverton Airport near Gloucester. There's a picture here of three planes and two hangars. It looks very smart.'

Gheeta settled herself in front of another computer.

'I'll do a company search and see what we can find out. You key into the Civil Aviation Authority and take a look at the South Western Air Taxi flight record.'

Palmer was surprised; he shouldn't have been, as Sergeant Singh's expertise at computer hacking had been used by his office many times, but he felt obliged to make his usual comment to cover his back.

'Shouldn't we put a formal request through to the Civil Aviation Authority for the records?'

'We can do sir, yes.'

Gheeta had a smile at the corner of her mouth. Palmer always played the dead straight, by-the-book card when he knew damn well what the answer would be.

'We can certainly do that, if you want to wait for about a fortnight for them to respond. Or you can go and have a coffee and we'll have the information in ten minutes when you return, sir.'

She passed Claire a small notebook from her shoulder bag hanging on the chair.

'Password for the CAA server is under A for Airlines.'

Palmer leant to look as Claire opened the book.

'I hate to think what that little book would be worth on the black market.'

Gheeta smiled at him.

'What little book, guv? Don't know what you're talking about.'

'Quite. I think I'll go and get a coffee. Anybody else like one?'

Chapter 31

Half an hour later, and all the information available had been downloaded.

'It seems a reputable company, guv; not even a CCJ against them. Owner is a Dennis Parks, and all its licences and paperwork are up to date.'

Gheeta sounded a trifle disappointed, 'So, why should our deceased pair be making calls to Dennis Parks on the day we paid them a visit?' Palmer asked as he sipped his coffee. 'Planning a flight somewhere?'

'Maybe they were getting ready to disappear?'

'So why didn't they then?'

Claire sat back in her chair.

'There's no Harry Robson or Finlay Robson on South Western Air Taxi passenger lists – no Robsons at all. Mainly sub-contract work for various national parcel carriers, with internal UK flights to Manchester, Southampton and such, plus regular ones to Calais-Dunkerque airport in France. All parcel delivery work; that seems to be their bread and butter.'

Palmer was thoughtful. He walked over to the progress chart and stood there, turning things over in his mind.

Perhaps Mooney and Hilton were the real crooks, using City Concrete as a cover… No, no that didn't add up; and anyway, Harry Robson wouldn't play second fiddle to anyone. No, Robson and Finlay are the top dogs – or were the top dogs. So who would kill them, and why? It had to be somebody in the know about the gold. Mind you, if word had gotten around about 'gold', some well-placed people with the knowledge of Robson's alleged past involvement with Brinks Mat would soon be on the scent. Maybe one such firm caught up with them and a deal wasn't struck?

And then there's Angela Rathbone, or 'Cherry' the receptionist. Why would she disappear? She turned up for work, gave a brief account of her movements the previous day, and then she was gone. But she definitely had somewhere to go, because she cleaned out her and her boyfriend Mooney's wardrobe – so he must still be alive, and if he is then Hilton will be too. Maybe Mooney and Hilton killed Robson and Finlay, picked up Angela and fled? So many permutations. Perhaps the Leytons had come for their gold? Not very likely at all, although Mrs Leyton was a feisty one. I wonder if she's a size six? And this air taxi service or whatever it is; certainly a quick way to put some miles between you and your pursuers. But who is pursuing who? Is there some third party involved that we haven't come across yet?

He took a long breath and exhaled loudly.

'Okay, let's get an early night and go down and take a look at the Air Taxi place tomorrow. Better let Gloucestershire CID know we are on their turf, but I don't want them doing anything; I don't want them anywhere near that airfield. If there is something going on there we don't want them frightened off. So plainclothes and softly softly is the order of the day tomorrow.'

'Hang on sir,' said Gheeta, pointing to her screen. 'There's a forensic report on Mooney's flat coming through from Reg Frome's department.'

'Is there anything interesting in it?'

Palmer was fed up with asking that, because it showed they were scrabbling for clues. She read from the screen.

'The trainers in the wardrobe were the ones that left prints in your front garden.'

'Really? So it was Angela Rathbone playing Knock Down Ginger, eh? Why would she do that?'

'Knock Down Ginger Sir? Sounds a bit violent.'

'Never mind, Sergeant. Is there anything else?'

'There are two sets of prints on the City Concrete safe handle – Robson's and Rathbone's.'

'Well, that would appear to be okay. They would both have access to it, I would have thought.'

'Yes, but the interesting thing is that the top print is Rathbone's.'

'Top print?'

'Yes, her print is partly over the top of Robson's; so she must have touched the handle after him.'

She pointed to an enlarged picture on the screen showing the safe handle and finger prints, accentuated by the graphite coating SOCO had applied. Print X was half over print Y. The text at the bottom read: *Robson Y, Rathbone X.* Reg Frome had written underneath *'interesting?'*

'She couldn't have her print over his, guv; he would have opened the safe and then he was killed. What's her print doing on top of his? She didn't go into the office the morning after when she arrived for work.'

'No, so she must have been there when it all went off the night before – or even after it had all gone off.'

Gheeta looked at Palmer, knowing the implication of that statement.

'Miss Rathbone seems to have a few questions to answer all of a sudden.'

'If we can find her to ask them, guv.'

'Oh, we'll find her. She'll be shacked up with Mooney somewhere.'

'We've got 'Stop and Holds' on them at all UK exits.'

'Good. Right then, let's get that early night.'

Claire looked quizzically at Palmer.

'Early night, sir? Something tells me there's something going on at the Palmer residence.'

Palmer wasn't one for early nights.

'You should be a detective, Claire. You're quite right, I have an ulterior motive. Mrs P.'s doing steak and kidney pie because the bloke next door's coming out of hospital with his new hip, and he won't have anything to eat at his house – and I'm blowed if he's going to get it all. I'll be waiting with my plate ready as it comes out of the oven.'

Gheeta was impressed.

'How considerate of her to look after a neighbour like that, guv. Very kind of her, isn't it?'

She also knew what Palmer thought of Benji and was winding him up. Palmer nodded.

'Isn't it just? But let me remind you, ladies, that the day I was brought home from hospital in an ambulance after that woman fell on me from six floors up in the Saturday's Child case, all I got was the local take-away menu left on the table, with a note saying *'gone to gardening club'*. So, if I don't get home early tonight there'll be another note this time, saying *'gone next door with the steak and kidney pie'*! Come on, close those computers down and let's go. Anyway, we need our sleep – off to Gloucester tomorrow.'

Chapter 32

'I'm DS Williams, Gloucester CID, sir. Hope you had a pleasant journey.'

He was in his mid-thirties, tall with cropped hair, and shook Palmer's hand as he and Sergeant Singh left the train at Gloucester station.

'I have a car waiting in the car park.'

Palmer introduced Sergeant Singh, and they all three walked through the pedestrian tunnel to the waiting squad car. There was another person already in the front passenger seat as Palmer and Singh got in the back.

Once they were inside, Williams turned from the driver's seat and explained.

'This is Mr Charles from Border Control.'

They all exchanged nods of greeting.

'We didn't want to say anything on the phone, when Sergeant Singh rang to say you'd be along today to have a look at Staverton Airfield and asked did we know anything about Dennis Parks and his operation. The answer is yes, we do know Mr Parks and we've been working on him for a few weeks; and like all these things the less people who know, the better chance we've got of getting a result. Walls have ears round here. Anyway, I'll let Mr Charles explain.'

Mr Charles, a portly chap in his early fifties with glasses and a goatee beard, turned and took up the story as DS Williams started the car and they pulled out of the station car park onto the busy Gloucester City roads.

'Six months ago, we got reports from various Border Control offices that some of the illegals that had been arrested and questioned had said that they were flown in on a small plane, landed in the country and then taken in large vans and dropped off in various UK cities; all those illegals came from the Calais migrant camp known as The Jungle, which is close to the French end of the Channel Tunnel.

'So, we did a breakdown of all the air traffic coming into the UK from the Calais-Dunkerque airport, which is a small one; close to the camp, and with no border control. We whittled it down to three possible air freight companies that could be involved in this trafficking. We got four positive IDs of Dennis Parks from the illegals, so we've been monitoring him and his flights since then.'

'Why not arrest him?' said Gheeta. 'You seem to have enough evidence.'

Charles nodded resignedly.

'It's a dual investigation with the French police. They asked us to hold back and let the scam go on until their undercover people inside the camp could pinpoint the traffickers at that end, and then we could roll up the whole lot in one swoop, here and over there.'

Palmer wasn't one to let another investigation get in the way of his. He explained that he was investigating a quadruple murder case, and that currently all roads led to Dennis Parks being involved.

'So, you can see at present it's all a bit circumstantial,' he concluded. 'Which is why we need a positive ID of Mooney, Hilton or Angela Rathbone to tie it all up; and then, Mr Charles, I'm afraid we go in and arrest them on suspicion of murder, which I think trumps Mr Parks's little trafficking of illegals caper?'

DS Williams was first to agree.

'Bloody hell, four murders and a quantity of gold? Christ! Yes, I think it does override Parks's scam.'

'And you, Mr Charles?'

Palmer wanted everybody on board.

'Well, yes – yes, I have to admit it's a bit above my usual cases. I suppose really I ought to get out at the next bus stop, leave you to it and go back.'

No way was that going to happen. Palmer had no reason to not trust Mr Charles, but the urge to tell his Border Agency pals about what Parks might also be involved in as well as human trafficking would be a great temptation.

'No, Mr Charles – you are onboard with us on this one. You said you'd got enough to pull Parks in and were just letting him run for the French side; so if we go in, you can take him too. You're not losing anything, are you?'

'No, no that's right,' Charles agreed. 'We could take him down now and prosecute if it wasn't for the French operation.'

'Good. One way or another, it looks like Parks is on his way to prison.'

'We are coming up to the airfield now, sir.'

DS Williams indicated an open stretch of land in front of them, a half mile down the road on the left. The Control Tower was visible standing tall on one side, with a main runway and several spurs off it with a few small aircraft parked up. Along the perimeter fence at the far end of the field, various hangars and buildings were spaced out. DS Williams pulled into a layby which gave a good view of the field.

'Which is Parks's bit, Mr Charles?'

Mr Charles pointed into the distance, where a single-storey office block stood with a medium sized hangar either side.

'That's his firm, South Western Air Taxis – right over in the back corner. Well-positioned for privacy.'

Williams turned to Palmer.

'What do you want to do now, sir? I can get nearer by going on the back perimeter road if you want to. There's an industrial estate with a car park right on the other side of the road behind Parks's hangars – we'd be able to sit there and watch. It's the nearest we can get without standing out like a sore thumb. There's a pair of binoculars in the boot, so we should be able to see any comings and goings.'

'Okay,' Palmer agreed. 'You know the layout of the land. Get us as close as possible.'

Chapter 33

The view from the industrial estate car park was a good one; they could clearly see the front of Parks's hangars and offices. It was getting darker as the late afternoon light faded and the evening mist began to rise across the airfield. Far away in the distance, the headlights of cars on the M5 twinkled in double lines. Williams started the engine and ran the heater.

'What's the plan, sir?'

Palmer hadn't really thought of one just yet.

'Well, first off I want to know just who is in there. We're banking on Mooney, Hilton, Rathbone and Parks. We need to make sure there isn't anybody else.'

'We'll need a few more bodies if you're thinking of a raid, sir.'

Gheeta was stating the obvious, but knowing how long it could take to supply extra uniformed officers she couldn't see anything happening that night; more likely Palmer was thinking of a surprise entry in the early hours.

'And arrest warrants,' she added.

Palmer nodded and thought for a while.

'Okay. Nothing going on at present is there, so it looks like they've finished for the day anyway. So I think...'

He was cut short as Mr Charles's mobile hummed.

'Excuse me.'

Charles took it from his pocket, answered the call and had a short conversation before putting it back.

'That's interesting. It seems Parks has filed a flight plan to Europe for tomorrow – he plans to leave at seven in the evening. The manifest says Freight Only, no passengers.'

'To Calais?' Palmer asked.

'Yes, his usual three parcel pallets are coming off there. but then he's going onto Spain – to Malaga Airport, which is the nearest airport to Alviria.'

'What's so special about Alviria? More parcels being delivered?'

Charles smiled.

'No, it's not a freight airport – mainly tourist package holidays. I don't think it's the sort of place on the Costa del Sol you and I would choose to holiday at, Chief Superintendent; full of ex-pat villains, and currently undergoing a turf war between the Brits, the Russian Mafia and Dutch drug cartels. Six murders in the last four months.'

'How do you know all this? That sort of action seems a bit off beam for Border Control.'

'Three of our 'most wanted' people traffickers fled there when we got close to them; sort of place a face can disappear into with no questions asked, as long as you've got the money to grease a few palms – human palms that is, not the plant type.'

He grinned broadly at his own joke.

'Looks very nice, sir.'

Gheeta passed Palmer her laptop. She'd pulled up pictures of Alviria and its beaches.

'I can just see you and Mrs P. in your deckchairs taking in the sun and sea air.'

'I don't think so, Sergeant – we are more Devon and Cornwall. Mind you, I must say it does look nice.'

He passed the laptop back.

'Right then, if Parks is off to Spain tomorrow on a flight which isn't his normal run, then we can surmise he's taking our three suspects and their ill-gotten gains with him, and they intend to, as Mr Charles said, 'grease a few palms and disappear'. They've certainly got the money to do that, and Parks probably has a contact or two out there to set things up for them. So, it looks like we'd better get a raid arranged for tomorrow afternoon.'

He looked at DS Williams with questioning eyes.

'I can do that, sir,' Williams said. 'What about firearms?'

Palmer wasn't keen on firearms, but then he didn't know what Parks was like.

'Okay, but the proper boys – Tactical Firearms Unit personnel only; nobody else to have weapons except the standard issue lasers and pepper spray. There are only four of them, not an army.'

Gheeta suddenly had a thought.

'Doesn't Parks have any staff? Seems strange if he hasn't got engineers and the like, or even a receptionist.'

Williams shook his head.

'No, the airfield has a number of qualified staff that do all the maintenance on any aircraft housed here, private or company. That way they can be sure all the safety work is done, and all the CAA certificates are up to date. If they didn't, and say Parks or any of the other companies operating out of here had a prang and rammed into a party of visiting school kids, they could be done under the 'Duty of Care' legislation. Same with the fuel, it all comes from the field's own tanks which are situated underground, away on their own in a far corner. They can't have tanks of aviation fuel all over the place for obvious reasons. The Civil Aviation Authority runs a very tight ship on its airfields; accidents are scarce.'

'Hello! We have some movement, sir.'

The office door had opened, and two people came out; one of them had very bright red hair. Palmer raised the binoculars to his eyes.

'Well, hello Angela Rathbone – and that chap with you could be Mr Mooney.'

The couple stopped, hugged, and kissed.

'Definitely Mr Mooney.'

Then they got into a Honda CRV and drove off along the perimeter road. Palmer lowered the binoculars.

'I think that's all we need, Sergeant.'

He turned and spoke to Williams.

'If you could get a team sorted for tomorrow – half dozen plainclothes, three uniformed, and whatever the Tactical Firearms Commander thinks he needs. In the mean time we'd better find a hotel, Sergeant; no point in us travelling back to London and then back here again in the morning. You alright with that? No pressing engagement for tonight I hope?'

'Yes, that's fine with me sir.'

'Good.'

He turned back to Williams.

'Can you organise a pair of eyes to watch this place overnight and tomorrow until we go in? Let us know if anybody arrives or leaves?'

'No problem, sir. I'll do it now.'

Chapter 36

Evening was falling fast as Angela Rathbone zipped the last canvas holdall shut in the back room of Parks's office building. There were four large holdalls, each with the gold bars inside.

Mooney came in, dressed in smart, new casual clothes.

'Bonjour senorita.'

He did a twirl.

'Oh, how very smart.'

Angela laughed, and they gave each other a quick kiss.

'But make your mind up whether to go to France or Spain, okay? Bonjour is French, and senorita is Spanish, you chump.'

He twirled again.

'We can go anywhere we like. Money opens every door.'

'Spain will do for now.'

'Tomorrow, my angel, we shall be on the beach drinking cocktails.'

'Or if it all goes wrong we shall be in a Spanish jail, awaiting extradition. Don't get too far ahead of yourself, young man. Steady does it.'

He hugged her.

'Nothing will go wrong.'

'How long have we got?'

Mooney checked his watch.

'An hour. We are still okay for a seven o'clock take off – Parks wants us ready to board by six thirty. When we get to Spain it will be dark, and he's got somebody coming out to the plane when it lands with overalls for us.'

'Overalls?'

'They've got a Spanish courier company's name and logo on them. We put them over our clothes and anybody seeing us around the plane or in the airport will assume we are workers with that company. Then it's into a large van with a few parcels and these four bags and bingo!'

Outside the sound of vehicles arriving at speed and slewing to a halt on the gravel forecourt was followed by loud shouts of 'POLICE!', and the front office door bursting open as the Tactical Firearms and uniformed officers swarmed in to put an abrupt end to their vision of nirvana.

Mooney reacted quickly, taking a key off the wall hook and thrusting it into Rathbone's hand.

'Here, take the bags and go out the back; this is the key to the perimeter fence gate. Your car's in the industrial estate car park opposite.'

'What? What about you? Come with me!'

'Just go! I'll keep them occupied here. If the gold's not here they won't have a case against me. GO!'

She lifted two bags, and with an anguished look back at him hurried through the back door into the evening gloom and across the five yards of grass to the perimeter gate. She was shaking as she opened the lock. Behind her she could hear the sound of scuffling and sirens as more police cars arrived. She left the bags and rushed back for the other two; the adrenalin coursing through her body made them feel lighter than when she had pulled them out of the City Concrete office.

Two at a time she pulled, carried and stumbled with them across the perimeter road into the industrial estate car park to her car and then heaved them onto the back seat. Holding back the panic in her brain, she drove out with no idea of where to go.

hundred yards start and then followed, keeping at a discreet distance.

Chapter 40

It was early the following afternoon that Palmer and Singh both arrived at the office in Scotland Yard. Having had a very late night at Gloucester Police HQ, Palmer had insisted they had a car back to London and was home in the early hours. It was just gone three when he slipped into bed next to Mrs P., and a full hour later when his mind stopped churning over the facts of the case and he actually slept.

He turned from updating the progress board in the team room as Gheeta entered and unslung her shoulder bag onto the desk next to Claire, who was still trying to find connections between the names in the case, but without any luck so far. Palmer smiled at Gheeta.

'I thought I told you to have the day off, Sergeant?'

'You did sir, but I may as well be here trying to make head or tail of this case as standing in my lounge doing the same.'

She moved over beside him.

'I just can't get a pattern in my mind, guv – it's like a jigsaw with a piece missing. Or am I just missing something obvious?'

'No, you're not. I go along with you.'

He pointed to the board and used his finger as a pointer as he spoke.

'We get Sidney Fenn turning up dead in a plastic bag in London; then we become aware of Charles Plant, who suffered the same fate in Brighton. Both tie into Harry Robson and Finlay Robson, who then both get killed themselves. The thread between them all is the Leytons' looted gold. Then there are two unknown principal players, Mooney and Hilton, who disappear a bit sharpish when we want to talk to them. Next, Angela Rathbone does a bunk. We then get information that she and Mooney are an item, so perhaps they, together with Hilton, are the murderers of all four victims. We catch up with them and Parks; Parks has had phone calls from both Harry and Finlay Robson on the day

Mooney and Hilton disappeared. Why? What has he got to do with it?'

Gheeta shrugged.

'All in it together maybe? Harry Robson afraid we'd get Mooney or Hilton, who would put the finger on him for the Plant and Fenn murders, so he arranges through Parks to get them into a safe house?'

'No, I don't buy that – not with the Harry Robson I knew in the game. If he thought anybody was going to drop him in it they'd be in a plastic sack under fifty tons of concrete themselves, and pretty quickly.'

'So, as he didn't do that to Mooney and Hilton it would point to them all being in it together.'

'Yes, possibly. But you saw how Angela Rathbone and Harry Robson were acting in the City Concrete office – nothing in their manner towards each other would suggest to me they were in harmony on anything. No, I think we have two strands here: Harry and Finlay, and Mooney, Hilton and Rathbone. Maybe it started off with them all in it, but I wouldn't mind betting there was a split.'

'And Mooney and Hilton killed the Robsons?'

'Why not? They've been put out of harm's way in Gloucester. Angela Rathbone gives Mooney a bell and says Robson's been taken in for questioning, so Mooney and Hilton think he might drop them in it.'

'Or, if he got bail, take the gold and do a runner,' Gheeta interrupted.

'Yes, so either way they then have a good reason to break cover and get the gold themselves, and then get Parks to fly them quickly out. I'm sure he'd be receptive to a bar or two for his trouble.'

'So, perhaps they all met up at the office by coincidence on the night of Robson and Finlay's murders, and battle commenced?'

'The timeline is right. Angela Rathbone phones Mooney when Robson is brought in for questioning – that was late morning. He and Hilton get on their way back to City Concrete to get the gold from the safe before anybody else can; Robson gets bail, and gets Finlay to meet him there too so they can get the gold and scarper – and bingo; as you say, all four end up in the office at the same time, a few heated words, and battle commenced.'

'Where's Angela Rathbone during all this? Is she involved?'

'No, she is keeping her head down. Then Mooney would have rung her to tell her they'd killed Robson and Finlay and were off. But, if she'd gone with them back to Gloucester then, and not turned up for work the next morning it would have set our alarm bells ringing. No, she played it very cool.'

Claire turned from her screen and interrupted their train of thought.

'Sir, there's something a bit wrong here.'

They both moved beside her.

'This is the immediate forensic report on Angela Rathbone's death. It wasn't an accident – the car was set on fire.'

'What?' said Palmer as he leant towards the screen.

'Petrol was used as an accelerant. Must have been poured into the car – it wasn't petrol from the car's petrol tank because that was still intact, and none of the pipes were broken. The brigade had the fire out before it could explode.'

Gheeta inhaled deeply.

'So where did the petrol come from?'

'And another thing,' Claire added. 'They've recovered gold bars from the wreckage and the ditch.'

'Good,' Palmer smiled. 'We'd have a few very rich firemen in the Gloucester Brigade if they said they hadn't.'

'Ten bars, sir.'

'Ten? Only ten? Are you kidding?'

'No, just ten bars. And there's none on the forensic team's contents listing from Parks's buildings or the aircraft's interior that they were going to fly off in.'

Palmer and Gheeta looked at each other as their minds took in the information and came to the same conclusion.

'There's our missing piece of the jigsaw, Sergeant. Our missing piece is an unknown person.'

Claire was puzzled.

'I don't understand. What person?'

Gheeta sat down.

'All the gold – and we know it was about two hundred and thirty bars – had gone from Robson's safe, and Mooney and Hilton are the only ones that could have removed it. They and Angela Rathbone scarper to Parks with it; we do the raid on Parks, and she gets out the backdoor with the gold. Then she crashes; we know it was a forced crash now, not an accident, because of the petrol. So somebody drove her off the road and set fire to her and the vehicle, but not until they had taken out all the gold they could see, leaving just the ten bars forensics recovered.'

'And they would have to be quick,' Palmer added. 'With all that police activity and blue lights at Parks's place, it would only be a short window of time before Rathbone would be chased when she got out the back. If we had chased her instead of going around the other way to block her off, we'd have nabbed the killer in action. Damn!'

'I'll go through the City Concrete employees again with a fine-tooth comb,' Gheeta said as she turned on a computer. 'They are all ex-cons, so I suppose it could be any of them.'

'No, it would have to be somebody close to the Robsons or Angela Rathbone. They wouldn't have broadcast they'd got their mitts on all that gold; somebody either sussed it out or was part of the team from day one and we've missed them somehow. Either that or somebody was playing a waiting game, and was forced to act when the raid went in.'

'But there isn't anybody else.'

'There is somewhere. We've missed them so far, but there's another person somewhere. Somebody burnt Angela Rathbone and took the gold. I've got interviews booked downstairs with Mooney and Hilton later on; with a bit of luck, when they realise it's all over and the gold has gone, we might get a name. I'm going for a coffee. You two want one?'

They both nodded. Then Gheeta's email pinged.

'Aha!' she said, pointing to her screen. 'I asked the industrial estate management company by the airfield to email me a copy of their CCTV that covers the car park entrance for the evening. Might be interesting.'

'And it might not. I need that coffee, I won't be long.'

He left as Gheeta downloaded the file and ran it. When he returned with the coffees five minutes later, Gheeta's wide smile told him she'd found something.

'What have you got then?' he said as he gave them their coffees. 'Your smile gives you away.'

'Well, there could be two people to fill our missing person gap. Look at this.'

Palmer stood behind her as she ran the grainy CCTV file on screen.

'There, see?' Gheeta pointed. 'There's Angela Rathbone coming through the perimeter gate from the airfield. She's got two big shopping bags, which must be the gold bars; they look heavy. We lose her now as she crosses the road and comes into the car park and goes under the camera's position. Then she goes back for the other two bags, and again we lose her under the camera's position.'

They waited as nothing happened and the camera showed the gate; then a car drove out and turned left.

'There she goes. I'll fast forward 'cause nothing happens for fourteen minutes.'

The picture whizzed through until Gheeta clicked her cursor to stop the *fast forward* mode as a car came into the screen from the left.

'And that is coming from the accident. Nobody passed us on that lane, and that is not Angela Rathbone's car.'

'Well it couldn't be, could it?' Palmer agreed. 'Her car is going up in flames down the lane. And seeing that nobody entered the lane from the end we had blocked off, that must be the killer; somebody who had been waiting for her down the lane, and seized the opportunity when she did a runner as the raid went in.'

Gheeta held up a hand to silence him.

'Hang on, watch…'

As the car passed by the car park and disappeared off the screen to the right, another car – no headlights – slowly came into the camera's view and exited from the car park to the right.

'So, who is that then? An accomplice? Doesn't seem to be as it isn't in a hurry, and left a good few seconds behind the killer's car going past.'

Palmer sipped his coffee.

'Could be following it then, keeping a safe distance.'

'It's a Jag,' Claire observed.

'How do you know that?' Palmer asked.

'My dad had one for years – mad on them, he was. I'll never forget the shape. That was a Jaguar, sir. Bet my mortgage on it.'

Chapter 41

Sylvia Fenn was tired, very tired. She sat at her kitchen table, looking at the four bags of gold bars she'd carried in through the back door under cover of darkness and heaved up onto it. She took a bar from a bag and put it on the table. A smile crossed her lips as she looked at it.

Funny how things work out – two hundred thousand in cash upstairs, and God knows how much here in gold. Always planned to steal Finlay's money, but the gold is a bonus – a bloody big bonus! Just have to sit tight now for some time, let it all cool down – keep playing the widow, and then when the time is right... hello, life of luxury.

A sharp ring at the front door bell startled her from her dreams.

Bit late for callers; nobody expected. Could be the police.

She quickly took off her coat.

She'd show them into the front room if it was; act surprised – just going to bed...

She walked through into the hall and opened the front door. Nobody there.

Bloody kids larking around...

She relaxed, shut the door and clicked the lock into place.

If they ring again, I'll ignore it. A nice cup of tea, and then a hot soak and into bed.

She climbed the stairs and went into the bathroom and turned on the hot tap in the bath.

Life is good. Better hide that gold though, just in case.

She went back downstairs and into the kitchen, and nearly jumped out of her skin. Sitting at the table was a lady in a gabardine coat and headscarf, her hands firmly holding a double-barrelled shotgun that pointed menacingly at Sylvia. She froze. Margaret Leyton spoke quietly but very firmly.

'Do sit down. Not on the chair – on the floor if you would, with your back against the wall. One silly move and I'll shoot you.'

Sylvia Fenn was shaking as she lowered herself to the floor and shifted back against the wall.

'Who are you?'

Margaret Leyton pulled a kitchen chair from the table and sat facing her.

'My name is Margaret Leyton. My husband is Stanley Leyton; you may have heard of him, he's an MP? No? Oh well, he's obviously not as well known as he thinks he is.'

'W…w…what do you want? Why…why…?'

'Why am I here? That's easy, I'm here to collect what is mine – gold bars that were stolen from me and my husband, and seem to have ended up on your kitchen table. These gold bars.'

She slid the bar on the table to the edge, and using one hand picked it up and put it back into one of the bags. Sylvia's mind was racing as she desperately tried to think of a way out. There was only one: sacrifice the gold.

'Take them… Take them all – just take them and go.'

'Oh, I intend to. You know, I would have thought it would have been harder to find you.'

'What do you mean?'

'Charles Plant. Remember him, the bullion dealer from Brighton? He and your husband Sidney worked together on several occasions.'

'Yes. Yes, I knew Charles. Not very well, but I met him a few times. Why?'

'He and I were… lovers.'

She laughed.

'Sounds a ridiculous name for two middle-aged adults, doesn't it? 'Lovers'. But we were – and we had plans too, such lovely plans. He and Sidney had hit the bullseye with our gold; shift it out slowly and nobody would be any the wiser. It was all going perfectly; and then your Sidney got greedy and got the Robsons involved, and it all went wrong. You had a thing going with the lad, Finlay.'

'I didn't, I…'

'Don't try to deny it. Charles knew all about it, and so did your husband. Oh yes, Sidney knew – he told Charles he knew. But he was going to let it go – keep the money coming in, and then sort out a divorce from you afterwards. Didn't you know? I thought you might have found out he knew, and that was why you and Finlay had him and my Charles killed, to keep all the money.'

'No, no I had nothing to do with any killings!'

'Really? Now why don't I believe that? It's all ended up rather well for you, hasn't it? Here you are, all alone with all the gold to yourself. Bingo, a full house.'

'I didn't plan this, I wasn't involved in any of the murders.'

'Really? What about the poor lady at the airfield – the one toasted in her own car?'

'I don't know what you are talking about. What lady? What airfield?'

Margaret Leyton laughed a cynical laugh.

'Oh, do give me some credence. I was there, I saw you.'

She took a deep breath.

'You see when Charles was killed, and my dreams killed with him, I wanted to know why. And then the Robsons paid us a visit and I realised why: greed, pure greed. We had the police come around and so I sat tight for a while. Then seeing the Robson's murders on the news, it was obvious things were moving along at a pace – and if I didn't act my gold would disappear quickly with somebody, and I'd never see it again.

'So, I came up to London to poke around a bit and see what I could find out. My husband has a flat in Charing Cross – one of the perks of a rural MP's life, the poor old taxpayer coughs up the rent each month. Anyway, I thought that secretary woman with the bright red hair would lead me to answers.'

'Angela.'

'Yes, Angela – Angela Rathbone; and lead me she damn well did. I followed her from the City Concrete place on the morning after the Robsons' murders; nobody noticed me, the place was swarming with police and the usual crowd of ghouls who race to any murder scene. I followed her to her boyfriend Mooney's place, and guess what? As I was sitting parked up, watching her load their clothes into her car, somebody else was watching too – you. I didn't cotton on until I followed her from Mooney's a few cars back; and then I noticed you in front of me, taking every turn she took; you even filled up before the M4 as she did. I had no idea who you were; first I thought you might be plainclothes police, but then two and two made four – especially when you parked up in the industrial estate behind the airfield. You had no suspicion that anybody else was interested in her did you, eh? You hadn't noticed me, also intent on them.

'You followed them to the restaurant in Gloucester and when they left you booked into a hotel; I didn't, I followed them back to the airfield after their meal. It was pretty clear that they had the gold and not you, so I wanted to stay close to it, just in case they moved it. I had a most uncomfortable night in the car in that car park; and then I watched all day, trying to work out how to get into the place, grab the gold and get away. Then guess what? All hell breaks loose as that Detective Palmer led a raid on them; and who should come out of the back door but Angela, with four large bags of gold bars. Well, I guessed that's what they were, the way she was struggling with them – and looking at these same two bags on the table, I guessed right. She came straight over the road and loaded them into her car – I hadn't noticed it in the car park. And off she went.

'Bit of a quandary for me. Should I follow her? Probably not, as the police would have sealed off that road further down. So there I was, tired, hungry, and now sure that she would be arrested and the gold would be found and go to the Treasury. But no! Suddenly there's a red glow in the distance down the lane; and then guess whose car comes from that direction straight past me, eh? Your car. I assume you'd been waiting for her?'

It was pointless for Sylvia to further deny anything.

'No, not really. I was parked in a layby so I could keep an eye on what was happening. Like you, I was trying to work out a plan to get the gold when the police raid happened. I saw Angela's car coming towards me in the gloom, no lights, so I guessed she'd got away with the gold; and like you, I thought the lane would have been blocked further down by the police at the main road. So I pulled out as she came round a bend to stop her, but she was going too fast, lost it on the gravel when she put the brakes on, and went into the deep ditch.'

'So, you did what? Caved in her head, took the gold, and set the car on fire with her inside?'

'No, no…'

Sylvia Fenn needed a solid explanation; Leyton couldn't possibly know what really happened in the lane. She could still save this situation.

'No, she was trapped inside and the tank had split. I tried, but couldn't get her out. So I got as much gold as I could, and knowing the police would see the flames I drove off the other way… Why don't we split it? Nobody will know.'

'Split it between us, you mean?'

'Yes, then go our separate ways. There's enough for two.'

'There is indeed. But why should I split *my* gold with *you*? Oh no, that's not going to happen.'

She patted one of the bags like a beloved pet.

'It's all going home with mummy. All of it.'

'Okay.'

Sylvia was thinking of Finlay's money hidden upstairs; time to cut her losses.

'Okay, just take it and go.'

'But what about you?'

'I said I don't want it. Just go – you won't hear from me again, I promise you that.'

'Oh, I can promise *you* that I won't hear from you again as well. It's time to say goodbye'.

Sylvia felt a surge of relief as Margaret Leyton stood and smiled down at her. From close quarters, the discharge from both barrels of the shotgun left a large cavity in Sylvia Fenn's chest where her heart and lungs had previously lived.

Chapter 42

'So, who is the missing link then?'

Mrs P. wiped round the kitchen bowl in the Palmers' kitchen sink, as Palmer put away the last plate and hung the wiping-up cloth over the oven handle . She feigned interest in his present case as she did with them all, but after forty years of marriage to Palmer there wasn't a lot left in the serial killer world that she – and he – hadn't seen before.

'You've missed a fork.'

She pointed to a solitary fork, waiting in the bowl to be dried. It was a long-standing ritual in their house that she did the washing-up and he did the wiping up. Palmer retrieved the cloth and finished the job.

'No idea. It's got to be somebody on the edge of all this who's kept a damn good low profile. We will find him – or her. We always do sooner or later.'

'Sooner, I hope. You've got enough bodies piling up already.'

Palmer had made sure he'd got home for his evening meal that day, as he'd seen the prepared moussaka in the fridge when he took out the milk for his bran flakes breakfast. Mrs P.'s moussaka was – like most of her home-cooked meals – well worth making the effort for; and after missing out on toad in the hole, he was determined the moussaka wouldn't get away.

Mrs P. gave the kitchen a once-over, seemed satisfied, and looked at the clock.

'Right, I'm off to see Benji; he's out tomorrow, so I said I'd pop into his place, put the central heating on low, and take him in some clean clothes. And while I remember, if you're home for tea tomorrow bring in a take-away; he's out at five and I said I'd pick him up.'

'Oh, how very neighbourly of you,' Palmer said sarcastically. 'I seem to remember when I was discharged from hospital with my leg and shoulder in plaster I had to get the bus home.'

'Justin, he's had a new hip; he can't walk far yet, and he can't put any weight on it. You only had half your leg in plaster – and anyway, you discharged yourself without telling us so how could we have picked you up?'

'I would have told you, if you or any of my wonderful family had bothered to visit the day before.'

'You were only in for three days, and you told us not to visit. You were very firm that you didn't want any visitors; you said you wanted a peaceful few days. So that's what you got. Anyway, I came the first day and all you said was 'did Barcelona win?' and then went back to sleep.'

Palmer thought silence the best option. His reasons for being home were, in truth, twofold: one, Mrs P.'s moussaka; and two, Barcelona versus Real Madrid on Sky, the first of the annual 'El Clasico' matches. He was thanking his lucky stars he wasn't expected to visit Benji too, or he might have had to feign some illness and insist she went alone. After his family, Palmer's loyalty list was Daisy the dog, Barcelona, Crystal Palace, and then his job; and sometimes he thought maybe Daisy the dog should top the list anyway.

Mrs P. disappeared and returned a few minutes later in a winter coat, outdoor shoes and a headscarf.

'Right then, if you get anything from the fridge make sure you close the door properly; and take Daisy round the block about nine o'clock. Poop bags are in the cupboard under the sink.'

A quick peck on the cheek, and she was gone. Palmer took a bottle of Stowfield cider from the fridge, making sure the door was shut afterwards, and nearly tripped over Daisy, who had seen Mrs P. leave and knew Palmer was an easy touch for a 'chewy'.

'Oh, I wonder what you are after you crafty old thing.'

He gave her a pat and a 'chewy' from the cupboard above the worktop, and together they padded into the lounge and flopped onto the sofa, where Palmer rescued the remote control from down the side of the cushion and flicked on Sky Sports.

He settled back, kicked off his slippers and farted loudly – something he didn't dare do if Mrs P. was around. The teams were coming out, the sofa was very comfortable, the cider was going down a treat. And the telephone was ringing.

Chapter 43

Gheeta and Palmer moved to the side of the Fenn front garden path and onto the unkempt small flower bed, as Sylvia Fenn's body bag was carried by two white suited forensic officers past them on a stretcher to the waiting morgue van.

'At least it's not a red plastic bag guv,' Gheeta said, catching his eye as it passed them. They made their way into the hall of the house which was a hive of activity, with SOCO and fingertip search teams going about their work. They put on shoe protectors and met Reg Frome as he came down the narrow stairs. Palmer shook his outstretched hand.

'You know Reg, the one constant in these murders is that you are always at the scene. Hope you've got alibis, 'cause we might try and pin them on you if we don't get a break soon; not having much luck so far. What have you got for me then?'

Frome laughed.

'Not a lot, Justin. Double-barrelled shot gun wound, weapon discharged close to the chest. Seems she was in a seated position against the wall in the kitchen. No motive other than murder. Doesn't appear to be anything taken but that's your job, not mine. We're dusting the place for prints to run through the system, and guess what.'

'There aren't any?'

'Don't know yet, but there are definitely footprints around the back door. Size six.'

'What? Same shoes as before?'

'No, unfortunately – these are shoes, not trainers. Same size though.'

'Who rang it in?'

'Newspaper boy was delivering one of those free papers along the street and noticed there was a flood of water coming out under the front door. He couldn't get an answer, so he went round the back and found the body. He's quite shook up, poor lad; they've got a WPC with him and she'll get a statement when he gets over the shock. The water was coming from the bath; the lady was obviously running a bath when she was interrupted and left the tap on.'

He slipped off his shoe protectors.

'Right then, I've been on since six this morning so I'm off home to bed. The rest of my team will finish up here tonight, and I'll get the results emailed to you asap tomorrow.'

They bade him goodnight and turned their attention to the house.

'Well, where do we start sir? And what are we looking for?'

'I've no idea, Sergeant; no idea at all. All we can say is that she was the wife of John Fenn who's been bumped off, and now she has too. Why? I don't know. Perhaps she knew too much and whoever is after this gold had to shut her up?'

An officer came to the top of the stairs and called down.

'I think you ought to come and have a look at this, sir.'

Palmer's heart sank.

'Not another body I hope.'

He turned to Gheeta.

'You go, Sergeant. My sciatica is playing up, and those stairs look a bit steep.'

Gheeta laughed and climbed the stairs. A young search officer checking the drawers on a small telephone table in the hall turned to watch her perfect backside as she ascended the stairs. Palmer tapped him on the shoulder and gave him his stone-cold stare.

'Don't even think about it sonny, or you'll be doing the Brick Lane night beat for the next ten years.'

The officer returned quickly to his task. Gheeta was gone from view for hardly a minute when she reappeared at the top of the stairs.

'Guess what, sir.'

'Don't tell me… gold bars?'

'No, but close. Two hundred grand in used twenties.'

Chapter 44

The team room was busy. It was ten o'clock the next day, and Palmer had called in all his regular team officers who were available off shift or could be pinched from other duties. They stood around, some looking at the progress chart, some drinking machine coffee from plastic cups and trying to get comfortable on hard wooden chairs; others kept on from the night shift stifled yawns, and hoped they'd get out on the road and clear up whatever they were going to be asked to do quickly and get home for some sleep.

Palmer brought them to order by slapping a clipboard onto a desk top.

'Right lads, sorry if calling you in has buggered up any plans, but I really want to get a handle on this case; and I know your wonderful expertise in crime-solving will help me get it.'

He smiled sarcastically at the barrage of raspberries and loud coughs that greeted this remark and continued.

'DS Singh has given you all a quick rundown on what's been going on, and to be honest we've not got any solid leads as to who is behind these murders. You've been split into teams of four, and this is the work load for each team. Team one?'

Hands were raised.

'Right, you do the house to house on last night's victim's street; if you don't get an answer make a note so we can go back later. Team two?'

Different hands were raised,

'You lot visit every shop and office on roads that lead into that street and get a look at any CCTV from last night, flag up anything that doesn't look right; and especially look for a Jaguar heading towards or from the street.

'Team three, you're all CID, so I want pressure put on your snouts. I want to know if there's any buzz about gold bullion, about some of the Brinks-Mat stuff surfacing; see who's suddenly got a bit active in that market – lean on the fences, see if anybody's getting quotes on shifting a few kilos.

'Right lads and lasses, that's it; pass back any leads, any new information, in fact anything – no matter how small – to DS Singh on your mobiles, so we can log it on the computer and send up a daily report to the top floor of more than half a page.'

A distinct murmur went round the room at the mention of 'daily report' and faces smiled. Palmer knew exactly what all that was about.

'Alright, alright, calm down. Yes, I know, I'm doing – or should I say, Sergeant Singh is doing for me departmental daily reports, and you all know my thoughts on them. But I've been hauled over the coals about them and their absolute importance to the force. Gives the top floor something to do all day,'

Agreeable laughter greeted that sarcastic aside.

'So, we need all the information you can get so upstairs can see how hard we work and come to their senses, so we don't have to spend important investigation time on writing flipping daily reports! Right, off you go – and be careful; five dead already, so don't you be the sixth.'

Wooden chair legs scraped the old lino flooring as the teams stood to leave; many who'd been roused from a long overdue sleep stretched their arms above their heads and yawned before shuffling out the door, clutching their files and donning their jackets. Palmer knew that if he bothered to walk down Victoria Street in ten minutes time he'd find half of them in Costa Coffee, waking themselves up with a dose of caffeine.

Sergeant Singh beckoned him over to the computer terminal she was working on.

'I've got Sylvia Fenn's phone records here, guv. GPS data says she made a call in Gloucester the same evening we were there; or at least her phone was used to make that call.'

'Did she now? A call to where?'

He slipped off his jacket and pulled up a chair beside her.

'Don't know where guv, but we know who to.'

'Who?'

'Rathbone.'

Palmer sat forward in his chair.

'You're kidding me.'

'No, Forensics got Rathbone's mobile from the burnt-out car and were somehow able to get her number and trace calls to and from it on her network's log history database.'

Palmer raised his eyebrows and looked directly at Singh.

'Forensics did all that, did they?'

She smiled, knowing she couldn't pull the wool over his eyes.

'Well… Forensics got the number; I got the data.'

Palmer knew damn well Singh had used one of her 'not altogether legal' bespoke computer programmes to hack into the mobile network's data.

'You ever heard of the Data Protection Act, Sergeant?'

Gheeta made a great show of thinking hard.

'No sir, can't say I have.'

'Hmm… funny that, 'cause neither have I.'

He gave a wink, then rose and went over to the progress board. Gheeta followed. Palmer picked up a felt tip and drew a line connecting Angela Rathbone to Sylvia Fenn.

'It's beginning to fall into place; the pieces of the jigsaw are coming together a bit now. Looks like Rathbone and Mrs Fenn knew each other. Rathbone was in with Mooney, who was partners with Hilton, and they were both part of the Robson gang. But what's two hundred grand doing in the bottom of Mrs Fenn's wardrobe?'

Claire swung road and called over.

'It's not her's, sir – it was Finlay's. Look at this.'

They both crossed back to Claire, who was scrolling down her PC screen.

'Reg Frome has emailed an advance Forensics report on Sylvia Fenn's place. Seems the wardrobe had quite a few shirts, a couple of suits and two pairs of shoes in it that belonged to Finlay; got his DNA all over them, as has the money.'

Palmer inhaled deeply.

'Well I'm blowed – the bugger was shacked up with Sylvia Fenn. No wonder he wanted Mr Fenn out of the way. How did we miss that?'

'Well, we didn't have him on our radar for very long, guv – before he was incinerated. But it all fits, doesn't it?'

'It does; a classic example of thieves falling out. But that still leaves somebody out there that pumped two barrels into Sylvia Fenn in her kitchen.'

He stroked his chin.

'Why didn't they take the money? The only reason is that they couldn't have known it was there, and they'd come for one thing, and one thing only – to kill her.'

'Hang on, sir.'

Claire was reading the screen.

'There are traces of gold on the kitchen table at Fenn's.'

'So that's what the killer came for; she had the gold at the house and somebody came to get it. Things got out of hand, and bang-bang.'

He crossed back to the progress chart and drew a line joining Sylvia Fenn to Finlay Robson.

'But that doesn't tell us who killed her.'

'This might, guv.'

Gheeta was working at another computer beside Claire. Palmer crossed back.

'I'll get dizzy going back and forth in a minute. What have you got now?'

'The current English Heritage tourist brochure for Sussex.'

'Very nice. Planning a holiday, are we?'

Gheeta ignored the remark.

'Sort of thing tourists pick up at their hotels or off the tourist information sites. But look closely; can you see what I can see? Guess who's on the front page in full colour?'

On screen was a colour photo of The Manor House, Hove – the Leyton's abode. Standing in front with their dogs at their feet, Stanley and Margaret Leyton smiled at the camera, Stanley's double-barrel shotgun hung over one arm. The strapline read: 'An English MP at Home'.

Palmer leant forward for a closer look.

'I can see the Leytons at home looking very friendly. What am I missing?'

'Corner of the Manor House.'

Gheeta flicked a pointing finger to the lawn beside the house, and beyond it to where a green car was parked. It was hardly visible in the picture, so she zoomed in on it. Claire leant forward and was sure.

'That's a Jag, sir. Hundred percent sure.'

Palmer looked at Gheeta in silence as he sat down, his brain racing to put the right pieces of the jigsaw in the right places.

'The Leytons? No, surely not.'

Gheeta didn't have the same regard for the English elite.

'Why not? It's their gold, their passport to financial stability, and their green Jag and shotgun.'

Palmer nodded.

'It would fit, would make sense.'

He paced the room.

'Okay, start digging; see what you can come up with on them.'

Claire leant forward again to examine the picture.

'That's a crap wig he's wearing.'

'Syrup,' Gheeta said.

'What?' said Claire, wondering what syrup had to do with it.

'Wig, syrup of fig – it's cockney rhyming slang,' Gheeta explained. 'Being a Cockney by proxy I know all the slang.'

Claire was laughing.

'Cockney by proxy, what's that?'

'Our DS lives in that well know Cockney area called the Barbican,' Palmer answered. 'So she's adopting the language in order to relate with the locals.'

He checked his watch.

'Anyway, I've got an appointment in the interview room with Mr Parks in five minutes, so I'd better get down the apples and pears or they'll be on the dog and bone. Can't leave the diamond geezer on his Tom Malone sitting on his Khyber pass, can I?'

Chapter 45

Palmer's interviews with Mooney and Hilton did not reveal anything new, as both had hit the 'no comment' button to answer all questions. He had hoped Parks might be more forthcoming; he wasn't.

'Mr Parks,' Palmer said, his exasperation at the *no comment* answers becoming apparent. 'Money laundering is a very serious charge. Transporting ingots of gold out of the country without customs or Bank of England clearance is called money laundering. Flying suspects wanted in connection with a murder enquiry out of the country, on a flight you listed as 'Freight', is also a serious felony. Both these charges, if proved – and I think you can see how easy that will be – could lead to a minimum jail term of twenty-two years. It would help your case substantially if you were to answer my questions. What was the nature of the phone call you received from Harry Robson, and the one later that same day from Finlay Robson? What did they want?'

'No comment'.

Palmer reached and clicked off the interview recorder and stood up.

'See you in twenty-two years, Mr Parks.'

He left the interview room and gave the coffee machine outside a frustrated kick. The coffee machine responded to the assault by releasing a torrent of hot water where a cup should have been waiting but wasn't, so it splashed out over Palmer's trousers. The duty officer in the corridor stifled a laugh.

Palmer climbed the staircase to his floor slowly, trying to focus on what move to make next in the case; usually by this time in a case the suspect had been identified and the chase was on. Assistant Commissioner Bateman's daily report sheet for today was going to be short; very short indeed.

He gave himself a smile and decided to make amends to the coffee machine in the basement by buying three cups from its brother in the corridor outside his team room, and treating DS Singh and Claire to a cup of the dishwater it dispensed under the guise of 'latte'.

Chapter 46

'Stupid, stupid people!'

Palmer was angry as he came back into the team room, his hands cuddling the three cups.

'What the hell does Park's think he's going to gain by keeping quiet, eh? He's going to be listed as a hostile witness and the judge will throw the book at him and send him down for a long time. Here.'

He passed the coffees out to Gheeta and Claire. Gheeta looked up from her screen.

'I take it Parks was no help then, sir?'

'None, absolutely none.'

'Could be that he, Mooney and Hilton think that's the safest thing to do; especially if they know Robson was connected with Brinks-Mat and he's been murdered. So if they think the gold's come from that heist...?'

Palmer nodded slowly.

'Good point Sergeant, good point. No reason to think they know about the Leytons though, is there? All they know is that a load of gold turns up from Robson and that Robson has previous with Brinks; and you don't mess about with the Brinks mob. Yes, a good point.'

Gheeta dismissed the thought with a wave of her hand.

'Anyway guv, I think there's something else you might want to chat with the Leytons about.'

'Something else?'

Gheeta nodded.

'I checked with the Treasury. The Leytons turned in three ingots.'

'Three.'

Palmer raised his eyebrows.

'They had ten left after Robson's visit, didn't they?'

'So they said guv, yes.'

Palmer took a long gulp of coffee and pulled a disgusted face.

'Yuck… You know, I'm trying very hard not to associate one of our English Members of Parliament and his lady wife to a series of murders over stolen Nazi gold bars. I really am trying very hard, but my head is telling me they are in it up to their bloody posh necks.'

'So is the evidence, guv.'

Palmer nodded.

'I think I'd better pop upstairs on this one. If we go after one of Her Majesty's Members of Parliament and we don't do it by the book, some smart-arsed lawyer will undoubtedly use that down the line as an excuse to get any case we might bring against them thrown out on a technicality.'

Palmer wasn't going to put himself in the position where, should things go wrong, he would take the hit. If he alerted Assistant Commissioner Bateman to what was happening and cleared it with him, then Bateman – being the senior officer – would take the flack. Nothing should go wrong, but MPs hadfriends in high places; and the public gravy train they all fed off always had a strong old boys network protecting its members.

Chapter 47

Palmer sat opposite Assistant Commissioner Bateman at the large modern desk in the AC's office.

'It's very circumstantial, Justin; no sightings of the Leytons at any of the crime scenes, no fingerprints or phone records.'

He raised his eyes from Palmer's file of daily reports.

'But it's very damning as circumstantial – very damning. I think there's enough there to at least have an official chat with them under caution and see what they say. Keep it low key; if the tabloids got wind of it, all hell would break loose.'

Palmer nodded. He'd never known Bateman back him before; but then he'd never asked him to before. He'd always thought of the AC as an administrator, not a copper. This was a different side of the AC, and a side Palmer liked – much to his annoyance.

'DS Singh has checked with the MP's office and he's at the House all day today, sir. I think I'll get an appointment for this afternoon and see what happens.'

'Okay, but softly, softly; and keep me in the loop.'

Chapter 48

'Bit cramped in here, isn't it?'

Palmer and Singh followed Stanley Leyton MP into his official House of Commons office; a small cramped room with four desks, several bookshelves all unevenly stacked with files, and every surface covered with various papers and more files. Leyton laughed.

'Three of us share this office Detective Superintendent, plus our researchers. I was all for taking over the Athletes Accommodation block at the London Olympics Park, as were most MPs; but the Treasury blocked that in their financial cuts, so this is where we work.'

He squashed himself behind a desk, using one hand to steady his wig as he ducked below a wall shelf and waved an offering hand at two rather old plastic and steel chairs.

'Do sit down. I would say 'make yourself at home', but I have no doubt your homes would put this place to shame, eh?'

He laughed at his own joke and sat down.

'Right then, what can I do for you? I've asked the other members I share with to give us half an hour.'

He sat back in his chair and made a steeple with his fingers, like a headmaster waiting for Palmer to explain his bad behaviour. Gheeta quietly pressed the record button on her laptop, guessing what was coming. Palmer was not one for beating about the bush, and hit hard straight off.

'Well sir, you do not have to say anything, but it may harm your defence if you do not mention when questioned something which you rely on in court. Anything you do say can be given in evidence.'

He paused for a second as Leyton's expression relayed shock, and the finger steeple collapsed.

'What have you done with the gold, sir?'

Leyton stammered out a sentence.

'I, err... what the... Err, hang on – the gold?'

'Yes sir, the gold.'

Gheeta noted Palmer was in cold steel mode – direct attack, and no prisoners taken.

'You said you had ten bars when we visited you, which you were going to deposit with the Treasury.'

'We did.'

'You deposited three bars, sir. What happened to the rest?'

'The Treasury people came and took them. I wasn't there, I was in the House the rest of that week; haven't been back since. We are very busy here at this time of year, rushing things through before the break. I have a London flat, I've been staying there. The wife and I moved into a hotel the day after your visit – didn't want the mother-in-law to know about all this; and when I spoke to Margaret she told me they had collected the bars.'

'They collected three bars, sir. Do you know a company called City Concrete and Demolition?'

'No, no I don't think so.'

'Or a lady called Angela Rathbone, or two chaps called Mooney and Hilton?'

'No, no I don't know them. What is all this about?'

'It's about five murders all connected to your gold. Do you have a double-barrel shot gun, sir?'

'Yes, used to shoot the grouse in Scotland. I have a shotgun licence for it, I haven't used it for… oh, at least four years.'

'And a green Jaguar car; do you own a green Jaguar car?'

'No, no that's Margaret's; her pride and joy. I'm not allowed to drive that.'

He paused as his brain took in the implications of Palmer's questions.

'Has something happened? Has it been stolen? Why are you asking about my gun?'

'The car has been caught on CCTV at several points during our investigation of the murders, sir – one of which was executed with a double-barrel shotgun. I'm waiting for the results of an ANPR trawl, which I believe will verify that the car was at the crime scenes beyond any doubt.'

'ANPR?'

'Automatic Number Plate Recognition. We have thousands of cameras all over the country, noting every car that passes.'

Leyton visibly slumped in the chair as the reason for the questions slowly became apparent.

'Oh my God. Margaret, what have you done? Oh my God, you stupid woman…'

Palmer and Singh exchanged a glance, before Leyton regained his composure.

'I think I'd better ask for a lawyer, don't you?'

'We will arrange it for you at the Yard, sir. Is your wife in London?'

'No, no she's in Brighton; she rarely comes up here.'

'Okay, so if you'd like to give Sergeant Singh your mobile phone and put anything you might need together you will accompany us now please.'

'Do I have to?'

The MP's bluster was returning.

'Am I under arrest? Have you a warrant?'

Palmer's eyes re-adopted their cold steel mode and bore into Leyton's.

'At the moment sir, you are helping us with our enquiries in a voluntary way. If you would prefer to be handcuffed and frog-marched out of here by a couple of uniformed officers then I can arrange it, and arrest you as a suspect in a serial murder case involving stolen gold. From what you have told us in response to my questions so far, I would advise you to keep quiet until we get you a solicitor at the Yard.'

It was pretty clear by Leyton's answers that he was not a serial killer, but Palmer had no intention of letting him contact his wife who, it appeared, could well be.

The journey to the Yard was made in complete silence. Leyton was processed by the duty officer in the Custody Suite, given access to a duty solicitor, as his own personal lawyer was in court all day, and was refused bail as his freedom could give him the opportunity to influence others in the case.

Palmer followed DS Singh into their office and flipped his trilby onto the hat stand like James Bond; only unlike Bond he missed and had to pick it up off the floor and hang it up by hand.

'Well, well, well…'

He sat at his desk and pushed his chair up on its back legs, so the top settled nicely into the groove in the plaster wall he'd made over the years, and swung his legs onto the desk before saying it again: 'Well, well, well…'

DS Singh flopped into her softer desk chair, unslinging her shoulder bag.

'It all happened today, guv. This morning we started with nothing, and this afternoon we have a chief suspect and enough evidence to make an arrest.'

'And tonight we'd better get down to Brighton and make that arrest, before Mrs Leyton cottons on that we're onto her.'

Palmer put on a Cockney accent.

'Funny old game, ain't it.'

'What, guv?'

'Jimmy Greaves.'

'Who, guv?'

'Never mind.'

He pulled open a desk drawer and searched for some change.

'Fancy a coffee? I'm parched. Then we'd better get moving down the A3 to Brighton. Give the Sussex boys a call and ask for a couple of uniforms and a Tactical Firearms Unit to meet us somewhere near the Leytons' place – not too near though, don't want her getting jittery with that shotgun. And I'd better give Mrs P. a call and tell her to expect me when she sees me. What about you? Anything planned for tonight you need to call anybody about?'

'Nah, nuffink planned mate. Was going to get on the old dog and bone and order up a Ruby Murray and then get off to Bedfordshire a bit early.'

She gave him a wide grin, which he returned.

Chapter 49

'Is this a sea mist?'

Palmer waved his arms to waft away the dank light fog that hung over them in the evening gloom. He'd been driven down to Brighton with DS Singh and was standing beside their unmarked squad car with two uniformed officers from the Sussex Force, DS Jones from Sussex CID, plus a Tactical Firearms Commander called Handly and two of his armed officers. Handly and the firearms officers were head to toe in combat dark uniforms and helmets with visors, but they'd left their weapons inside their unmarked van. They all listened intently as Palmer explained the situation.

'So,' he concluded. 'She might well just be an easy arrest; no problem, just in and out. We do have the element of surprise on our side. Or, on the other hand, she might flip and start banging off that shotgun in a panic. The entrance to the Manor is five hundred yards down the road here, so I will go in by car with DS Singh and the uniformed constables, and hopefully come out with Margaret Leyton without any trouble. But just in case it goes pear-shaped, I want close back up from your lads please, Commander.'

Handly nodded.

'We'll keep out of sight by the gate, sir. Hopefully you won't need us, but at the first sign of that shotgun hit this.'

He handed Palmer a pressurized air horn the size of a felt tip.

'Press the button and hit the floor; it'll scream loudly, and we'll come in fast shooting at anybody standing, so hit the floor.'

Palmer took it and put it in his pocket.

'Right then, let's go.'

He got into the front passenger seat as DS Singh got into the back, and the driver took the car slowly towards the Leyton's drive, followed by the uniformed officers in their panda car.

They turned into the drive slowly and cut through the fog, seeing the eerie shape of the Manor House emerging from it in the distance.

'Looks like its empty, sir.'

Gheeta leant forward between the front seats, peering intently through the windscreen.

'Not very inviting, is it?' Palmer noted. 'Like one of those places from a Hammer film.'

'What film, sir?'

'Hammer… Never mind, you're too young. No lights on, so perhaps she's out.'

Gheeta grimaced at the weather swirling around them.

'Mad to go out on a night like this.'

Palmer checked the facts.

'They have moved back from the hotel, haven't they?'

'Yes guv, I checked,' Gheeta assured him. 'They left it the day after the Robson's murders; must have seen all about it on the news and thought *'Whoopee! We're safe now'* and come back here'.

The driver pulled up in front of the imposing stone porch, with the panda car stopping behind them. They all got out. Palmer pulled the lapels of his coat together.

'Blimey, that sea breeze cuts through you doesn't it, eh?'

DS Jones laughed.

'Healthy for you, sir. Blow away the big city cobwebs.'

'More likely to blow away my hat,' Palmer said, grabbing the brim of his trilby before the wind made off with it. 'Right then, let's see what we can find here. You take a constable and go round the back, in case anybody tries to slip out that way. I'll take Sergeant Singh and the other uniform and try the front. Remember, if anything goes off, no heroics – hit the floor. This lady could be a killer already. Understand?'

Jones nodded and crunched over the gravel, with a constable disappearing round the side of the Manor.

Chapter 50

Gheeta had watched as the Jaguar disappeared up the Manor House drive with her boss at the wheel. Handly stood next to her.

'We can stop it at the end of the drive?'

Gheeta was adamant.

'No way. You saw what I saw – she's got a gun at his head. Let them pass. We can find them again.'

'We can?'

'Yes.'

'Okay.'

He gave the order to let the car go on its way into his radio. It was acknowledged.

Gheeta ran back to the Manor and hurried inside the hall, where she shook the rain from her coat and hat like a dog after a bath. She put her shoulder bag on a large hall table and slid the laptop out and switched it on. Handly and the others watched as the screen lit up and she tapped the keyboard. She clicked on one of the many apps that showed up, and the screen changed to blue with a box asking for a password. She typed one in. She was impatient.

'Come on, come on…'

Handly understood her impatience.

'This is rural broadband country down here, no fibre optic fast speed. Still on the old copper phone wire.'

Gheeta smiled.

'Yes, I can see that.'

The screen changed to another and asked for another password. Handly was intrigued.

'What are you doing? Hadn't we better get after the Chief?'

'That's exactly what I am doing.'

She thought she'd better explain.

'We had a case not so long ago where I got kidnapped by an irate killer and was left chained to a radiator in an old warehouse. Not a very nice experience, so we can now trace where I or DS Palmer are on a computer at all times.'

'He's got a tracker bug on him?'

'No, not quite – but the same principle. What I did was to add a tracker chip to his mobile phone SIM card that gives out a signal – providing the phone's on – that is picked up on the satellite GPS system. But this laptop isn't powerful enough to take the signal direct, so I've had to key into our powerful computers at the Yard using a Team Viewer programme that I adapted and encrypted that allows me to basically take over the work computer from here; and what we are looking at now is that screen.'

She tapped the keyboard.

'Put in the Superintendent's code, and… hey presto!'

A flashing dot appeared at the top right corner of the screen.

'That's him. Now where are you, guv?'

A map of Europe appeared, with the dot flashing in the south of England. Gheeta zoomed in, and like a rocket descending from space the picture took them down and down, with the landscape below becoming larger and larger and more detailed until she released the zoom button as the screen showed a number of streets and buildings. The flashing dot was behind one of them.

'The Lanes. Does that ring a bell?'

Handly peered closer.

'Brighton. The Lanes is in the main shopping area on the outskirts.'

'That's where he is then. Let's go.'

They hurried to their vehicles.

'Lucky he had his mobile turned on then,' Handly called as he got into the TF SUV.

Gheeta smiled back as she got into the front passenger seat of the squad car. She opened the window and shouted back.

'That's why I was waving mine at him; he has a habit of turning it off. I know what he's like.'

She tapped her nose with her finger.

Chapter 51

Palmer edged the car slowly into the dark alleyway between the shops.

'Left into the backyard,' came the order from the rear seat.

He turned left through a narrow entry into the backyard of what used to be *CHARLES PLANT, Antiques & Jewellery's* rear yard. It was dark with high walls on three sides and the back of the shop building on the other. In the far corner to the right was a large shed that Palmer assumed was Plant's old smelter. He pulled up close to a wall and switched off the engine. The incessant rain beat on the car roof.

'Lights out.'

He did what he was told and heard Margaret Leyton get out of the car behind him. She opened his door and stood back, the shotgun pointing menacingly towards him.

'No need for that. I'm not likely to try and run, am I? Wouldn't get very far.'

'No, you wouldn't.'

'Jesus, Margaret! What are you doing with him?'

It was a male voice with a high degree of panic in it. Palmer hadn't noticed the figure come quietly out of the shop's back door; as it moved into the cloud-reflected light of Brighton he recognised Mr Stanley Leyton, MP – an extremely worried Mr Stanley Leyton, MP.

'It was the only way I could get away, Stanley. The police arrived at the Manor about five minutes after you called, I didn't have any time; had to use him as a hostage to get away.'

'I rang as soon as I was released. Oh my God, what do we do now? What do we do with him?'

Palmer could hear the trepidation in Stanley Leyton's voice and sense his utter confusion at the situation.

'We stick to the plan, Stanley. The boat's ready to go.'

Palmer raised his eyebrows.

'The boat? What boat?'

Margaret Leyton smiled a knowing smile.

'Oh yes Chief Superintendent, we have a motor boat; thirty foot and very powerful. Be across the Channel and landing somewhere in Europe before they can put a trace on us.'

Stanley Leyton clearly was not as confident as his wife.

'I don't know, dear. Now the gold's gone, perhaps we should have another think about this. It's all getting a bit heavy, a bit serious.'

'The gold hasn't gone Stanley, I got it back. That's what I've been doing this last week while you've had your head stuck up the PM's arse. It's in the car – well, most of it is; enough to set us up for good anyway. God, Stanley! You are such a bloody wimp. If Charles was still alive he'd be champing at the bit to get going.'

Stanley Leyton regained his composure.

'Well Charles Plant is not alive, is he? And we are heading for a lot of trouble I can tell you – the police have got you and your car tied into murder, Margaret! And what's more, bloody Charles bloody Plant started it all!'

Stanley Leyton was getting very worried about his lofty position in life, and a jail sentence would finish his political aspirations for good. Palmer saw a chance to open a rift between them. He raised his eyebrows in a 'now I know the situation' way and spoke to Margaret Leyton.

'So, *you* were the lady seen socialising around with Plant then, were you? We got reports about her, but I never thought it was you. The reports had the two of you as an *item*.'

Stanley Leyton looked a little numbed by that. He swivelled his gaze between Palmer and his wife; the wig was clinging on as best it could, what with the swivelling and the rain.

'An *item*? What do you mean by that, Superintendent?'

Margaret Leyton spoke out.

'An *item*, Stanley. Charles and I were an *item*. Did you think I'd sit by the fire and knit with the WI, while you were fawning around your political hierarchy in London?'

Stanley Leyton looked like he'd been hit with a sledgehammer. He stood perfectly still, the rain running off from his flattened wig down his face and dripping from his nose and chin.

'I… I… I don't understand.'

'We were lovers, Stanley. Charles was full of life and wonderful to be with.'

She dismissed that track of conversation with a flip of her hand.

'Anyway, that's all gone now – water under the bridge. So we are where we are, and we'd better get going. Come on, move! The police will be here soon.'

Palmer nodded like an old sage dispensing wisdom.

'And when they get here you'll both be off to jail. Not a very nice place is jail, Mr Leyton; full of thieves and cheats and liars. Just like the House of Commons, eh?'

He couldn't resist it.

'People who will stab you in the back – only these people use real knives; especially if they think you've got a pot of gold stashed away somewhere. Some of them will want to beat you up until you tell them where it is, and others will want to protect you from the beatings for a big share of it; and when their mates on the outside don't find that share, they'll beat you up too. Not exactly a win win situation, is it?'

'Shut up!'

Margaret Leyton brought the shotgun stock round hard into Palmer's back so hard that it sent him sprawling in the muddy wet ground of the yard. His already grazed and stinging hands took another hit as they softened his fall.

'Just shut up! Not another word from you. Stanley, open the shed door.'

She gave him a padlock key. Leyton stood fixed to the spot, his mind gone totally blank.

'Now, Stanley. *Now!*'

He stumbled to the shed and opened the padlock that clattered to the ground. Palmer could guess what she had in mind for him and played for time.

'You've set my sciatica off.'

He winced as the pain shot down his right leg as he slowly heaved himself up from the quagmire that the yard was fast becoming as the rain intensified.

'What?'

Margaret Leyton was confused by the remark.

'My bloody sciatica, you stupid woman, I've got a couple of dodgy discs, and that thump in the back hasn't done them any good at all.'

'Then shut up, or you'll get another one.'

'Assaulting a police officer was just added to your list of offences.'

Flashing blue lights permeated through the night rain, from the main street up along the alleyway outside the backyard. Stanley Leyton was shaking.

'The police are here.'

Margaret Leyton stopped short.

'How the hell did they know where we were?'

She peeped slowly around the corner of the yard down the alleyway. At the end of it, the road was lit up by police car headlamps. Blue lights flashed and figures cut shadows in the light as they moved to and fro.

'Shit!'

She turned to Palmer.

'Take off your coat.'

'What?'

'Now! Take off your coat. Stanley, swap coats with him.'

As they did so, she leant into the Jaguar and retrieved Palmer's trilby and gave it to her husband.

'Put this on. And now you can go into the shed, Chief Superintendent.'

She motioned with the shotgun towards the shed door. Palmer moved slowly to it; he'd guessed this was her plan.

'Your husband doesn't look anything like me, it won't work. Best if I drive the pair of you.'

Margaret Leyton wasn't in the mood to be argued with. She prodded him sharply in the stomach and he fell backwards over a raised step into the shed. She slammed the door and hooked the padlock into place.

'Stanley, you're driving. Get in.'

Margaret Leyton got into the back seat behind her husband.

'Right, let's go.'

She pulled Palmer's trilby down as far as she could on her husband's head and placed the shotgun barrels against his neck.

'Drive out slowly and keep looking forward. Don't show your face. They don't know you're here, so they'll think it's still the Superintendent driving. Come on, let's go; we're in too deep to give up now.'

Leyton executed a shaky three-point turn in the yard, and very slowly brought the car into the alleyway and towards the bright light of the road.

Chapter 52

DS Singh stood beside Handly and DS Jones as the Jaguar approached them down the alley.

'I can get a clear shot at her when they turn from the alleyway into the road.'

'No, no way,' DS Singh was adamant. 'Let them go.'

She wasn't going to take a chance that something might go wrong and end with the back of Palmer's head receiving two barrels of shotgun pellets; and anyway, decisions like that were way above her pay grade. She really needed a local DSI to arrive and take command, but that wasn't going to happen; and she knew Palmer had full confidence in her being able to handle the situation.

'Let them pass and then follow at a discreet distance; not too close but near enough to make them aware of us being there. Keep the blues on too.'

The Jaguar was given clear passage through the cordon of police vehicles and accelerated off again, with Singh and Handly's squad car in pursuit and the other pandas led by Jones following.

Half a mile on and Gheeta realised a swap had been made.

'Pull over!' she said, patting the driver's shoulder quite hard. 'Pull over! Palmer's back at the shop. Wave the other cars on and then turn back.'

'What?'

Handly did the waving as they pulled up and the pandas sped past. 'He's driving that Jag.'

'No, he's not. Look.'

She showed him her laptop. The flashing tracker dot was still flashing at Charles Plant's old premises.

'He's still there.'

'So who's driving the Jag then?'

'I don't know, but I have a good idea. Come on, we need to get back in case the guv is injured. Fast as you can please, driver.'

Back at the entrance to the alley Singh and Handly jumped out of the squad car and ran into the shop's backyard. A loud thumping was coming from the smelting shed door as Palmer back-heeled it from within. Handly tried the padlock but it was shut, and the key not with it or on the ground around the door. He called out loudly to Palmer.

'It's Handly here, sir. Get well back, as I'm going to shoot the padlock off.'

'Okay,' Palmer's muffled voice came from inside. 'Hang on… Right, off you go.'

A staccato burst of gunfire from the semi-automatic transformed the padlock into a jagged misshapen lump of metal, and sent it whirling through the air until it hit the back wall and jangled to the ground.

'All clear, sir. You can come out now.'

Palmer emerged, shielding his eyes from DS Singh's torch light.

'You okay, sir?'

'I'm fine, Sergeant. She's got Stanley Leyton with her.'

He was brushing off the dirt and dust from his trousers that had stuck to him when he squashed himself in the shed's far corner before Handly shot the padlock off.

'I guessed that when your tracker stayed here, sir. He fooled us for a while with your coat and hat.'

'Where are they now?'

'Don't know, but I can call in and find out. We've got cars on their tail.'

'Good. She said they have a motor boat and she'd got it all ready to get across the channel with the gold.'

'I hate to tell you this sir, but we haven't got any cars on their tail.'

Handly had called in for an update.

'What?'

Palmer stopped brushing the floor dust from the shed off his trousers.

'They lost them in the estates. We've a helicopter up looking now.'

Palmer thought for a moment and then asked Handly: 'If she's heading for a boat – a decent size boat – where would she keep it? Is there a marina around here?'

Handly pursed his lips in thought.

'Probably the Brighton Marina; it's about the only place for that size vessel, and it's open twenty-four hours. I'll get our duty people to contact the harbourmaster and see if Leyton's got a berth there.'

He used his radio as they made their way back to the squad car. They were well on the way to Brighton when the call came back to Handly. He took it, thanked the caller and turned to Palmer.

'The Leytons have got a berth at the Brighton Marina, and Mrs Leyton was there all day yesterday filling the tank and taking on provisions, plus two extra barrels of fuel. She told the harbourmaster they were going up the Channel and across the North Sea to Holland, and up the Rhine for the Beer Festivals.'

'Right then, step on it driver. Brighton Marina, as quick as you can. Sergeant, radio DS Jones and tell him to keep well back; not to go anywhere near the marina and ground that chopper. I don't want the Leytons to think we are onto them and to get going faster than they have to. I want them thinking they're a jump ahead of us and have got away.'

He ran his hand through his hair.

'And I want my hat and coat back, or I'm in trouble when I get home.'

Gheeta laughed.

'Could have been worse, sir. He could have swapped your trilby for his syrup.'

Chapter 53

The rain had ceased as Palmer, Singh, Handly and the firearms officers moved quietly and stealthily along the quayside of the Brighton Marina. The wet concrete reflected the flickering night lights of the boats moored alongside, as they jostled each other on the lapping waves hitting against the harbour wall like a wet flannel hitting tiles. Upfront with Palmer, the harbourmaster moved slowly along in a crouched position; being of a similar age to Palmer, their stooped walking position was not doing either of their sciaticas any good.

'That's her on the end of this row.'

The harbourmaster pointed forward along the line of moored boats stretching in front of them.

'The one with the Jag parked on the quay.'

Palmer patted his back.

'Thank you, and sorry to have disturbed your evening. You'd better go back and let us handle it from now on.'

'Didn't disturb my evening Chief Superintendent, good Lord, no. Never did like that chap Leyton – bit of a know-all about everything, he is. They call him Captain Snooty round here. What's he done then, what's he up to?'

Palmer put his finger to his lips.

'National Security, can't tell you –sorry. But now you'd better get back to your gatehouse; keep anybody else well away would you, that would be very helpful – don't want any boat owners walking in on us. I'll make sure those at the top know how helpful you've been.'

'Oh yes, you can rely on me, sir. Bloody spy, eh?'

He tapped his finger on his nose and gave Palmer a knowing wink before making his way back at a stoop.

'Sir,' Sergeant Singh said as she moved up beside Palmer.

'Yes, Sergeant?'

'Will you make sure those at the top know how helpful I've been too, sir?'

She and Handly couldn't control their smiles.

'Of course I will, Sergeant. I'll highlight it in my daily report to Bateman.'

Handly's radio, which he'd put onto silent mode, vibrated; he took the call and listened.

'Okay, good work,' he whispered before hooking it back onto his belt and turning to Palmer. 'The Border Control chaps have their cutter Valiant waiting out of sight a mile off shore. If the Leytons get out of the harbour they'll pick them up and arrest them before they get into the main Channel.'

Palmer was impressed with the way Sussex Constabulary was handling the situation.

'Well done, lad. Let's hope we can get them here; high speed chases up the English Channel are alright in Bond films, but I'd prefer a nice easy arrest and home to bed with a cup of cocoa.'

Gheeta gave him a disbelieving look.

'As if.'

They edged forward until the tall hull of the boat next to the Leyton's motor boat was the only cover left. They were about twenty feet away from the pair; Margaret Leyton was sitting in the driving seat, head turned and watching as Stanley Leyton loaded the last of the three bags of gold onto the boat whose engine was chugging quietly.

'Okay?' Palmer whispered to his people.

All gave affirmative nods, and the Firearms Officers took off the safety catches.

'No firing until I give the order.'

He stepped into the light and walked openly towards the boat with the officers behind him, their weapons pointing at the boat.

'Cut the engine Mrs Leyton and just step off the boat this way please,' Palmer shouted loudly. 'I have four armed officers with me as you can see, so don't be stupid enough to even pick up your shotgun.'

He indicated the Firearms Officers, each with their automatics held up and now pointing at her. Four laser dots speckled her chest.

Time seemed to stand still. Margaret Leyton froze as her mind evaluated the situation. Stanley Leyton froze, as his privileged world crumbled before his eyes.

'Stanley, cast off. *Now, Stanley!*' she shrieked at him. '*Now!*'

As if in a daze, and on auto-pilot himself, Stanley Leyton unhooked the shank of rope from the boat and it slid over the edge, splashing into the harbour.

'Don't be stupid, Mrs Leyton,' Palmer was shouting as she hit the accelerator and the boat moved off at speed. 'There's a Border Patrol ship waiting outside the harbour. You won't get far!'

They saw her lift the shotgun from the floor and swivel it towards them. The blast echoed around the harbour, bouncing off the walls, and the shot tore into the hull of the boat tied up to the harbour wall next to them; she couldn't get still enough in the swaying motor boat for a good aim as the waves tossed it up and down.

Handly shouted to Palmer as he and Sergeant Singh scurried back for cover behind the large hull for protection.

'Shall we take her out or the boat, sir?'

His men knelt waiting for an instruction as Palmer thought quickly.

'The boat – don't hit her or Leyton, just stop the boat. Sink the bloody thing.'

He thought it far better to pull a wet member of Her Majesty's Government and his wife from the water than two bodies riddled with police bullets. Less paperwork involved.

'Fire at the outboards!'

Handly had hardly given out the instruction when four repetitive bursts of gunfire followed their laser red guide dots towards the rear of the boat. The noise of the gunfire was tremendous. Tactical Firearms don't use silencers; their job is to frighten the enemy and overwhelm them, and noise helps. But the noise they made was nothing to that made by the first barrel of extra fuel that went up like a barrel bomb with a terrific *whoomp* and sent a wall of fire spiralling into the sky.

Gheeta thought she saw Stanley Leyton through the fireball either dive off the boat or be blown off it by the blast; the next blast as the second barrel went off blew the boat to smithereens. The petrol whooshed upwards in another white fireball, the dazzling light reflected from the sea. The heat could be felt by Palmer and Singh a good fifty yards away.

'Christ!' was the only word Palmer could utter as small bits of the boat fell from the sky all around them. A gold bar fell and clanged to the ground beside him. A few more hit the quayside flagstones among a shower of mixed wood and metal that was until a few moments ago part of an expensive motor boat,

'Cover your head, Sergeant!' he shouted to Singh as they squatted, their arms protecting their heads as more gold bars hit the quayside and others plopped into the harbour waters in front of them. As quick as it had happened, it was all over. Slowly Palmer and Singh stood up and looked out onto the harbour where the burning base of a once expensive motor boat was all that was left floating on an oily sea.

Handly and his men were attending one of their own, who had taken a hit on the legs from the flying wood.

'Is he okay?' Palmer asked with concern.

'Yes, fine sir. He'll be a bit bruised and have a couple of stitches in a cut, but other than that no problem. Not the worst injury we've ever had, sir.'

'I don't doubt that,' Palmer answered.

'I don't think there's going to be much left of the Leytons though. I can't see anybody surviving those explosions.'

'No,' Palmer said, thinking the same thing. He turned to Singh. 'You okay Sergeant?'

'Yes sir, I'm good.'

'Right, radio Jones and tell him to cordon off the whole harbour; absolutely nobody to come in. Then tell him to get an Underwater Search team down here pronto – two or three teams if he can. Warn them that there are two bodies – or what's left of them – and two hundred gold bars in that water somewhere. Oh, and get the Border Patrol boat to come in and seal off the harbour entrance from the sea – no vessels to be allowed in or out. The whole place is a restricted crime scene now.'

He stood pensively looking at the burning remnants bobbing on the waves.

'What a bloody awful end to the case. Just shows you what greed can do.'

He stooped and picked up a gold bar off the quayside and turned it over in his hands.

'Pure greed.'

'Guv, look.'

Gheeta nodded towards the water lapping the harbour wall at their feet, where Palmer's battered trilby was gently rising and falling on the waves. Next to it, a sodden wig was doing the same.

Chapter 54

'Isn't it lovely? I'll put it away until he's old enough to appreciate it.'

Mrs P. was showing Palmer a gold link bracelet with '*GEORGE*' engraved on the name plate.

'It must have cost Benji quite a lot you know, it's not a cheap one.'

It was a token of Benji's appreciation for Mrs P.'s help in his 'hip replacement' hour of need: a small thank you present for their latest grandson, one year old George – their tenth grandchild. Palmer wasn't impressed.

'He does know George is a boy, doesn't he?'

'Of course he does. Boys wear bracelets these days, Justin. You're so out of touch.'

'That could have been made from stolen gold.'

'Shut up, Justin. So could your teeth fillings.'

Palmer hadn't thought of that. How ironic would that be, eh? Him being one of the detectives on the edge of the Brinks-Mat gold heist caper, and now having some of it possibly filling his teeth. He smiled; he could live with that. But what if he was an FBI Agent with gold fillings? Could he live with that, knowing that a fair proportion of the US gold reserve was from recovered Nazi loot? And we all know where a high proportion of that came from…

END

CASE 6: I'M WITH THE BAND

Chapter 1

Stag George was on autopilot. With forty-two years of touring
with the band behind him, his body went through the live
show from start to finish on autopilot. The crowd in front of
the stage were just a tangled, frantically excited, jumping
mass of out-of-focus heads and waving arms; it was all a blur.
Perhaps he ought to have contact lenses fitted, or laser eye
surgery; the band's manager, Solly Brockheim, had been on at
him to have one or the other for ages. Stag raised his guitar up
into the air in front of him as he launched into his lead solo.
He didn't need lenses or surgery for that; he could play that
damned solo blindfolded, same as he could play all their
songs blindfolded come to that. One day he would count up
how many live shows they'd played in the forty-two years the
band had been going. Was it really forty-two years? Seemed
like only yesterday that he and Rob Elliott on bass guitar
started up their rock band and decided on the name
Revolution. The name came from their intense belief that they
were going to set the rock n' roll world alight with their
music. They hadn't done too bad over all – five number one
albums, and so many sold-out tours Stag had lost count; and
still the fans filled the major venues to see them. And it began
all those years ago, in Rob's dad's garage. It seemed like
yesterday.

Stag's left arm was really aching. Thank God it was
the final number. *This bloody guitar is getting heavy now,
holding it up in front for the solo. It never used to feel heavy,
but then I never used to have an arthritic elbow. Getting too
old for all this…*

Out of the corner of his eye he caught sight of Rob
Elliott sidling up on his left, and Charley Frost the rhythm
guitarist moving in on his right – both getting set for the big

finale. Charley was on wages, like the drummer Sid Harley and the keyboard player Jon Madley, brought in over recent years to replace the other original members who had left; retired with their millions or packed off to an expensive rehab unit by their wives before all the money disappeared up their noses. There had been plenty of changes to Revolution's line up over the years, but the fans didn't seem to mind and still packed venues when they toured. *I'm going to make this the last live tour* was always the predominant thought in Stag's mind, at the end of every live gig of every tour for the past ten years; but the internet and music downloads had made the band accessible to a whole new generation of fans and given them a whole new income stream, which was very nice. Stag had never been able to say *no* when Solly waved the promoter's financial guarantees in front of him. *Okay, just one more – then finish.* And then there was always another one being offered. *But this has got to be the las*t… It never was.

The last bars of the finale were coming up, and all three guitarists hit the final chord in unison and raised their guitars above their heads as one; standing godlike as the pyrotechnics blasted out fire behind them, and compressed air cannons blew thousands of pieces of coloured tinsel into the air above the masses that floated down over their screaming heads.

The stage lights dimmed, and from the wings the roadies hurried out to take the instruments off the band, while others draped thermal wraps round their shoulders and led them quickly off and away down a long dressing room corridor; out of the stage door, through a small autograph book-waving crowd, into the stretched limo and off back to the hotel suite. Another one done.

There was never much chat in the limo on the way. After forty-two years and hundreds of gigs, there wasn't anything new to say between the band members. Solly was usually the bouncy one, telling them what a good show it had been and how fantastic the merchandise sales were, and how the back catalogue sales were leaping up during the tour. Not that it really mattered when you'd got a few million in the bank already.

Chapter 2

Peter Brown looked out of place amongst the stage door autograph hunters. He stood at the back as they held out their books in the hope that one of the band would stop and sign. None of them ever did; the band was quite aware that most of the publicity photos being thrust towards them with a biro or felt tip were being held out by autograph dealers, and if they did sign one it would probably be up on eBay within the hour. So they never signed, which of course made their autographs more valuable, and the hunters more determined.

Peter Brown knew this. In fact, he knew just about everything there was to know about the band. He knew how they formed, how they played for five years in the local pubs for nothing; how they had had to use their day job wages to put diesel in the first old van they bought so that they could play venues further away; how they had slept in it for a fortnight when they played nine grotty clubs and pubs in London for no money, on the back of false promises from record label A &R men that they'd '*come and have a look.*'

Peter Brown knew all this because Peter Brown had been their mate and manager – their *first* manager. Just a mate from school who liked the thought of being in 'the music business' and had taken care of the bookings, scamming free rooms for rehearsals, walking the streets and pestering the pubs and clubs to give them an 'open spot', usually an unpaid ten minutes somewhere in the evening; probably between the stripper and the filthy comedian who always closed the show in those days. He built their website too, ran it, and used most of his wages as an IT technician on keeping the old van running, and coughing up cash when an instrument broke or meals were needed.

Peter Brown lived for that band. Now he was killing them.

Chapter 3

There was always a sense of emptiness at the end of a tour. Stag had never been able to fill the void that hit him every time he walked back into his fifth-floor apartment on the Battersea embankment and shut the door behind him. It was warm and inviting, and everything was just as he had left it eight weeks ago. He had a cleaning company that came in every week and gave it the once-over while he was on tour and made it ready for his return; they made sure the boiler hadn't burst, the fridge was full of his favourite snacks, and things were all in order. But it still took him a few days to come down from major celebrity status to being just a bloke who liked a pint at the local and a take-away in front of the telly with his feet up and on his own.

He stood looking out of the panoramic window over the Thames to Chelsea, where the night lights and neons flashed and beckoned. Not tonight though. Tonight, he would relish his own king-size bed, instead of a hotel bed that could range from the equivalent of sinking into a large marshmallow to laying on concrete. Then tomorrow? Well, that was the problem. What would he do tomorrow? Not a lot, that's for certain. Perhaps go down to the local pub and catch up on the neighbourhood news, or take a stroll down the Kings Road. He wouldn't be recognised – not after the wig and hair extensions had been removed by the band's make-up artist after last night's gig. He smiled to himself. In reality, Stag was as bald as a badger's arse – or, in these days of political correctness, he was follically challenged. His trademark three foot pony tail was, in fact, completely false, and usually lived in his wardrobe with his ties. Quite a few times on stage, too much headbanging had started it to move around towards the front of his head, and Rob had had to catch his eye and signal with a little nod towards it. Stag would then move slowly to the back of the stage out of the main light glare, and a roadie would reposition the errant tail in the dim light.

Rock n' roll, eh? False hair, make-up, tight leather trousers that had to have talcum powder liberally sprinkled inside or he couldn't get in or out of them, fake tan spray over the chest and any other visible body parts, embrocation rubbed into his dodgy knees before every gig; and now he had a skin-coloured elbow support bandage to aid lifting the guitar for the big finale. Yes, it was definitely time to pack up; he'd more than enough money to see him through his remaining years in good comfort. Better give it a day or two, and then tell Solly; and don't let him talk you out of it this time, he told himself. His thoughts were interrupted by the doorbell. He'd ordered a prawn and chicken biryani on his 'Just Eat' phone app on the way home – his favourite late night meal – and there was bottle or two of Chardonnay in the fridge to go with it, as well as several episodes of *The Bridge* to watch on 'catch up'. The evening was sorted.

Stag's doorbell rang again. *Okay, okay, hang on*, thought Stag. He'd detoured through the kitchen on his way to answer it, plucking a bottle of the Chardonnay from the fridge and a glass from the kitchen cupboard to save time. But it was not his take-away that smiled at him when he opened the door.

'Fucking hell! Pete Brown.'

Stag recognised his old manager at once.

'What brings you here?'

'Hello, Stag. I was just passing, and I know the last tour just finished and I guessed you'd be taking it easy for a few days. If it's inconvenient I'll go, I only called on the off-chance.'

'No, no,' said Stag, pulling the door open wider. 'I was just about to sit down. Thought you were the delivery chap – got an Indian ordered. Come in.'

He beckoned Peter Brown inside and through to the lounge. *What the hell does he want after all these years?* thought Stag. *The parting of the ways wasn't exactly amicable. Hope he's not on the cadge – skint and looking for a handout. Not going to go down that path. Christ, it's been what – thirty years? Must be.*

'So how's life treating you then, Pete?'

Shit, probably shouldn't have asked that...

'It's okay, pretty steady... I'm good, can't grumble.'

'That's good to hear.'

The bell rang again.

'That'll be my take-away, excuse me a moment.'

It was the take-away. Stag returned from the door with his meal in a hanging bag and put it on the table next to the wine, which he opened. Peter Brown was out on the small balcony, looking out over the Thames.

'Nice view, Stag. Good view of the boat race I bet, eh?'

Stag laughed and joined him.

'Yes, it's not bad. You must come up and watch from here next time if it interests you. Can't say it excites me much.'

'No, nor me – but the wife is ex-Cambridge.'

Peter Brown was putting his carefully thought-out plan into operation.

'Wife? Are you a married man now then, Pete?'

'Yes.'

Peter Brown leant over the hip-high railings of the balcony and pointed down towards the pavement five floors below.

'She's waiting down by the street door. I wasn't sure you'd be in, and if you were you might not want to see me. It wasn't exactly a happy parting of the ways all those years ago.'

He gave Stag an embarrassed smile.

'But that's all ancient history now, eh? You can see her down there.'

Peter Brown leant over the railing and waved to somebody out of Stag's view. Stag was beginning to wish he hadn't invited Pete in, not if he'd now have to invite in the wife as well; all he wanted was a quiet evening in with a meal, wine and 'catch-Up' TV. He leant over beside Pete, thinking he'd better show willing and beckon the wife up.

It was a mistake. Quick as a flash, Peter Brown was behind Stag and bending down, he clasped both Stag's legs with his arms, and straightening up, propelled him over the railings. A split second later, a quick glance over confirmed the plan had worked. Stag's body was impaled on the security railings at the front of the building between the basement flats and the street.

Brown ducked inside quickly, took the meal bag from the table and pouring half a glass of wine, put them both on the small balcony table. Next, he took the wine bottle and emptied most of it down the kitchen sink, before putting it next to the glass and meal. Then, after wiping the glass and bottle clean of any prints, he was out of the apartment and down the stairs as fast as he could go. At the ground floor, he walked quickly along the residents' corridor and exited the building from a side door a hundred yards away from the main entrance. He glanced back to where a small crowd was gathered around Stag's body, and someone had had the decency to cover it with a coat as they waited for the police, ambulance and fire brigade.

Peter Brown felt elated, alive, and very happy. He laughed out loud. Job done.

Chapter 4

Peter Brown talked to himself inside his head quite a lot. *They didn't care about you, they left you… All you did for them and they left you… They wouldn't be anywhere without you… It's your money, and they stole it… They deserve this, they deserve to die – they do, they really do, it's only fair and right…* And by talking to himself, he only ever got a reply that agreed with him.

This continual fixation of his right to some of the band's financial success and status had grown over the years, and over time had morphed into his life's obsession. It was like a court case: he'd put his case, argued his right, and then – being the victim, the judge, and the jury, he'd passed sentence. They had to die; the complete payback, the only justifiable verdict. No appeal would be allowed.

He angrily remembered that awful time when the record label had called him in to say they wanted an experienced, professional manager for the band, and thank you for what you've done Pete, but goodbye. He was shocked, speechless at that – never had he imagined that could happen. They were a band of brothers; they'd survived the con artist promoters, the pay to play venues, the A&R rejections; and then, when they'd broken the surface and the air tasted good, what did they do? *They killed me off. No other word for it, Your Honour, they killed me; and so, as murderers, they must pay the ultimate price.*

Two of them already had. Original band members Maurice Jade and Frank Moss were dead. Peter Brown had no quarrel with the newer members, just the original ones he'd spent eight years working his arse off for; eight years driving them around, hassling for gigs, taking the rejections on the chin and sugar coating them for the band: *'Their A&R chap was at the gig and I rang him this morning. He says we are nearly there, and he'll keep an eye on us – maybe do a pitch next year'* – the truth being that the chap hadn't even bothered to turn up. Eight years of spending all his time and money on their shared dream. And then came the nightmare ending:

'Thanks for what you've done Pete, but goodbye.' Not even the offer of a roadie's job; a complete end.

Tonight, he sat in his dismal bedsit in a three-storey terraced Victorian worker's house off the Walworth Road. His four walls housed a gas stove, gas fire, bed, table and chair. He thought about Stag in his luxury apartment. Several times in the past, when he couldn't sleep because of the continual voice in his head telling him it was justice to kill them – that it was his right, that he was the victim, that his was the retribution they deserved – he'd walked through the night up to the Elephant & Castle, down to Nine Elms and along the Embankment, to sit lonely on a bench and watch the fifth floor windows of Stag's apartment, now and again being bothered by a down-and-out after a fag or a few spare coins. He'd hear their pneumonia-based coughing in the shadows as they struggled to sleep in an old box or filthy sleeping bag; brothers in the same world, each having had some catastrophe throw them from normal life into the trash bin of discarded people; the bin Brown felt at home in now, sitting there alone with his repeated thoughts of revenge.

Chapter 5

A year Earlier

Maurice 'Mo' Jade had left the band in 2014 after thirty years as the drummer, or 'banging the cans' as Stag would humorously describe Mo's musical input. He'd enjoyed those years, but the early days of non-ear protection had taken their toll on his tinnitus and in the end he'd had an implant to relieve the continual buzzing. The consultant had told him he was a fool to carry on drumming and to do so would cause increasing damage over time, probably resulting in total deafness. So, with two broken marriages behind him the life of an irresponsible wealthy bachelor on the loose appealed to Maurice Jade. An end to the continual touring and rehearsing appealed more – a time to unwind, to put the feet up and sample the good life; time to spend more time building up his Chinese porcelain collection. He had one of the best collections of the Jiajing period porcelain in the country, and yet he really didn't know why he had such a collection. He wasn't an expert, and had gotten the *collecting* bug after doing an 'expert with a celebrity' antiques program on TV, where he'd been ferried around Dorset for a week with two hundred pounds to spend buying antiques, guided by an expert; the idea being that they made more money when their wares were auctioned at the end of the week than the opposing team, and all profits went to a charity of his choice. In a classy antiques shop in Wareham he'd been really taken by a lovely goldfish vase, which was from the Chinese Jiajing period and priced at ten thousand pounds – far above what the program allowed. But money was not a problem for Mo, and two weeks later he was back at the shop on his own, and the vase was his.

And so, his love for the Jiajing period ceramics grew; and with online auctions making it far too easy for him to buy pieces while on tour shut in a hotel room anywhere in the world via his laptop, his collection grew as well. A lit and locked display cabinet in the lounge housed it, and of an evening when he was home, Mo would sit and wonder at the craftsmanship each piece showed. Now, if he retired, he could really learn more about the period and attend the sales himself; the Chinese market was soaring, but when you are on the road ten months of the year you don't spend much money and the bank balance soars as well. Even after the alimony payments to the exes, Mo was still a wealthy man; and, of course, even in retirement the royalties would keep coming in from record sales, publishing rights, PRS and a host of other income streams that Solly had arranged. Mo had thought of leaving Revolution for some time, but the hearing issue was a perfect excuse as he'd get the sympathy of the rest of the band and the fans. Perfect!

And so, he had retired. His exit made double-page spreads in the *NME* and *Rolling Stone*, and he was interviewed solidly for a fortnight, warning up-and-coming musicians about the dangers of excessive noise levels. The back catalogue took a very healthy rise in sales as fans bought in order to have the 'original line-up' releases in their collections; even the now useless cassette tapes had a field day on eBay. And then it was over; a big farewell party thrown by the record company at The Dorchester, lots of hugs and tears – mostly of the crocodile variety – a few last words for the music press and MTV and then… peace.

He purposely hadn't taken advantage of a free suite offered by The Dorchester, and Solly had booked him a room at the nearby Hilton. He knew that if he had stayed at The Dorchester he'd have been kept in the bar until daylight by his peers; and even then, when he finally got to go to bed, he would probably have had to fend off the groupies who always seemed to evade security and find the band's rooms in whatever hotel they were in anywhere in the world.

In the next six months Maurice Jade, rock star became Maurice Jade, normal human being. He enjoyed living a life of quiet solitude in his country house on the Cornish coast near St Ives; the house was not a mansion, as was usually associated with rock stars, but a nice four-bedroom Edwardian rectory in two acres. His first act was to use the outside incinerator to burn his stage suits of brightly coloured sequinned silk, the leather trousers, the boots and the fake gold chains – you never wore real gold on stage in case the crazed fans got through the front of stage security men and got to you before you and the band could get off. He had his hair cut to normal length, and his body reacted to having decent food prepared by his housekeeper – or eating at one of the local restaurants – by gaining two stone in three months.

Mrs Armitage the housekeeper came in two days a week and cleaned and kept the place tidy for him. She was in her sixties and probably should have retired as well, but she wouldn't hear of it. '*When you retire, you seize up. When you seize up, you die – like a car stuck in a garage for years. No thank you!*' She cooked meals for him on those two days she was there, and made sure the fridge and freezer were stocked up with healthy microwave meals and the fruit bowl full for when she wasn't. Maurice's parents had died ten years ago, both within months of each other; Maurice was convinced his dad had died of a broken heart when his mother passed on. But at least he'd been able to give them the trappings of a good life in their last years – nice house, world cruises, anything they wanted, and a lot they didn't. Mrs Armitage reminded Maurice of his mum, always fussing about him. *Was he eating enough? Had he got his thermals on when it was cold outside? Did he want anything from the shops as she was going into Penzance later with Mr Armitage?*

Mr Armitage was the male equivalent of Mrs Armitage – late sixties, and even at that age fitter than Maurice would ever be. He did the gardening and kept the shrubbery at bay; the shrubbery being half an acre of rhododendrons that some past occupant of the rectory had planted many decades ago, which now provided an ongoing battle for Mr Armitage to prune and cut back each autumn – a pruning that only seemed to spur the bushes on to get their own back by bursting out in an amazing and beautiful array of colour come the next summer. Mr Armitage was a magician in the garden, and Maurice had often told him so.

Maurice liked the Armitages, but he'd had to tell them some news that he didn't want to tell them the week before. Maurice had done something that he had been meaning to do for decades – he had spoken to his son in America. Maurice's first marriage had ended in divorce when he succumbed to the rock star life in the throes of the band's early success and had an affair with an actress, who turned out to be a gold digger and sold the story to the media. His son was only six months old then, and the lawyers had come to a fairly amicable agreement that his wife – who was an American – would go back to live in the States with the boy, and Mo would have unfettered access in return for a whopping financial settlement that would make her secure for the rest of her days. The problem was that Mo hadn't kept in touch. The continual touring and working had pushed his son into the back of his mind; but as he got older he began to feel guilty and had made some contact, if only on birthdays and Christmas by phone. Even when the band toured the States they had avoided each other by agreement; neither wanted to upset the mother who had a successful second marriage and two more children.

So, it was only when Mo had hung up his guitar and sat down to rearrange his post-rock star life that he bit the bullet and made contact with his son, James – now a man of twenty-three and doing well in the financial area of business. They had met in New York a couple of times, and also in London when he was over for a banking seminar. James had extended his stay and spent a week with Mo at the rectory, which he'd fallen in love with. He told Mo how he was married, and that Mo was now grandfather to three little children under the age of eight, and how they'd absolutely love to come and stay at the rectory in their summer vacation.

This put Mo in a quandary. He had told the Armitages that he intended to move to a serviced apartment in London for his retirement, and that they would get the rectory as a thank-you for all their years of service. Now he had to tell them he was staying put, and had changed his Will to bequeath the rectory to his son, who was now sole beneficiary

Gheeta put a coffee down in front of Claire, crossed the corridor into the office and put Palmer's on his desk in front of him. He looked up from the papers he was reading.

'Lovely job, thank you.'

He sat back in his chair.

'How was your serial killing informant? Stood between two blokes in white coats, was he?'

Gheeta ignored the remark and pulled out her notebook as she sat at her desk.

'Ever heard of a band called Revolution, guv?'

Palmer took notice and raised his eyes.

'Yes, of course I have. Real strong rock band, very big a few decades ago – in fact, I've probably got a couple of their LPs at home in the back of the garage somewhere. On a par with AC/DC. I saw them at the NEC, supporting Status Quo.'

He smiled at the memory.

'That was a good night. They must be getting on a bit now, though – more likely to lead a dog than a revolution.'

He laughed at his own joke.

'Only one of the original band members left now, guv. Three dead, and according to their manager, in suspicious circumstances.'

'Drugs or booze probably – par for the course in rock-n' roll. Put money on it.'

'No, according to Solly Brockheimer…'

'Who?'

'Their manager, Solly Brockheimer.'

'Cockney lad?'

She ignored it.

'According to him, they were a very ordinary bunch of lads with no bad habits who stayed on the straight and narrow. It does seem a bit peculiar that three of them met unnatural ends though, doesn't it? I might just take a look at it if you agree.'

'How *unnatural* were their ends?'

'One was killed while being robbed, one fell off his fifth-floor balcony onto railings, and one emigrated to

Madeira and fell over a cliff edge, despite being a vertigo sufferer who wouldn't go anywhere near a cliff edge.'

'That's three. I seem to remember Revolution was a four-piece band.'

'Correct, one left; and Solly Brockheimer is very concerned for that chap's safety.'

Palmer leant his chair back into what he unkindly called Perkin's Groove, a deep rut in the wall caused by years of banging back against it that he had named after the maintenance foreman, Charley Perkins, who had given up repeatedly filling it in a long time ago. He put his hands behind his head and thought for a few moments.

'Okay, take a look at it Sergeant. It does sound a bit funny, doesn't it? See if all the reports on the deaths and forensics make sense; shouldn't take too long. See if we can't put Mr Brockheimer's mind at rest.'

'Thank you for your support,' Mrs P. said with a withering look.

'I didn't mean it like that. I meant that neither of you have any experience of election campaigns, and you'll be up against the Labour lefties and the Tory well-oiled party machine.'

'Exactly, and local people don't want either of them, do they? They want a councillor who is local and knows what local people want; not a political numbskull dropped in from some other area and quoting party policies like a robot. They want somebody who is on their level, treating each local concern with an open mind.'

'I beg to differ, my dear. What local people in Dulwich want is three Mediterranean cruises a year and a brand new car every two years – and there's only one local who has that: Benji.'

'Well, like it or not, Justin Palmer, he's got my support; and the support of the Gardening Club and the WI.'

'He must be spreading bribes around. What's he offering, a free half hour in his hot tub?'

'No, he's supporting the extension of the council allotments and making the library reading room and internet computers free to all local clubs.'

'As I thought, bribery. I'll have to have a word with the local Fraud Squad.'

'You mark my word, Justin Palmer, that when Benji does get elected – and he will – there's going to be a revolution in our local council.'

'Ah, that reminds me. Do you remember going to the NEC many moons ago and seeing a band called Revolution?'

Mrs P. laughed.

'Course I do. That was the time you tried a bit of headbanging and your glasses fell off and you trod on them.'

He ignored it and ran through the day's events.

Chapter 8

'There you are, I knew I'd have one somewhere.'

Palmer gave a triumphant smile as he walked into the Team Room the next morning and proudly placed the Revolution LP – 'Storm the Barricades' – on the desk in front of Claire and DS Singh.

'Box in the back of the garage labelled Rock. Full of memories.'

Claire picked it up.

'Good looking lot, weren't they? All that hair and leather.'

'I thought there were four in the band, guv? There's five in the picture,' said Gheeta, pointing at the sleeve.

Palmer nodded.

'There *were* only four; the other one must be your Mr Brockheimer.'

Gheeta took a closer look.

'If it is he's changed a lot over the years. Did you have long hair like that, guv?'

'I wish. I don't think Hendon Police College would have appreciated Cadet Palmer wandering in looking like Noddy Holder.'

'Looking like who?'

'Never mind.'

AC Bateman came into the room, with Lucy Ross from Press and Media in tow. He didn't look happy.

'Ah, there you are Palmer.'

'Good morning, sir. Morning Lucy, haven't seen you for a while.'

Lucy gave them all a smile, while Bateman gave them a perfunctory nod.

'It seems you've embarked on a case that has no clearance.'

Palmer shook his head.

'Have I, sir? I don't think so.'

Bateman took the copy of the music paper Lucy was holding and spread it on the desk beside the Revolution LP.

'Take a look – front page news. I see you've got their record as well.'

Palmer, Singh and Claire leant over to read the print. *'REVOLUTION DEATHS, Murder suspected. Scotland Yard Serial Murder Squad take charge.'* It then went on to tell of Brockheimer's meeting with DS Singh, and how *'the serial murder squad were going to examine the deaths again.'*

'That story didn't come through my department, Justin,' said Lucy.

Palmer nodded and straightened up.

'Or mine, Lucy. This Brockheimer chap came in off the street yesterday and told us about these suspicious deaths. That was the first we had heard of them. My Sergeant had a conversation with him and we said we'd have a look at the case files; and bearing in mind the coroner's verdicts, it was unlikely we'd go any further. And that's as far as we have gone; in fact, so far we haven't even looked at the files. So that's why I haven't sent a clearance request up to your office, sir. There's nothing to get clearance for yet.'

Bateman was disappointed; he wanted to put Palmer on the spot and hadn't been able to. There wasn't a lot of love between the pair of them, never had been; Palmer being an old school cop who worked the beat and worked his way up to CDS status, and Bateman getting a few bits of paper at university and being fast-tracked along the managerial rails to the top floor. You could almost cut the heavy silence as Palmer and Bateman eyed each other. Lucy finally broke it.

'I had the paper's editor on the phone asking for details and confirmation. I said we had no knowledge of it and it wasn't an ongoing investigation, and where did the story come from? Apparently this Brockheimer chap was out of here and down to their offices double quick after he'd spoken to DS Singh; he'd already told the paper about his suspicions before he came here, and they had set the type and were ready to print as soon as he confirmed he'd met somebody from the Squad. Can I put out a denial?'

DS Singh looked at Palmer, who caught her gaze.

'No, don't do that. I think that we have a duty to Mr Brockheimer to at least take a quick look at the case files and let him know if we think further investigation is necessary. And it might well be,' he added quickly. 'It certainly seems a strange series of events.'

AC Bateman being the typical political creep who wanted to keep everybody on his side – especially at this time as there was the possibility of a Commissioner vacancy coming up soon – could see danger looming. His current superior had blotted his copybook with their political masters by denouncing the latest round of police budget cuts as 'totally stupid', so Bateman didn't want to rock the boat of any of the other forces whose Superintendents had a vote on the next incumbent by Palmer putting his size elevens into their closed files and coming up with anything that wasn't done correctly. He eyed Palmer, thinking '*I'll make this as difficult as I bloody well can.*'

'Right then, before you even ask for those files from any other force Chief Superintendent, I need a request from you to open the investigation, and on what basis you have reached that decision; then, and only then, I'll request the case files from the appropriate force through the correct channels. Understood?'

Palmer nodded.

'All by the book, sir.'

'Correct, all by the book.'

Bateman nodded to each of them and left.

'Sorry Justin,' Lucy said apologetically. 'My boss went bananas at Bateman when this broke; we didn't realise it was all conjecture by this Brockheimer man. I'll put a release out that Brockheimer *has* spoken to us, but that no decision has been made and no case reopened. That should pour a bit of cold water on the flames. Is that the band?'

She bent over to look at the LP cover on the desk.

'Good-looking lot, weren't they?'

'The governor was a fan,' DS Singh said, with a nod towards Palmer.

'No, really!' Lucy feigned surprise. 'Never had you down as a rocker, Justin; more of a Mod. You know, Crombie overcoat and a Vespa; bank holiday punch-ups on Brighton beach?'

Palmer ignored the remark.

'He had a Twisted Sister as well,' Claire added, causing the three ladies to collapse in laughter.

Palmer raised the palms of his hands in front of him to bring order.

'Alright, alright, calm down. Twisted Sister was the name of a band – they had a massive hit called 'We're Not Gonna Take it', and now I'm not *gonna* take any more of this from you three, so back to work. Thanks, Lucy; let me know how it goes in case Brockheimer turns up again. If he does, I'll read him the riot act.'

Lucy Ross bade her farewells and left. Palmer took a deep breath.

'Right, I'd better sit and work out an investigation request to get Bateman to ask for those case files.'

Gheeta looked at Claire with a guilty look as she spoke.

'Do you mean these files, guv?'

Claire tapped her keyboard and the case file from the Hammersmith CID investigation into the death of Stag George scrolled down the screen, followed by the Cornish CID Maurice Jade file, and the Portuguese Madeira Force file on the death of Frank Moss, translated into English. Palmer gave a false frown that turned into a smile.

'I won't ask how those files came to be on our computers.'

'No sir, best not to.'

'But I would like a printout of them.'

'Yes, sir.'

He rose and walked through into his office, the clicking of the printer audible behind him.

Palmer had pulled in many favours to get Gheeta Singh transferred to his unit, after his HOLMES program had suffered a glitch that had made it practically useless and the

IT unit had sent her to repair it. Not only had she repaired it, but she had added a few of her own programmes that had linked it to the European Interpol database and the USA Ergonomic database; both of which were thought to be one hundred percent secure by their operators. Palmer was impressed and talking to Singh had realised what a bonus to his department her knowledge would be. And so it had been; five mainframe computers were established in his Team Room with 64-inch screens on the wall above them, as well as normal-sized desk screens. All his team had had Gheeta's bespoke app installed on their work mobiles, and could interface with the Team Room and pass information to and fro on an encrypted Wi-Fi IPS through any of three major networks; the SIM cards were altered to provide GPS tracking of the phones and therefore their users twenty-four seven. The IT that Gheeta had at her fingertips now gave the squad a window into most of the UK and European databases that they were ever likely to need; totally illegal of course, but Palmer used the mantra '*ask no questions, get no answers*', and purposely ring-fenced himself away from Gheeta's cyber domain so that if it did all come tumbling down, he could express total ignorance.

The more Palmer read the case files, the more his copper's instinct told him something was wrong. It was all too easy to put the obvious conclusion to each death: Stag George had just happened to lean too far over the balcony wall and fallen; Frank Moss had fallen down a cliff although he got vertigo on a pavement kerb; and Maurice Jade didn't appear to put up a fight with an intruder stealing his prized possessions. And in Palmer's limited experience of antique theft, it was very unusual for porcelain or china to be lifted except if stealing to order; more likely to be gold or silver, which could go into the smelter and 'disappear'. He put in a call to George Gregg at the Arts and Antiques Theft Unit. Yes, Gregg remembered the case, and they had a list of the stolen items and pictures that had been provided by Jade's insurance company; and no, not one of the items had turned up anywhere in the time since.

'But there was something that I couldn't understand on that theft, Justin. It kept bugging me at the time.'

'Go on.'

'Jade had a bloody good CCTV system that covered the drive, the house and the rooms inside. Apparently he didn't turn it on that day, and there was no disc in the recorder; local CID said he probably ran out of discs and couldn't be bothered, and if I remember rightly, his housekeeper said he sometimes just forgot. But it recorded the day before and the whole week before that. All those discs were there. Strange that, isn't it? I mean, he could have re-used a disc. Very strange.'

'Isn't it just. Why would he forget to put a disc in on that precise day, the day he was murdered?'

'Exactly my thoughts, Justin. But the murder wasn't my case – out of my jurisdiction; and you know what Bateman's like if you wander off the patch.'

'Indeed I do, George. Thanks for that, I'll keep you in the loop if we take the case. With a bit of luck, a name you know might come up in the enquiries. Talk to you soon.'

'Okay, Justin. Good luck, mate.'

Palmer put the phone down and leant back. Yes, this case was already running around his brain and he was going to pull it into his department and have a jolly good look at it. It just didn't look right. *Right, let's get into gear then*. He felt the flame ignite in his head, the flame that ignited every time a new case started. First thing to do was get a clearance, which Bateman couldn't refuse to give. Things just didn't add up when you put them all together. A single coroner's verdict of Accidental Death wouldn't raise eyebrows in the local CID; but if they'd known of another Accidental Death and a 'Murder by Persons Unknown' verdict relating to close friends of their victim, it probably would have raised a flag; but the three deaths being in two separate force's patches and one overseas meant no suspicions were likely to be raised. Solly Brockenheimer might just have kick-started Palmer on a journey to finding a very clever murderer.

Better get DS Singh to tell him the good news that we are taking an interest and arrange a meet with him. I bet he's got a few names to give us for starters.

When Palmer collated the files' information and passed it upstairs, AC Bateman wasn't too pleased; but the reasons were solid enough, so he reluctantly gave clearance and sent advice notes to the senior officers at Hammersmith and Cornwall CID departments, and then through Interpol asked the Judicial Police at the Criminal Investigation Department of Funchal – Madeira's main town – for any paperwork they could provide on the death of Frank Moss.

In the Team Room, DS Singh gave the progress boards a wipe and stuck up pictures of the three victims and Rob Elliott. She stood back, and the visual message the board sent was pretty clear. She turned to where Palmer was reading the case reports.

'I think we might put some protection in place for Rob Elliott, guv. The pattern is pretty obvious.'

Palmer looked at the board.

'It is, isn't it. Give your man Brockheimer a ring and get Elliott's address and contact number, and we'll pay him a visit.'

'With Brockheimer?'

'No, without Mr Brockheimer; after all, at this moment in time he's also a suspect. And while you're talking to him, I want a listing of all the band's contacts since day one – that should keep him occupied and away from the press for a while.'

'Band contacts, guv?'

'Yes, any record company personnel who dealt with them – especially ones they dropped. Then there's roadies, producers – again, especially ones they dropped; musicians they used on tours and then dropped…'

'He's going to be busy isn't he, eh?'

'Exactly, and it should keep him off our backs for a while. A band going that long must have made a few big enemies along the way, and being their manager he would have been the one delivering the *'thanks but we won't be using you again'* messages. I want to know who was really upset and angry with them. Hopefully this Rob Elliott can help with that, too.'

Chapter 9

'I think he's gone off into cloud cuckoo land.'

Rob Elliott was sitting in his lounge on a red leather button-studded antique armchair opposite Palmer and Singh, who shared a very large sofa of the same type. Brockheimer had given Gheeta Elliott's telephone number, and a meeting had been arranged at his ultra-modern designer-built house on the edge of a very selective golf course in Berkshire. The house was set in its own two-acre grounds on an incline overlooking the course; his personal privacy was assured by the whole of one side of the house being one-way glass. The furniture was classic, antique and minimal. Palmer knew he was looking at a three million-pound home; probably more.

'I mean, if the deaths had all been within a couple of months then okay, might be something in it. But there's two years between them. I think Solly's being paranoid.'

Palmer nodded.

'Could be, but there are a couple of things that don't make sense. Nothing that might not be explained by our investigation, but things that cause us some concern and make us want to take a closer look.'

'What things?'

'Missing CCTV pictures; and, of course, the fact that Stag George managed to fall over a balcony that nearly came up to his chest.'

'Probably pissed,' Elliott observed in a matter-of-fact way. 'He liked the sauce, did Stag.'

'Not a drop of alcohol in his stomach. And why would Frank Moss – who suffered chronic vertigo – even go near the edge of a cliff?'

A phone rang in another room. Elliott gave a fed-up nod in its direction.

'Bloody press, I've had call after call since this story came out. They say all publicity is good publicity, but I don't think so – bloody pain in the arse. I'll kill Solly when I see him.'

He paused and smiled as what he'd just said dawned on him.

'Better retract that last sentence, eh?'

Palmer smiled back and nodded.

'Well, it would have been better if he'd not talked to the press until we'd taken a good look at the files. Anyway, Mr Elliott…'

'Rob.'

'Rob. Could you rack your brains and see if you can come up with any episodes in the band's history that might make somebody extremely angry with you all?'

Elliott laughed.

'Christ! That'll be a long list of people.'

'I don't mean a fan who never got an autograph,' Palmer explained. 'Nothing trivial like that. If there is a killer out there knocking the band off one by one, then he or she was hurt in a big way – big enough to hold a grudge for years; and the cause of that grudge happened before Frank Moss died two years ago. He was the first suspicious death; and at the moment we have to remember that's all they are – suspicious deaths.'

Elliott nodded.

'Trouble is that everybody was – and is – very nice to us in the band 'cause they all want something off us; like record companies who want back catalogue rights, and publishing companies after our publishing rights; promoters who want a tour. They all creep around us, send gifts; but we are all wise to that. Solly would be the one who gets the flack and the nasty words – we make the decisions, yes; but he's the one who tells them to sling their hook if we don't want them. He'd probably be better at doing that sort of a list than me.'

'He's already doing one for us, but we'd still like one from you. We might find a few matching names on your lists.'

Elliott was impressed.

'Yes, you might at that. What a bloody good idea – be an interesting comparison. Okay, I'll have a good think and get to work on it.'

Gheeta passed him her card.

'If you could email it to me when you've finished and then send any others you might think of later, that would be good.'

He took the card.

'Okay, I'll get my thinking cap on.'

Palmer stood up.

'Right then sir, I think that's about it so far. We will keep you informed of any progress. Oh,' he added as an afterthought. 'You might notice increased police patrol activity in the area, just to be on the safe side.'

'You're scaring me now.'

'No need to be scared; but Brockheimer's decision to go public might jar the killer – if there is one – into action earlier than he or she had intended. This is a private gated estate, so pretty secure; but just be a bit careful.'

'I take back my earlier retraction – I will kill Solly.'

They walked towards the front door. Palmer was inquisitive.

'One thing, Rob; and it's nothing to do with this case.'

'Yes?'

'Where are all your gold discs and awards? I know you have a lot, and when we've been in celebrity houses in the past they have them on display on the walls – pride of place on the hall table and so on. Have you got a separate room for them all?'

Elliott laughed.

'They are in boxes in the garage. I've been doing this for forty plus years, Chief Superintendent; it's a job. The glitz and all that award crap wears off after a few years, and to be honest with you, when I close that front door behind me after a tour, the last thing I want to be reminded of is Revolution. I'm just a sixty-something old man at home, enjoying golf, taking my dog out, and having my friends' company. When I go onstage, I am a totally false Rob Elliott; one in tight leather trousers that irritate, press-on tattoos, and a pony tail on elastic – by the way, it's upstairs hanging in the wardrobe in the bedroom if you wondered. I wear more makeup than Barbara Cartland did, and I gyrate like a whirling dervish on speed, even though I've now got a new hip and a new knee. So why do I do it? I ask myself that question after every tour, and I know Stag and Mo were asking it too. Mo has a son in the USA, product of a failed marriage; I know he wanted to reunite with him – hadn't seen him for over twenty years. I'm glad he got together with the boy before he died, that was good. So, as I'm the only original left, I reckon I might just morph into that sixty-something gent and enjoy some personal time, eh?'

'Sounds good to me.'

'Just don't tell Solly I'm thinking of it, or he'll go into panic mode.'

They said their farewells and Palmer and Gheeta walked down the short drive to where the squad car was waiting.

'What a nice chap, guv.'

'He is, isn't he? Very down-to-earth. Mind you, I wouldn't want to be Solly Brockheimer when he next meets him. He's in for an earful.'

Chapter 10

Solly Brockheimer didn't get an earful. He didn't get anything. Solly Brockheimer was dead.

Palmer stood beside DS Singh on the edge of the platform at Baker Street tube station as they looked down onto the tube rails. Brockheimer's body had been removed, and Palmer was thankful for that; viewing mangled human remains wasn't his favourite pastime. The British Transport police had closed off the station and were taking witness statements in a room off the booking office. A British Transport Police Inspector came along the platform and joined them.

'Be about an hour by the time we get all the statements. Some of the witnesses are a bit shook up.'

'I think I would be too.'

Gheeta looked down to where Brockheimer's blood had mixed with the oil and detritus in the pit under the raised lines.

'Pity he didn't fall into the pit.'

The Inspector nodded.

'Some do. Then they usually raise their head and the first carriage link knocks it clean off.'

Gheeta grimaced.

'Ouch!'

The Inspector smiled; it was all in a day's work for him.

'You get used to it. Twenty-six last year, that's about average. Most are suicides. This one wasn't.'

Palmer gave him an inquisitive look.

'It wasn't?'

The Inspector pointed to the CCTV camera along the platform.

'My Sergeant tells me the staff monitoring the cameras saw him being pushed. They have it all on disc.'

Palmer and Singh exchanged glances. A breakthrough?

'Could we have a copy of that, and a copy of the witness statements once they are completed?' Palmer asked, feeling his heartbeat quicken.

'Of course, I'll get it all over to you. Was this chap a serial killer then?'

The Inspector obviously had been told who Palmer was.

'No, more than likely a serial killer's victim.'

'Your job sounds a bit more interesting than mine, Chief Superintendent.'

Palmer smiled.

'Not always, I can assure you. Serial killings generate more paperwork than a suicide on the tube.'

Gheeta had a thought.

'Is there CCTV at the street entrance to this station?'

'Yes, every station has it. I can guess where you're going with that; I'll get that disc copied for the half hour before and half hour after the… I was going to say accident, but perhaps murder might be more relevant?'

'Poor bugger…' Palmer said as they turned and left. He felt sorry for Solly Brockheimer. Gheeta spoke as they travelled up the escalator.

'*Accidental death* doesn't ring true now guv, does it.'

'No, not one bit. Somebody is very angry with Revolution, very angry indeed. Give Berkshire a ring and make the coverage on Rob Elliott's place twenty-four hour, with two Firearms Officers inside with him. Nobody goes in or out of that gated estate without an ID, and without Claire checking them through our data programmes; and then, if they aren't residents, they have an escort until they leave. And you'd better ring Elliott himself and bring him up to speed. He's not to go out anywhere alone, and anytime he does go out he's to inform the uniform on the gate where he's going, and use a squad car with two of our chaps for company.'

Peter Brown sat on his bed, still wearing the hooded top and gloves, reading the news about Brockheimer on his laptop. It was reported as just another Underground death – suicide not ruled out, and not ruled in. No mention of his relationship with Revolution. There should have been; the media must know. So the Met were keeping that quiet, were they? They knew it was murder, of course they did – and he knew they knew. The Serial Murder Squad were on the case, and they had no clues and no leads; and he was in control.

He had that elated feeling again. He smiled; in fact, he hadn't stopped smiling since the push – the push that sent Solly Brockheimer off the edge of Baker Street Tube Station platform two Metropolitan Line and under the 17.35 train to Aldgate as it roared in. *So where did you think getting rid of me all those years ago would get you Solly, eh? Bet you didn't think it would get you under a tube train, eh? Bastard. You should have been nice to me – offered me a job, kept me on; but oh no, not you… Just take all my hard work – all those years of just getting by, all that – and when it comes good, you and those other bastards just thought you could kick me out, eh?*

Shouldn't have gone to the papers, Solly; stupid thing to do. Got the police involved – trying to get me caught, were you? Stupid thing to do, stupid – you made it easy for me to choose. Elliott was going to be next but you leapfrogged him, Solly. You didn't even notice me on the platform. Stag didn't at first, either – just another bloke… I waited outside your office for two days, Solly; waited for you… You kept me waiting, you bastard… It wasn't going to be you next – but you went to the papers and got the police involved. You shouldn't have done that… It's your fault… Stupid, stupid, stupid…

They won't catch me anyway, Solly – not a chance. I'm too clever for Mister Plod, they'll never catch me. I don't leave a trace, I'm just a forgotten face from way back – no way they'll trace me… Just one more of you bastards to go and my job's done. Just one more.

He tapped his keyboard.

This will make you sit up and respect me, Detective Chief Superintendent Palmer. Oh yes, I know your *name – but you don't know mine. But it's time to say hello…*

Chapter 11

Palmer knocked on AC Bateman's door and walked in after getting the 'come in'. Bateman was behind his large, impressive-looking desk.

'Got a message you wanted to see me, sir.'

'Sit down, Palmer.'

'Been sitting all day, sir. I'll stand if you don't mind.'

He hadn't been sitting all day, far from it; but he'd long ago sussed out that the chair offered in front of the desk was much lower to the floor than the one Bateman occupied behind it, giving the AC a sense of power over you.

'Please yourself.'

Bateman eyed him suspiciously. The distrust was mutual.

'Right, I just want to impress on you Palmer – and you on your staff – that although we have the clearance to re-evaluate the files of other CID units in the Revolution death cases, I do not want any comeback against those units if you find obvious clues that they missed, or any sign of slack procedural work on the cases. Just carry on and complete your investigations. No pointing fingers.'

'You think I'm going to find some poor work then, sir?'

'No, but as you may be aware the Commissioner is retiring in a few months and I have been advised that my name – together with others, of course – has been put forward to our political masters for consideration for that position. So I would really be very grateful for a smooth run-up to that election with no inter-force arguments erupting.'

'Congratulations, sir. Good luck.'

Bateman knew Palmer didn't mean this. Palmer's dislike of fast-tracked university types straight to management level in the Met was well-known; and Bateman's numerous attempts to get Palmer's squad integrated into CID, and Palmer retired, was also well-known. But Palmer wouldn't take the early retirement offered; he loved his job, and more to the point what would he do all day? Mrs P. had made it very clear that her lifestyle of various WI committees and Gardening and Dog Clubs would go on, and he would have to work his retirement around them. Bateman had even looked into offering redundancy, not a tool the Met usually employed to get rid of staff; but Palmer had served for so long the payment would be astronomical, and there would be questions from the political masters as they liked Palmer, which Bateman could never understand why; the truth being that they liked Palmer because he caught killers, his record was exemplary, his officers loved him, the press liked him, and he was a big brick in the wall at New Scotland Yard. Bateman acknowledged Palmer's good wishes for the election.

'Thank you, Palmer.'

'If you need any help sir, I could give you Dotty Watkins's number.'

'Who?'

'Our local florist; she's organising the local campaign for our neighbour who is running in the local council election – same sort of thing really. She may be able to give you some pointers, sir.'

Bateman had to stop himself from smiling. He could see the laughter in Palmer's eyes.

'I'll bear it in mind, Palmer. Off you go – and remember, don't rock the boat.'

'Me, sir? No, never.'

Palmer took the stairs down to his floor. He didn't like the idea of Bateman getting the top job; another stuffed shirt paying more attention to cutting costs than to cutting crime figures. But he did like the idea of Bateman not being his boss anymore. Mind you, better the Devil you know.

He gave a little jump of glee off the last two stairs, and immediately wished he hadn't when his sciatica stabbed into his left thigh as a reminder of his age; too old for gleeful little jumps.

In the Team Room Claire and DS Singh were tapping away at their keyboards as usual.

'Nothing happening here, guv,' said Gheeta. 'We haven't really got a starting point – needle in a haystack job.

We've got the tube station footage though. It was definitely a push on Brockheimer, not an accident.'

'Okay,' he said and sat beside her. 'Let's have a look.'

They watched the screen as the tube station platform filled up with commuters. Gheeta had put a red arrow marker that followed Brockheimer as he came onto the platform from the escalator, and a green arrow that followed his killer who looked to be a man – or maybe a woman – in jeans and a hooded top. The platform was full of the rush hour crowd, so it was difficult to see the two of them entirely; the man stood two people behind Brockheimer, who was at the front of the platform. The train came in and the killer made his – or maybe her – move, barging forward between the other passengers and giving Brockheimer a heavy push, sending him over the platform edge and down onto the line. It wasn't subtle or disguised, and it was obvious to all the passengers nearby what had happened. Shock permeated them into a frozen state; hands were raised to mouths, and a stillness overcame the immediate throng; except for one person – the hooded assailant – who barged his or her way through them back to the rear of the platform and disappeared through the arch leading to other platforms and public exits.

'That's it,' Gheeta sighed loudly. 'Didn't stand a chance, did he? I've sent a copy to Forensics to see if they can enlarge the picture and maybe get a face shot or something that identifies the killer. Don't think we have much chance though, as he or she was well-covered. I've got the CCTV from the entrance, but he doesn't show on that, either entering or leaving; so he might have come on another train and left on one going the other way on the Metropolitan line and got out at any of the stations along the route. Or he could even have changed lines somewhere and then got off anywhere on the whole Underground system.'

Claire sat back in her chair.

'The Sergeant's right, sir – finding a needle in a haystack would be easier. Where do we start cross referencing people? As far as I can find out from the net so far, all the band had the same social circle. Their Facebook pages are just about identical; they knew all the same people, and so presumably they had all the same enemies too. I'm checking out all the fans that have left condolence messages on the Facebook memorial page first, and there's a lot of them.'

Palmer was surprised.

'That's a bit off, isn't it? A memorial page...'

Claire shrugged.

'It's the done thing these days – any celebrity popping their clogs seems to get a memorial page on Facebook.'

The phone rang and Gheeta answered it.

'Okay, yes that's fine. Bring him up, please.'

Palmer raised inquisitive eyebrows as Gheeta stood up and went to the door.

'Rob Elliott has turned up; hopefully with his list of enemies of the band.'

She went and met him at the lift and brought him in. Pleasantries were exchanged, and Claire introduced.

'Sit yourself down, Mr Elliott,' Palmer said. 'Tea, coffee?'

'No, I'm fine thanks; and please call me Rob.'

He looked around.

'So this is where it all happens, eh?'

Palmer smiled.

'No, it all happens outside. This is where we try to make head or tails of it.'

Elliott pulled a folded piece of paper from his inside pocket.

'I've brought a list for you like you asked. Not a very long list, I'm afraid. As I said before, Solly did all the hiring and firing and we just smiled apologetically when people left, making out that it was beyond our control.'

He caught sight of the case progress board on the wall with the pictures of the band members taped to it and walked over. Under the pictures of Stag George, Maurice Jade, Frank Moss and Solly Brockheimer were the words 'dead'. He turned to Palmer.

'Christ! That brings it home doesn't it, eh? Then there was one…'

'Which is why we have you under protection, sir.'

Palmer moved beside him and patted him on the shoulder.

'Don't want you on the memorial page do we, eh?'

'What memorial page?'

'The one on Facebook.'

'I didn't know there was one.'

'We presumed your record company put it up.'

'If they did they didn't ask me.'

Gheeta pulled it up on her screen.

'Have a look.'

Rob Elliottt sat beside her and looked at the black-edged screen with a series of band pictures, followed below by various messages from fans. He wasn't impressed.

'I don't like that. Bit cheap and tacky isn't it, eh? No, I don't like that at all. I know the lads wouldn't want that sort of thing.'

He pulled out his iPhone, flipped it open and tapped a speed dial number.

'I think that can come down pretty quickly. Awful…'

He spoke into the phone.

'Shirley? Hi, Rob Elliottt… Yes, fine thanks… Yes I know, we will all miss him. Shirley, I'm looking at the band memorial page on Facebook; it's pretty awful, cheap and tacky, and I'd like it taken down. I wasn't consulted… You didn't… Okay, I'll hang on.'

He covered the phone and addressed the others.

'She's our PR lady and knows nothing about it. She's finding out who in the Social Media Department sanctioned it.'

They waited a minute or so and then Shirley came back.

'They didn't? Really? Okay… Yes, please go ahead. Thanks Shirley, talk soon. Bye.'

He shut his phone and sat back.

'They didn't put it up; nothing to do with the record company. They're having Facebook shut it down. Usually takes a day or so.'

'So, who did put it up then?' Palmer asked.

Rob Elliottt shrugged.

'No idea. I suppose it could be a fan?'

Palmer turned to Gheeta.

'Anything we can do to find out?'

'I can trace the original IPS of the person who posted it? Hang on.'

And she was away, tapping her keyboard and hacking into the page's data. She had a thought.

'Claire, get on the front page and bring up the list of 'friends' and print it out before they pull it down.'

'Okay.'

Claire brought the page up on her computer and started the task.

'There's lots of them.'

Rob Elliott laughed.

'At our peak we had a hundred and thirty-eight thousand members of the Fan Club.'

'Christ!' said Claire, looking aghast. 'Hope they aren't all 'friends' on here. I'll be here all night.'

Palmer was lost.

'Friends?'

Gheeta explained as she worked.

'If you have a Facebook page guv, people ask to be able to see it and post things on or make comments on anything you post by becoming your 'friend'. They click an icon and then it asks you if you want them to be your 'friend' and see what you post and be able to post back. You can say yes or no.'

'Sounds a good way to waste a lot of time to me.'

'It is,' Rob Elliottt agreed.

Claire gave a sigh of relief.

'There's only six hundred and eighty-two 'friends' on the memorial site, I'm glad to say. I'm downloading the list into a PDF file in case it's taken down before I can print them all out.'

Gheeta nodded.

'Yes, good idea. Well, I'm sorry to say we aren't going to get to know who put the site up as they obviously don't want anybody to know. It's been routed through proxy servers in Eastern Europe and a mousetrap.'

Rob Elliottt looked at Palmer who shrugged.

'No, I have no idea what she's talking about either. But I take it we've hit a brick wall.'

Gheeta nodded.

'We have, guv. Whoever put this Facebook site up did it through eight unregistered servers in Romania and Bulgaria, and linked them together so that when you finally get to the last one it sends you back to the first one again, and that just repeats and repeats the process *ad infinitum*. It's a well-used system on the dark web – a brick wall, known as a mousetrap.'

'Clever bugger, eh? But why would they want to do this? The content seems okay; nothing nasty about the band or anything like that.'

'They could be bootleggers, collecting the Facebook addresses of the genuine fans so that at a later date they can offer them fake band memorabilia or illegally pressed live recordings – bootlegs.'

Rob Elliottt nodded.

'We've had that in the past. Usually they have recordings of live shows and flog them outside the venues; got so bad in the early nineties we had security people checking bags at the concerts for recording gear being smuggled in.'

'Well, well, well!'

Claire spoke slowly and sat back in her chair.

'Look at this. Here's a surprise *friend* on the list.'

'Somebody we know?'

Palmer was hoping for a lead.

'You bet.'

'Who?'

'A certain DCS Palmer.'

They all turned and looked at him. You could have heard a pin drop.

Palmer thought for a moment.

'I don't have a Facebook page, so it can't be me.'

'You have now, sir.'

She clicked on his name in the friends list on the memorial page and up came the DCS Palmer Facebook page. The header picture across the top of the page was the cover of the Revolution LP 'Storm The Barricades'.

'And you only have one *friend.*'

'I have?'

'Calls himself *'Just Desserts'*. Bit ominous, isn't it? Considering what's been happening.'

Palmer nodded.

'He's our man then, got to be; and he wants to play a game of 'catch me if you can' by the look of it. Silly boy – putting his head above the parapet like this and coming out into the open, gives us a target'.

Gheeta had been tapping away.

'Both your site and his are non-traceable, guv. His site is just a blank colour wash, nothing else; so he must have set it up just to be able to write on other sites like the memorial one and yours. Why would he do this?'

Palmer rubbed his chin.

'Recognition, any criminal profiler will tell you that; he's after recognition. He's done four murders, and none were reported until Mr Brockheimer gave the story to the press. Our killer is a star in his own mind and wants to be lauded as one by other people. He wants recognition for what he thinks are the perfect murders; and that's when this type of killer trips themselves up.'

He pointed to the 'Barricade' picture.

'He's gloating and threatening at the same time; he's showing us the three members of the band he's killed plus Brockheimer, while at the same time putting Rob in the picture which is the threat.'

He looked at Rob Elliottt who leant forward and pointed at Brockheimer in the picture.

'He's got the wrong bloke then. That's not Solly, that's our first manager Peter Brown.'

The silence was deafening. Palmer looked at DS Singh and raised his eyebrows. She shook her head.

'He's not on our check list guv, and he's not named on the record sleeve or we'd definitely have him on the list.'

'He wouldn't be named on that sleeve,' Rob Elliottt explained. 'We'd cut that record and done the sleeve photo, and then he was sacked just before it was released. No time to have another picture taken, so all they could do was erase his name from the credits on the back.'

'Sacked?' Palmer said, all ears. 'What was he sacked for?'

'Nothing bad, nothing like that. Pete was a school mate who'd been with us since we started out, but we'd got to a level where the powers that be at the record company wanted a professional management company to take over; it was all getting a bit too much for Pete to handle. One day he was there, and the next they told us he'd left and Solly's company was taking the reins.'

'Did he stay in touch?'

'No, but we would see him now and again in the audience at gigs. But he never came backstage or anything like that. Shame, really.'

'Where did he go, what did he do?'

'No idea, but he was into IT and very good at it; he built our first website and stage sound systems. Good ones they were, too. So, I imagine he probably got into computers or software as that was his pride and joy, as well as his Mercedes SL280 car. He renovated it from basically a heap of scrap. He loved that car, sprayed it bright red. Everybody in the business knew it.'

'Recognition principle again,' Palmer said softly. 'He wanted praise for his work. The band was getting all the plaudits and attention and he wasn't because nobody recognised him as the manager. So, by driving a stand-out bright red car they would.'

Gheeta spoke softly.

'Being so good at IT and web building he'd know all about Facebook and the dark web and how to use them, wouldn't he.'

Rob Elliottt went quite pale.

'Oh my God, you think he put the page up. You think he's the killer.'

Palmer gave him a reassuring pat on the back.

'We don't know – bit early to make that assumption. But we'll check him out at CRO and hope he comes back clean. In the meantime, I'll get a car to take you home; and don't worry too much, you've got officers outside your place and two will be inside with you twenty-four seven, so just carry on as normal. Only difference is you'll have company. If you need to go anywhere, you'll have two of our chaps with you all the time.'

He gave Elliott a fatherly smile.

'Hope you're not courting? Could be a bit awkward.'

'Courting? No way. I've two broken marriages behind me and I'm not going down that road again.'

He froze.

'You don't think one of my exes could be…?'

Palmer laughed.

'No, not a chance. If you think of anything connected with Peter Brown give us a call, okay?'

'Okay. God, I can't believe it would be Pete. He's just not the sort.'

Palmer shrugged.

'People change and do strange things when jealousy or the thought of revenge starts to eat into their minds; and if he's had thirty years of it in his head it might just have built and built until it pushed him over the edge. But, let's hope it's not him and we can clear him from the picture, as he sounds quite a nice chap.'

He nodded to Gheeta, who stood and steered a rather thoughtful Rob Elliott out of the room and down to street level for his ride home.

Palmer sat deep in thought, looking at *his* Facebook page and wondering just what *Just Desserts* was planning as the next move. Obviously, it had to be something that would get him close to Rob Elliott; close enough to kill him, which was made harder now that he had shown his hand to the police. So why had he? Was he hoping to control Palmer's moves? Send him on wild goose chases? Or was it the usual egoistic drive of the serial killer to have recognition?

Palmer thought hard. *How shall I play him? Make contact online and play him along? Annoy him so much that he breaks cover? Or perhaps just sit tight and make no comment so he thinks we haven't noticed him? That might annoy him even more.*

Gheeta came back into the room.

'He's off with two armed protection officers for company. I hope they like heavy rock music.'

She sat at her computer.

'Right. I have an idea, guv.'

'Go on.'

'We can log into *Just Desserts*'s ISP server – that's his Internet Service Provider, like Yahoo or BT – and I can flag up his unique customer code so that we get a heads up whenever he logs onto Facebook. Being a clever so and so with IT knowledge he will be using a mobile phone to log on as a landline is easily traced; so, when he logs on we need to keep him online long enough for me to hack into the ISP, get the mobile number and then run it through the service provider's customer bases, which will give me a postcode for the area he's logged in from – and postcodes generally only cover about half a dozen addresses.'

Claire nodded her head in admiration.

'The girl's a genius.'

Gheeta smiled.

'I am, aren't I.'

Palmer took a deep breath.

'I have no idea what you are talking about, but will it take us to our killer?'

'It might, if it all works.'

'And the words *hack in* were mentioned.'

He raised his eyebrows questioningly.

'I take it that I might well end up in front of a disciplinary hearing if word of our *modus operandi* for your little trick became public knowledge?'

Palmer was well-aware that some of Sergeant Singh's methods of information gathering were not quite legitimate; and he also knew he'd get the usual answer she gave him whenever he questioned them.

'I couldn't possibly comment, sir.'

'Okay, carry on.'

He left the Team Room and went over to his office, leaving Gheeta and Claire putting various links and programmes onto their computers in readiness for when *Just Desserts* logged in.

Peter Brown was smiling, a big smile. He was sat in the bedsit, watching both the Revolution Memorial and the Detective Palmer pages on Facebook on his iPhone. The Revolution page had shown Palmer log on and then click through to the Palmer page.

Come on, come on, you stupid copper, type something. Say hello… You waiting for me to start a conversation, are you? Not yet… No, not yet… You know when? When I kill Elliott, that's when… Are you worried? Of course you are. You know I'm more than a match for you, Detective Chief Superintendent Palmer – much more than a match for you… You didn't protect the others, did you? I got them, didn't I? You won't protect Elliott either –you wouldn't even know I was here if that stupid manager hadn't blabbed to the press, would you? Wouldn't even know I was here. It would all have ended and nobody would be any the wiser – just a few deaths of old rock musicians. People would have thought they were probably high on crack or pissed at the time – open and shut cases. But then you poked your nose in... and I'm going to give you a bloody nose...

He switched off the Facebook app, shut down the phone and lay back on his unmade bed, smiling to himself.

That's long enough... You think I don't know you'll have your cyber geeks tracing my calls? I've forgotten more about the web than they'll ever learn. Tomorrow the fun begins... tomorrow...

Gheeta had put a bell call onto the final programme once she and Claire had loaded and stringed together the various codes and apps to make it all work. If *Just Desserts* signed in on either the memorial page or Palmer's page, they'd get a loud 'ping'. She guessed that he wouldn't sign in until he saw Palmer was signed in; no point really. He was obviously trying to outwit Palmer, so he'd wait until Palmer was signed in so he could text him. She briefed Palmer on her thoughts on that, and he agreed that it was the most likely way *Just Desserts* would act.

After Claire and DS Singh had left for home later that afternoon, he stood in front of the progress board, looking at the happy faces of the deceased band members as he put on his coat and trilby. *I'll get the bastard, lads; don't worry, I'll get him.* Tomorrow would do fine for starting this cat and mouse game with *Just Desserts*, and a quiet evening at home to gather his thoughts would go down well.

He took the train home for a change, Victoria to Herne Hill, and walked through the pedestrian tunnel to Milkwood Road. He bought an evening paper at the stall under the bridge that had been there since he could remember and was still run by the same husband and wife team. They must be in their eighties now but were still up at five every morning to sort the papers coming in off the train, and there until eight at night selling them; no life really, was it. He strolled past the Half Moon pub where he and Mrs P. had often sat in their courting days with their drinks, sharing a packet of cheese and onion crisps while watching a local band make a right mess of a current top tune. He turned right past the famous old cycle track – all changed now, sold off for 'executive homes' – and along into Dulwich Village. Ten minutes later, he was home. Benji's poster was still in situ on the garden wall, and his eyes seemed to follow Palmer along.

Daisy the dog greeted him in the hall, with one of Mrs P.'s shoes in her mouth. Daisy never had got the '*bring me my slippers*' command right.

'You'll have to get something out of the fridge for tea, Justin. I'm canvassing tonight.'

Mrs P. appeared from the kitchen, sporting a rosette the size of a dinner plate with Benji's face beaming from it.

'You're not going out like that surely?'

'And why not?'

'You look like one of those Cliff Richard fans of a certain age.'

She bristled.

'What age?'

'Over twenty-one.'

He smiled at her. *And approaching sixty*, he thought to himself.

'Local politics are very important, Justin Palmer. Your money pays the rates that the council spend, you know. We need to have a face on the council keeping an eye on them and what they're spending it on.'

Palmer pointed at the rosette.

'Yes, but not *that* face.'

'Benji is a very community-minded man. He does a lot of voluntary work in the neighbourhood, as you well know; and he was in business, so he won't have the wool pulled over his eyes on the finances. I wouldn't be surprised if they didn't make him the council leader.'

'Steady on, he's not been elected yet. You'll have him running for PM next.'

'Could do a lot worse.'

'What if he doesn't get in? I suppose he'll be sulking for six months.'

'He *will* get in, Justin. Dotty Watkins's campaign is working well; we've had lots of local newspaper and radio coverage. You should get involved in politics more.'

'I'm a police officer, I can't be seen to take sides.'

'You'd be the first one out there on the streets if they banned steak and kidney pie or toad in the hole.'

'Too right I would – but that would be important. Benji mincing round the Council Chamber isn't.'

Mrs P. nodded her head in exasperation.

'I give up on you, Justin Palmer. Just make sure you turn the TV off if you go to bed before I get back.'

Chapter 12

'I think we ought to have a word with Maurice Jade's son.'

Palmer had given the case a great deal of thought during his evening alone at home.

'You think he knows something, guv?'

Sergeant Singh was Googling the names from the memorial site.

'Being away from his dad for so long he couldn't know much, could he?'

'Probably not, but it's just niggling me that Jade was killed so soon after a family reunion. Perhaps somebody saw that as a threat.'

'A threat?'

'Yes, I don't know how but it could be. For instance, what if Jade had a girlfriend and she saw the son coming back into the fold as having the potential to upset things?'

'How?'

'I don't know, it's just a thought.'

'I'll gladly fly over to Manhattan on expenses guv, and have a word with the son.'

'I bet you would. And visit all those relatives of yours over there at the same time, eh?'

Gheeta laughed.

'You can read me like a book. I'll arrange an Intranet hook up.'

'A what?'

'It's like the internet but just for selected people – like a video conference call but more secure. We can do it through the Cyber Administration department downstairs.'

'Okay, get it set up.'

The NYPD 17th Precinct was hooked into the Met's Intranet line, as were the main police HQs of most of the United States and basically all the major law enforcement main offices worldwide; it gave a super quick way of getting things done. If an absconding criminal managed to board an outbound flight from the UK, a quick call on the Intranet to the police station nearest to his destination and a welcoming party would be waiting on the tarmac when he disembarked.

James Jade was more than willing to talk to Palmer, and was grateful that his father's murder file was being raised and examined. *No*, he didn't think there was any special lady in his father's life; *no*, he couldn't think of anybody with enough of a grudge to murder him; and *no*, he didn't think that their reunion had changed anything in his father's life. On the subject of Maurice Jade's Will, which Palmer had to bring up for obvious reasons, *no*, he didn't think his appearance had caused his father to change it; most of the money went to various members of the family and a few charities, although James had been surprised to find he'd been left the house, as he thought that was going to the old couple who had looked after it for over twenty years when his father was away touring.

The alarm bells that started ringing in Palmer's brain at that bit of information would have drowned out Big Ben!

Pete Brown sat in his car, parked fifty yards down the road from the gated entrance to Rob Elliott's estate. He sat very still, so he wouldn't be obvious to a quick, cursory glance from anybody. How he was going to get inside the estate had set him a problem. He watched as the gates swung open when a resident's car pulled up and closed after it had entered. Must be a button on fob switch; he couldn't see a way of getting one of those, so his plan was to pull up quickly behind a resident's car as they were about to enter and follow them through, giving a wave as though he was a resident. He'd then kill Elliott and exit using the same procedure.

Time to have a dry run. It was late afternoon, and residents were returning from business and going through the gates into the estate quite frequently. The weather was gloomy, so he could have his headlights on which would prevent the driver of the car he followed in from seeing him clearly. His hands were sweaty with excitement as he started his car and waited.

Soon an oncoming vehicle signaled to turn across the road and into the estate. He moved slowly forward – got to let them in the gate first and then follow in quickly. It was a BMW... *Shit!* It was Elliott's BMW – the personal number plate RE1 gave it away; and there were two other occupants who were definitely not music people, big hefty chaps... *Shit, he's got police protection... If he's got them in his car then he's got them in his house... Shit! Shit! SHIT!*

He banged the wheel with a clenched fist and drove straight past, as the BMW waited for the gate to swing slowly open. He'd have to think of a new plan.

'It was very interesting.'

Palmer was relaying the gist of his chat with James Jade to Sergeant Singh and Claire in the Team Room as they continued to check the memorial page *friends*.

'His mother and Maurice Jade divorced, and when they split she took a hefty wad of money and went to the States. Poor kid was only five.'

'God, that must have been an awfully traumatic time for a five year old,' Gheeta sympathised. 'To be pulled away from your dad at that age. Poor kid.'

'Well, he seems to have survived it well – he's financial controller of a cable TV network now. Said he was most surprised when his dad made contact. He reckoned that when Jade packed up the band and had time to assess his life, he probably felt a bit bad about not keeping in regular touch with him. It was just birthdays and Christmas that they heard from him, and then it was usually a delivery of toys and a card; no phone calls or physical visits. But the most interesting bit of the conversation was that he thought the Armitages were getting the Old Rectory in his dad's Will, and he was pretty sure that his dad had mentioned that to him at some time; and so he was most surprised when he got it, and a bit embarrassed when he had to go and get the keys off them to give to an estate agent who he'd instructed to sell the place.'

Gheeta was confused.

'So, I assume that you saying that that was the most interesting bit of your chat with him means you see two more suspects with a motive: the Armitages.'

Palmer shrugged.

'It's a thought, isn't it. The fact that Jade's CCTV was not operating that day has niggled away at me. I can't see a good reason why he would not use the system on *that* day, that particular day; and if he did switch it on and put a disc in, where is it? Where's the disc, who removed it? And if it was removed, it's got to be somebody who knew it was there in the first place.'

'Yes, that has bothered me too, guv. But with *Just Desserts* making an entry into the case as prime suspect, I assumed that – with what we know about his expertise in IT – he knew about the system if he'd taken a look at the place before he did the murder; or if he didn't he would have seen the cameras at the house on the day, and realised there was a system operating which would show him arriving. So he found it, turned it off and removed the disc when he left after he'd killed Jade.'

Gheeta thought for a moment.

'On the subject of CCTV, I wonder if the local force checked the local shops for their CCTV of that day, if they had any operating? If there's a Post Office they'd have one for sure. It's a long shot, but maybe our killer went in to get a sandwich or a drink.'

Claire tapped her keyboard.

'I'll check the file. By the way, some good news: I checked the airline passenger lists for flights to Madeira for up to three days prior to the death of Frank Moss, and then the passenger lists for return flights for the three days after, and guess what?'

'Mr Brown was on one of them.'

Palmer waited with baited breath, as a wide smile appeared on Claire's face.

'A Mr P. Brown was indeed on them. He travelled with Monarch two days before Moss fell off the mountain, and back the day after.'

Palmer spread his hands.

'Okay, that's enough – he's definitely our man. No doubt about it now. Sergeant, put out a wanted note to all forces on him, mug shot to follow if we can find one; and put out a stop and detain notice to all airports, ports and places of departure.'

A loud 'ping' from Sergeant Singh's computer interrupted their conversation.

'We have lift off, guv.'

Gheeta pulled the Palmer Facebook page up onscreen. The side bar showed Palmer and *Just Desserts* as both being logged on.

'I've had you logged in all day guv, in the hope he'd notice and take the bait. You just talk to him as though he's here, and I'll type in what you say onto the page for him to read. Keep him talking if he does talk back so we can trace the call, as he's bound to be using a mobile phone or iPad; he's not stupid enough to use a traceable computer.'

She nodded to Claire.

'Claire's into that part of the programme and reducing the options by hand, so the longer time we get with him online, the better chance to isolate him.'

Claire was already working away on her keypad. Palmer nodded.

'Okay, I understand. Let's try 'Good afternoon Mr Brown' for starters.'

Gheeta typed it in on her keyboard.

Nothing…

'Oh, come now Mr Brown, you can't be shy. After all, you set this page up so we could talk… didn't you?'

An answer came texting back across the screen.

'Good afternoon Superintendent Palmer.'

'*Chief* Superintendent Palmer, if you don't mind. It took me a long time to get to this rank by catching murderers, so show respect.'

Palmer thought that would wrong-foot Brown, as the reason for putting up the site was for Brown to get what he mistakenly thought would be respect for himself, not Palmer demanding it.

'Palmer you don't deserve respect you couldn't catch a bus let alone me.'

Palmer moved onto his next ploy.

'Why would I want to catch you, Mr Brown? You haven't done anything. You're just a nutter, living in a fantasy world. You need help, Mr Brown, not arresting. You don't seriously believe I think you had anything to do with the Revolution deaths, do you?'

'I killed them! I killed them all. I pushed Frank Moss off the footpath, I pushed Stag over the balcony wall, I killed Jade in his posh house and I pushed Brockheimer under the tube train. I DID IT ALL PALMER and I'm going to get Rob Elliott too, doesn't matter how many coppers you surround him with I'll get him.'

There was anger in the text. Palmer liked that; he'd pushed Brown out of his comfort zone pretty easily.

'Mr Brown, you are delusional. Frank Moss fell because he suffered from vertigo and had an attack while out walking on a cliff path. Stag George had a belly full of alcohol and toppled off his balcony. Brockheimer was suicidal, and Maurice Jade was attacked when he found burglars in his home. So, stop this silly charade and get some medical help for yourself.'

'That just shows how good I am Palmer I killed them all and you stupid coppers can't see it even when I confess. The perfect murders... I committed the perfect murders... You wouldn't even be investigating now if Brockheimer hadn't shouted off his big mouth to the press, and Elliott would be dead by now too. They had it coming to them for what they did to me. I made them, without me they wouldn't have amounted to anything... not anything, it was me Palmer... I made them and they dumped me, kicked me out with nothing. They deserved to die Palmer didn't they... they deserved it...

and I did it…me…and there's one to get before I finish and you won't stop me.'

And with that he logged off. Gheeta sat up.

'He's logged off, guv. Just waiting for the other programmes Claire's working to interface and give us a postcode on the phone signal. I think we had enough time for them to adjust and sort it out.'

'We did, we did!'

Claire clicked her 'return' key and the large screen on the wall above her terminal showed 'SW1Y5BJ' superimposed on a map of the UK. The postcode homed in on the map as it increased its picture from the whole of the UK to the South, then to London, and then to its final destination.

'Got you Mr Brown!'

But then Claire's face dropped.

'Where is he?'

Palmer squinted at the screen. He could see it was London, but where in London?

'Trafalgar Square.'

'Blast.'

Gheeta slumped back into her chair.

'Oh, he's a crafty one, guv. He was texting the Facebook page using his iPhone from Trafalgar Square.'

Palmer nodded.

'Crafty bugger – but we now have a full confession from him, so print out that conversation before he realises and deletes it.'

He sat down and thought for a moment.

'Okay, look – take the LP cover and see what a police artist can do to take Brown's face and age it thirty years, both with and without hair. Then send that out as an addition with the stop notices. I'm going to get the old original evidence box on the Maurice Jade murder sent up from Cornwall.'

'You're not happy with that one guv, are you?'

'No,' Palmer said. 'The CCTV being conveniently off is still bugging me.'

Peter Brown was both angry and elated; so elated that he was giggling to himself, causing passers-by to give him a wide berth as he walked down Whitehall to the bus stop. He tried to control the giggling when he noticed people were looking at him.

That told you, Palmer... Now you know you've got a real opponent – a clever one. So, you didn't think I did any of the murders, eh? All just accidents? Well, now you know they weren't just bloody accidents... Stupid coppers... Now you know they got what they deserved and I did it... Have all the programmes running, did you? Bet you did – thought you'd trace me, eh? Thought I didn't know all about phone traces, eh? I would have loved to see your face when Trafalgar Square came up – disappointed, I'll bet...

So, now you know I'm good, aren't I? Better than you lot of stupid coppers... Did Elliott tell you I was good at IT? Did he? I can run rings round your lot, Palmer – you've no chance against me. Elliott is as good as dead already, and he will be in a week's time... You might have him all surrounded in his house, but I know him... I know him, and I know something you don't know... He's dead in a week... I promise...

Chapter 13

'We're winning.'

Mrs P.'s voice from the kitchen had a happy lilt to it.

'How do you know that?'

Palmer was sitting on the bottom stairs in his hall, taking off his shoes and giving Daisy the dog a cuddle at the same time, as Mrs P. was dishing up his meal in the kitchen.

'By what people say when we knock at their doors. They like Benji, they think he'd be good for the district – a good independent voice on the council'

'They don't know him.'

He threw a shoe up the hall for Daisy to fetch back, which she didn't. She looked up at him as if to say, '*a ball fifty yards in the park, maybe – but a shoe eight-feet up the hall? Nah.*'

'He comes out with us and meets them, they can talk to him. No other candidates are out.'

'They've got more sense.'

'You've no sense of adventure, Justin Palmer – and definitely no community spirit.'

'Okay, so tell me why a bloke would want to put himself forward to be elected to a council where they'll all be arguing, one half won't like the other half, and probably none of them will like Benji – plus all the voters who didn't vote for him won't like him as well. Not exactly a win win situation, is it?'

He pulled on his slippers and ambled into the kitchen.

'What are we having? Smells good.'

'Moussaka.'

'Burnt cheese on the top?'

'You have the most unusual tastes, Justin. Yes, burnt cheese on the top - of yours.'

He pulled out a chair from the table, sat down and tucked in.

'Wouldn't it be easier if all the candidates had a public meeting, put forward their agendas and took questions from the great unwashed?'

'I don't think the residents of Dulwich would like being called '*the great unwashed*'; and yes, it would be a good idea, but you'd never get them all to agree to do it.'

'They do it in America. Trump and Clinton did it.'

'And what a shambles that was.'

'Well, what do you expect? A washed up has-been with financial scandals against a grade one knobhead.'

'I don't think you'd be very good in the Diplomatic Corps, Justin.'

They both laughed.

'I do hope that Benji gets in, though,' Palmer said seriously.

'Do you mean that?'

Mrs P. was a little taken aback at this.

'Yes.'

'Why?'

'Because if he doesn't there's an election coming up in three months for the local Police Commissioner's job and I'd hate to think he might go for that.'

Chapter 14

Peter Brown sat and watched as the CD played on his laptop. He'd watched it a few times since that day he drove down to Cornwall. The screen split into four, and showed all four recordings taken by Maurice Jade's four security cameras on the day that he was murdered.

The bottom left screen showed the hall and front door as Mr Armitage was greeted by Jade and entered. Both walked out of view into the lounge, where the top right screen picked up the rear view as Jade walked into his lounge and was attacked from behind by Armitage wielding an iron wrench. Jade fell forward to the floor, where another final blow was dealt. As this was happening, the top left screen showed Peter Brown's unmistakeable red Mercedes 280SL pulling up on Jade's drive behind Armitage's car, and Brown getting out. The screens showed Brown entering the house, walking through the hall and into the lounge as Armitage stood up from Jade's prone body.

They faced each other, Armitage raising the wrench and threatening Brown, who waved both hands in front of himself in a calming motion to Armitage. Armitage lowered the wrench and the two of them seemed to be talking for a few minutes, before Brown left and returned with two large plastic boxes from his car. Armitage then used the wrench to smash open the glass china cabinet and they removed the china pieces into the boxes, and the boxes out and into Armitage's car boot. They talked for a further few minutes before Armitage drove off. Brown then re-entered the house and was seen in the hall opening a small wall cupboard, and then the screen went blank.

Peter Brown sniggered to himself as he ejected the disc and held it up. *Silly old fool, Armitage... you'd be doing life now if I hadn't come along and removed this... You were so angry that you weren't getting the house that you forgot about the cameras didn't you, eh? Well, this little beauty is my insurance policy on you. You think I'd let you take the credit for the murder? No way, old man – Jade was mine, and*

you stole the joy of my day of revenge from me… But you'll
never be able to tell anybody – or sell that china until I say
so; not while I've got this. His killing is on my list, and there
it will stay…

The evidence box from Cornwall duly arrived. In the Team
Room, Claire put on latex gloves and laid its contents out
along a table as Palmer and Singh put on their gloves and
watched.

'Not a lot there is there,' Palmer noted in a
disappointed voice.

Gheeta nodded in agreement.

'Mostly blood-stained clothes and crime scene
pictures.'

'And the box of security camera discs,' Claire said,
pointing out the box.

'Minus the one for the day of the murder.'

Palmer opened the box and looked at the discs.

'Any comments on these from Cornwall?'

Gheeta thumbed through the forensic case reports.

'Just says Jade's prints are on them. The people
shown on the discs are himself, the Armitages, and various
delivery people. All checked and cleared.'

'So, it seems that only Jade had access to the security
discs if nobody else's prints are on them. Perhaps we are on a
wild goose chase, Sergeant. Perhaps he just ran out of discs
that day, and didn't have another one to put in.'

'No guv, according to the report there are ten used
discs in here from the previous month, and twenty used for
the current month of the murder. So, looks like he re-used
them once the month was over.'

'Seems logical; no point in buying new ones if you
can re-use them.'

Gheeta pulled out two discs in separate covers.

'And these are the CCTV discs from the village Post
Office and the local garage for that day.'

She traced her finger down the case report.

        'Of no interest, according to the local forensic report. The people in the Post Office disc are all known locals and accounted for, while the garage is basically the same, but with seven unknowns. But being a holiday destination and in the middle of the holiday season that was to be expected.'

        Palmer took a deep breath and thought for a moment.

        'Okay, seven unknowns – so our killer could well be one of them. When the aged Peter Brown drawings come back from the artist do a comparison with the seven unknowns on the disc, and see if we can get a near likeness.'

        'Be nice if we do, guv.'

        'Wouldn't it just.'

Chapter 15

Gheeta had just relaxed in her living room when her computer pinged. It was Thursday – she had forgotten it was Thursday. Thursday was the day Aunty Raani in New York and her mother in London had a conversation on the family website; the family website that Gheeta had built, and sometimes wished she hadn't. But the Thursday family thing had become a 'must do', and anyway, a few minutes on the web with them was better than having mother 'pop round'.

She sat in front of the screen and logged in. Mother, Aunty Raani, and seventeen year-old cousin Bavinda were in conversation when her picture popped up alongside theirs.

'Hello Mother, Aunty Raani, Bavinda.'

They acknowledged her presence.

'Are you well, dear?' her mother asked. 'You look pale.'

'She is working too hard.'

Aunty Raani, who was always quick to find something detrimental to say about Gheeta's police career, was quick to seize the opportunity.

'The life of a policewoman is not a good one for a lady.'

'It's a very good one, Aunty,' said Gheeta, knowing what would come next.

'No – no, at your age you should be settled as a mother and wife. I cannot understand you Gheeta, I really can't. Where is the man in your life?'

'There is no man in my life, Aunty. Only Palmer.'

Aunty Raani perked up.

'Palmer? Who is this Palmer? Does he come from a good family? Are they in business? What business? Have you met his parents yet?'

Gheeta interrupted her.

'He's my boss, Aunty. He's over sixty and happily married for forty years.'

Aunty Raani was shocked.

'You are having an affair with an older man?

Gheeta turned to her mother for support.

'Mum, explain please.'

'Raani, listen,' her mother explained. 'Mr Palmer is Gheeta's boss – that is what she meant by him being the man in her life, nothing more; it's purely work. She doesn't want a man in her personal life. Why should she want one? She's doing very well without one.'

'You have one,' Aunty Raani addressed her mother. 'I have one. It is not healthy. I keep giving you introductions to very good family businessmen in London Gheeta, but you never contact them. Bavinda is waiting with her sisters to be your bridesmaids.'

'No, we are not,' said Bavinda, looking amazed. Aunty Raani ignored her.

'They are wondering why you are not married and giving them nephews and nieces.'

'We are not.'

Bavinda had witnessed this conversation many times.

'We couldn't care less. Stop trying to arrange a marriage, Mum; it's so old fashioned.'

She turned her attention to Gheeta.

'Any good murders lately, Gheeta?'

Gheeta took the chance to steer the conversation away from marriage.

'Working on one now, Bavinda. Members of a pop group being knocked off one by one.'

'Wow!! I hope its One Direction.'

Gheeta laughed.

'That's not a very nice thing to say.'

'I know, it's just that my sisters play their songs over and over and over – drives me mad. It's not as though they are any good; just another manufactured talentless boy band.'

'I think you should pursue a career as a music critic, Bavinda,' Gheeta laughed.

Aunty Raani had decided she had to refute that earlier assumption.

'I am not trying to arrange a marriage, certainly not.'

Mother knew otherwise.

'Yes, you are; you were always sending young men round with gifts to me when we were younger. Those old customs are dead now, Raani; you have to forget them. Young Indian women of today are worldly wise and run their own lives, choose their own careers, and choose their own husbands too. If we were African, you'd probably still be advocating FGM.'

Aunty Raani was taken aback.

'Good God – never!'

'What's FGM?' asked Bavinda.

'Nothing,' said Aunty Raani, looking embarrassed. 'I just think Gheeta is such a lovely young lady that she may be missing out on her social life by being single.'

'Gheeta, tell me more about the murders.'

Bavinda was the centre of attention when she regaled her college friends with an update of what gruesome killings her cousin Gheeta – who was, according to Bavinda, in charge of the London Murder Squad – was working on.

'We have to go. We have some of your father's business people coming round soon.'

Aunty Raani thought that any details of murders would be inappropriate for a seventeen year-old daughter, who she still thought of as a little princess of the Disney kind; whereas Bavinda actually behaved more like a little hoodlum of the Godfather kind.

'Dad never told me people were coming round. Are you sure?'

Bavinda was disappointed, but Aunty Raani didn't want any details of gruesome murders, thank you very much.

'Yes, I am sure. See you all next Thursday. Take care.'

She gave a little wave. Gheeta and her mother waved back.

'Say goodbye, Bavinda.'

'Bye Aunty, Bye Gheeta.'

She turned to her mother.

'What's FGM?'

'Have you finished your homework?'

Their screens went blank.

'Sometimes my sister drives me mad. So, how are you Gheeta?' said Mother, sounding more relaxed now. 'Is Mr Palmer okay?'

'Yes, he's fine; and I'm fine too, Mum. I do wish Aunty Raani wouldn't turn every conversation we have into a discussion on my marital status. Judging by the men she's tried to introduce me to in the past, I'd do better sticking a small ad in Mr Patel's corner shop window.'

'Don't do that, whatever you do,' Mother laughed. 'You have to understand – Raani is the eldest female in the family; *her* marriage was arranged, and thankfully it has worked out. But I know many friends from my school days whose arranged marriages are just a sham; on the outside it seems alright, but inside it's broken. It is such a waste – a good loving relationship between two people is made in Heaven.'

'Don't you start.'

'No, no, you know your father and I have let you and your brothers lead your own lives; and we are very proud of you all. We would never interfere. But you know we are here if you need us.'

'Yes Mum, I know that.'

Chapter 16

'Is that him? It doesn't look like him.'

Gheeta squinted closer at the screen.

'It doesn't look like the *'him'* the art department gave us, but it's him alright. Nobody else would be filling up a red Mercedes 280 SL in the village on the same day as the murder, would they?'

Palmer straightened up from viewing the CCTV footage from Cornwall CID.

'Well done for spotting the car, Claire. He's certainly changed a lot from the bloke on the LP sleeve. Get a still from the disc and put it out to all forces and the Border Patrol.'

Gheeta stood up.

'Well, at least we know who we are looking for now. It's a good clear image.'

'Unless he's changed it – grown a beard, shaved his head; couldn't tell from the tube station pictures. Bloody hoodies, they should ban them. Other than the burka, they're the easiest *'off the shelf'* disguise villains ever had.'

Palmer hadn't any time for personal human rights where criminals were concerned.

'It was that twat Cameron who said *'hug a hoody'* wasn't it? Yes, hug him as he plunges a knife into your chest and nicks your wallet. Great advice that was.'

'Bingo! He's still got the car as well.'

Claire was tapping her keyboard.

'DVLA has that registration number belonging to Peter Charles Brown, Top Floor Flat, 28 East Street, Walworth.'

Gheeta was on the internal phone straight away.

'Shall I get a car, guv?'

'Yes, an unmarked one; and two plainclothes Firearms Officers with it.'

East Street off the Walworth Road was quite a busy outdoor market. Stall holders shouted out their wares as Palmer's car edged forward amongst the throng of punters.

'Would be a market day, wouldn't it. I think we'll hoof it from here, come on.'

Palmer opened his side door.

'Be all day at this rate. Park it up where you can driver and wait for my call. Come on you lot.'

He got out and couldn't help but notice the sideways glances and quick disappearance of several stall 'workers' when they caught site of Sergeant Singh's uniform and the two burly plainclothes officers that joined him on the pavement. Things hadn't changed much since this area had been part of his patch as a young detective. The triangle between the Old Kent Road and the Walworth Road had been a hot bed of petty crime, with a few big players amongst them; old school villains who were on first name terms with their 'mates' in the Met, their 'mates' being officers who turned a blind eye to various escapades and made phone calls prior to making raids that never found anything; and all for the brown envelope of ten pound notes slipped to them once a month.

Palmer hadn't particularly liked being part of the cleanup teams set up by Commissioner Sir Robert Mark but had realised at the time that the bribery and corruption in the Met had gone too far. By the time the new Commissioner Sir Robert Stephenson came in, the clean-up had forced four hundred and seventy-eight officers to leave the force with disciplinary bad marks against them. Palmer had made himself unpopular with some bent CID units for calling for the usual 'get out' of a *bent* officer being able to take early retirement on full pension to be stopped, and the officer to stand trial like any other criminal. So unpopular was he that at one stage he had armed protection officers at home. He smiled at the memory; the Met had changed but the criminals hadn't.

He looked at the nearest door.

'That's number fourteen, so this way.'

He led them along the crowded pavement, stepping over boxes of vegetables stacked over boxes of fake designer clothes, perfumes, trainers and God knows what other contraband and stolen goods, all waiting to be moved on, sold, or fenced. East Street market was a known outlet for such goods; it used to be said that you'd have your watch pinched by the time you'd walked twenty yards into the market and be able to buy it back off a stall before you reached the end.

'This is it, guv,'

Gheeta pointed to a doorway with 28 scrawled in paint alongside it.

'Doesn't seem as though Peter Brown is living the high life, does it.'

'No, it does not. No wonder he's a bit miffed at the band's success if this is what he's come down to. I can understand his anger now.'

He turned to the two Firearms Officers.

'Right lads, easy does it. But remember he's a multiple murder suspect, so any funny business from him just take him down fast.'

The officers nodded as they followed Palmer into the dim hallway. Old paint was peeling off the walls and busted children's toys parked or dumped along it created an obstacle course. Gheeta flicked a wall light switch, but the solitary hanging bulb stayed dead.

'Right then, better start to look for him. Top flat, the DVLA said.'

Palmer led the way up a bare wooden staircase with a wonky banister that creaked annoyingly. The first floor yielded two more doors, and at the end of the landing a small flight of six stairs leading to the top flat. There was a bell with the name BROWN on the dirty label. Palmer pointed it out while motioning the others to be silent. No security peephole in the door that he could squint through, so he gently knelt down and slowly pushed open the letter box flap and looked through. All he could see was an empty room, except for a couple of chairs, a TV, a sofa and a low table. It looked very clean and orderly.

Straightening up he gave a few taps on the door. No answer, and no sound from within. He tried again.

'Mr Brown? Are you there, Mr Brown? This is the police, open the door please.'

Nothing. Palmer took two steel pins from his pocket, knelt down in front of the door and picked the lock.

'Amazing what skills you can pick up in the force.'

He stood up as a gentle push slowly opened the door.

'Oh look, Mr Brown's left the door open. That's handy.'

Peter Brown walked along East Street and crossed through the crowds to his building.

'You've got visitors, mate.'

The stallholder from the fake designer clothes stall pitched outside his street door nodded towards it as he hung a bundle of coats on a mobile rail.

'What?'

Brown didn't understand the comment.

'Rozzers, three plainclothes and a uniformed bird. Went in a few minutes ago. What you been up to then, eh?'

Brown understood that alright.

'Thanks, mate.'

He turned and quickly mixed into the crowd, and made his way back to the end of the street; then down a narrow vehicle entrance between two shops and into a resident's parking yard surrounded by lock-up garages. He unlocked the up and over door on his garage and swung it up, just enough to bend under and go inside before lowering it behind him. Sitting in his car he took out his iPhone and brought up Palmer's page on Facebook and tapped a message.

'Hope you've got a search warrant Chief Superintendent. All breakages must be paid for. Now it's time to complete my quest and get back to the status quo, bye bye.'

Then he sat, deep in thought. He was so near to finishing the job, so near. Just one band member to go, and his mind would be free from all the hate and stress. Just one. He had to get away and complete the job. *Can't stay here, the neighbours know I've got a garage. They're bound to be questioned by the police… Got to get away now… One more day, that's all I need – one more day.*

He left the car and took a small wooden box from the shelf at the back of the garage which he put into the car boot; then he lifted the garage door before getting back in the car and driving out into the yard. He stopped, got out, shut and locked the door, and drove out of the yard onto the road and headed for the M5.

'Cheeky bugger – *all breakages to be paid for.*'

Palmer looked at the message Sergeant Singh was showing him on her laptop.

'Can we get a fix on it?'

'Claire's doing that now, guv.'

'Must be close, otherwise how would he know we are here? He must have seen us come in.'

'He might have a webcam in here somewhere, guv. Then he'd be able to watch the room from anywhere on a laptop or mobile.'

Gheeta was busy looking for it.

'But I can't see one.'

'So he's possibly watching us now?'

'Yes, could be.'

Palmer immediately thought that installing one in his hall at home would be a good idea; he could sit in the local pub and monitor when Mrs P.'s Gardening Club or WI meetings were on and stay there until they had finished, rather than being banned to the kitchen with Daisy and a takeaway.

'I don't think there's one here, guv.'

Gheeta straightened up from checking under the low shelves.

'It would have to have a good view of the room and would be fairly obvious.'

Her mobile rang. It was Claire. She listened and thanked her before turning to Palmer.

'You were right, he was close. Postcode puts him in the same area as us, not more than a hundred yards away.'

'He won't be there now. Be miles away by now. He's not stupid is he, and we know he already knows we can pinpoint him. Right, not a lot we can do here. Get SOCA to go over the place; tell them what we are looking for, anything to do with Revolution or its members. I'll have a word with the local CID and get them to do a house to house with Brown's picture and see if we can turn up anything from the neighbours.'

'Might be worth me checking the other residents of this building now, guv. I only noticed four doors so wouldn't take long.'

'Okay, good idea. Take the plainclothes boys with you and watch your back. I'll see you back at the office.

Back at the office in New Scotland Yard Palmer fed the coffee machine in the corridor with his loose change. Loaded with two coffees, he went into the Team Room and passed one to Claire who was busy at her terminal.

'That's very welcome sir, thank you. Looks like you nearly got him at East Street.'

'Yes,' Palmer said as he slipped his coat off and sat down. 'Perhaps I should have put a surveillance team on the place and waited. How did he know we were there?'

'Probably just saw you and bolted.'

'Yes, in his special car no doubt.'

'A red Mercedes 280SL. I've got a camera request ongoing with Traffic and Transport for London. They're checking the street cameras in the area to see if we can pick it up.'

'Good, well done.'

He sipped his coffee and pulled a face.

'Christ! This stuff is awful. Trade descriptions should prosecute whoever calls this *coffee*. Glad I didn't spill it – take the shine off my shoes.'

He stood up.

'Right, I'm going in the office to write up the daily case report that Bateman insists on having – bloody waste of time. Hope he gets the Commissioner's job, maybe the next incumbent won't be so fussy.'

He went across the corridor to his and Sergeant Singh's office and settled behind his desk, took a deep breath, and started filling in the report.

Half an hour later he'd rewritten it three times and was about to make more changes when Sergeant Singh arrived back.

'We found his garage. guv.'

'And his car?'

That would be too good to be true.

'No, and not much evidence really; just a few tools and empty oil cans. But I've got SOCA going in when they finish with the bedsit. You never know.'

Peter Brown was feeling a little worried as he drove up the M1. Every time he saw a police patrol car he tightened up inside. He really didn't have any reason to feel like that, as the first thing he'd done when he had got clear of East Street and up the Walworth Road was to take the Borough High Street from the Elephant and Castle, park his car in the basement of a NCP car park, and hire a basic Ford Fiesta at the rental garage.

I'm not stupid, Palmer... not stupid enough to travel around in my own car. The only way you could have traced my home was from the car – who told you about the car, eh? Fucking Rob Elliott, got to be... Well, Mr Elliott... make the most of your last days alive...

When he got to the M6 he turned onto it, and then half an hour later into the Coventry Premier Inn for the night. He felt better now.

Chapter 17

'He got in.'

Mrs P. greeted Palmer with a great smile.

'Who got in, Trump?'

He settled into a kitchen chair and loosened his tie. It had been a hard day.

'I told you he would – people's choice. Like Brexit.'

'Benji got in – or should I say *Councillor* Benji. He got in by a landslide.'

Palmer faked utter disappointment.

'Oh no, you can't have people like him on the council.'

'Why ever not?'

'Fake tan and pony tail?' he said, then putting on a posh accent: 'Not the sort of thing we expect of our councillors in Dulwich.'

'*We* will just have to get used to it then, won't *we*?' replied Mrs P. with an equally effected voice.

'Well, I hope he remembers all the hard work you and Dotty Watkins put in. Tell him I think he should lower the rates band for this house as a thank you.'

He suddenly thought of something and quickly left the house, then returned a couple of minutes later struggling with the large Benji poster from the front garden wall.

'Don't have to have this up anymore then, do we?'

Mrs P. took it from him and stood it against the wall, admiring it proudly.

'It's a memento of a great day. What shall we do with it?'

'Burn it.'

Chapter 18

The next afternoon in the Team Room Palmer and Singh looked at the CCTV results from the traffic department that Claire had printed out.

'So, he went up to the Elephant and down the Borough High Street and that's it?' Palmer asked.

Claire nodded.

'That's it. He doesn't show on any cameras from then on; to all intents and purposes, he disappeared.'

'No, he didn't do that. He stashed his car somewhere. He knows we know what he's driving and it's not exactly going to blend in, is it? So he dumped it somewhere. But the important thing is, what did he do *then*?'

Sergeant Singh moved to the back wall and looked at the large-scale map of London.

'I'll have a word with the local station in the Borough guv, and impress on them the need to find this car; get them to check around a bit, have a word with the local garages.'

'Not heard from him at all, have we? No messages on the page?'

Palmer was hoping for a lead.

'Nothing, sir,' said Claire. 'All quiet.'

'Where is he then? Where are you, Mr Brown? What are you up to now?'

He walked over to the progress chart and looked at it, hoping some inspiration might come from it. Nothing did.

Sergeant Singh's mobile rang and she took the call. Her smile told Palmer good news was about to emerge.

'Got him!' she said, shaking her fists in the air.

'In custody?'

'No guv, but after you'd left Brown's bedsit yesterday SOCA found his cheque book in a drawer and I put in a request to his bank for details of any cards he might have and a trace on their use. He's got just the one debit card, and he used it yesterday afternoon at Euro-Rental in Waterloo where he hired a Ford Fiesta, and then again this morning at the Premier Inn in Coventry. I've got the vehicle number, so

I'll put a 'find and watch' call out to West Midlands and get them to see if it's parked at the hotel still.'

'Plainclothes; don't want any uniforms frightening him away if he is still there.'

'No, guv.'

'And get a car for us; I think we'd better get up to Coventry. I don't think he's going to come back to East Street anytime soon – seems he's off to somewhere else. Would be today wouldn't it, eh?'

Gheeta reached for the phone to order a car.

'You got something booked for tonight then, guv?'

'Mrs P.'s toad-in-the-hole, followed by Barcelona versus Real Madrid on Sky, 'El Clasico'; an evening of heaven just gone down the pan.'

He rose, went across the corridor to his office and returned with his hat and coat.

'If the great British public knew the sacrifices I make to protect them, they'd make me a Saint.'

AC Bateman walked in, having heard the last comment as he did so.

'Certainly wouldn't be Saint Palmer of the Paperwork, would it Chief Superintendent? Any chance of *yesterday's* daily report being on my desk sometime in the foreseeable future?'

Palmer stalled for an answer.

'Ah… Well, I was just putting the finishing touches to it sir, when we got word that our killer has been located; and we are just off to hopefully arrest him now.'

'Saint Palmer of the Excuses might be a good fit too. Update me on the case before you go please, Chief Superintendent.'

Bateman sat down, and Palmer brought him up to date as fast as he could.

'Okay, you'd better get going then. Media tells me the newspapers are getting restless on this one; rather not have any 'police incompetence' stories in the Sunday papers if we can avoid it.'

Palmer agreed.

'Not when something might be happening on the fifth floor, sir. Any news?'

'Not the kind you'll like, Chief Superintendent. Unfortunately for both of us, I was unsuccessful.'

Palmer felt genuinely sorry for Bateman.

'Oh, well, I am sorry, sir. I really am. I know you wanted it, and in my book you'd be the man for the job.'

'Yes, well, in other people's books I wasn't. Never mind.'

He turned to leave and stopped briefly at the door.

'Perhaps I should have employed Dotty Watkins after all.'

They exchanged smiles as he left. Gheeta eyed Palmer suspiciously.

'I think you're secretly glad he didn't get that promotion, guv. I reckon you've got a bit of respect for Bateman that you try to hide.'

'He's okay – and better the devil you know,' Palmer said as he slipped his coat on. 'With any sort of hierarchy in the work place you sort of reach a plateau of agreement after a time; you know how far you can go with the boss and when to stop. I've got that with Bateman, so although I don't actually like fast-tracked university nerds who have never arrested anybody running the force, I know how to play the game. It's a bit like marriage; I know the things that would make Mrs P. bristle, so I don't mention them.'

'What things?'

'Oh, anything to do with her appearance that isn't complimentary. Like the time she had a blue rinse and perm; she looked like Marge Simpson in a gale, but I couldn't say anything or she wouldn't have talked to me for at least a month. And any *toad in the hole* would have been a definite no no.'

Chapter 19

Brown had left the hotel by the time the local CID got there. The receptionist confirmed it had indeed been Peter Brown from his mugshot, and the hotel CCTV showed him driving out.

Palmer sat back on a sofa in the hotel lounge as Sergeant Singh checked the vacated room and sealed it for SOCA to examine. She came back and joined him, their driver, and two local CID officers who had ordered coffees.

'He hasn't left anything in the room, guv. SOCA will go over it, but I don't think it will give us anything; just an empty hotel room.'

'Do you think we've had a wasted journey? Where's he gone now, what's he up to? He must have come up here for some reason.'

'Red herring, guv? Is he clever enough to realise we'd find his bank details and be able to track him through his card, so he's dragged us up here on purpose and then perhaps doubled back to have a go at Elliott on his home turf?'

'That sounds a bit involved, but you never know – he's a clever bugger. Give our people at Elliott's place a call and tell them to be on their toes; keep him inside for the time being. Better safe than sorry.'

He stood and looked down the foyer to the outside of the hotel while Gheeta made the call.

'Dark now,' he said, checking his watch. 'Nine o' ruddy clock already; the match will be just about over. Oh well, should get back for the highlights on the late news. Great.'

'Governor.'

The tone of Sergeant Singh's voice sent a warning signal as he turned towards her. She was cupping the mobile in her hand, and her expression said all was not right.

'Elliott's gone to the NEC. He's doing a guest appearance at a Status Quo concert tonight.'

'What? That's just up the road. Oh Christ, that's where Brown's heading then, got to be.'

'Well, we did tell him to carry on as normal. He's got two of our protection chaps with him.'

'Come on, that's got to be where Brown's going to have a go at him.'

He looked at the local officers who were gulping down their coffees.

'How long to get there from here?'

'Thirty or forty minutes.'

'Right.'

They hurried to the car.

'Blues on driver, and foot down.'

As they raced towards the NEC, Gheeta remembered something and checked Palmer's Facebook page. There it was, staring up at her.

'Guv, do you remember the last message from Brown when we were at his bedsit? He said: *time to complete my quest and get back to the status quo.*'

Palmer nodded.

'He couldn't have made his intention much clearer, could he? I should have had Elliott's protection crew keep us up to date on his movements too. If Brown knocks him off tonight, Bateman will have my guts for garters.'

Earlier that afternoon, Peter Brown drove slowly into the NEC complex and recalled being there with Revolution all those years ago. It was much bigger now; twenty halls and acres of more car parking space, but luckily the giant directional posters advertising the Quo show led him to the main hall. He parked up, took his small wooden box out of the boot and made his way with the throng of early arrival fans towards the entrance. Then he veered off and slipped through a line of small metal barriers to the back of the hall, where all the big tour lorries were parked up and an army of 'roadies' unloaded and wheeled the giant amps, instruments and other gear down the wide stage entrance corridor and up onto the stage.

Brown stood in the shadows and peered carefully around until he found what he was looking for: a long wheel base transit van with the Revolution logo on the sides and back. One of the back doors was open, and Rob Elliott's current roadie was inside working on a guitar. Brown crossed to it and silently stepped inside, pulling the door closed behind him.

'What the…'

That was all the roadie managed to say before Brown had him round the neck and slammed his head into the van's side, knocking him spark out. Using a roll of gaffer tape, he gagged and tied up the unconscious roadie and dragged him out of sight from anybody opening the back doors.

Brown smiled as he noted the guitar the roadie had been tuning was a Gretsch G9201 Honeydipper; a metal one, the type Rob Elliott had used all his career. He'd checked the latest tour photos on the Internet to make sure Elliott was still using that type of guitar a fortnight ago, as it was an integral part of his murder plan. He took off the roadie's pass that hung around his neck and put it on, then pulling off the chap's Revolution logo bomber jacket and beret he slipped them on too, then left the van carrying Elliott's guitar and his wooden box. Walking slowly, he approached the security gate where two uniformed security personnel barred his way. He flashed them the pass.

'I'm with the band.'

They nodded him through and he walked slowly down the wide corridor towards the back stage without any more challenges. He smiled to himself. It felt good; just like the old days. But this wasn't just like the old days at all. This was a 'one off day', a day of final revenge.

He walked up the ramp onto the stage area, past other roadies heaving up various props and amps on bogies, and there he spied the floor manager. His heart was beating fast; if Elliott's roadie was known to the floor manager this could be a problem. The floor manager was talking into a walkie-talkie and checking papers on a clipboard. Brown waited as the man finished his conversation and turned to him, eyebrows raised in '*what do you want?*' mode.

Brown raised the guitar.

'Rob Elliott's gear. Which amp do you want it plugged into?'

'I thought you were bringing your own amp?'

Brown thought fast.

'No, nobody said that. I haven't brought one with me.'

'Shit…'

The floor manager checked his running order plan.

'Oh good, that's okay; your guy's only joining the band on stage for the final number. Good, that helps… Right, use that one over there.'

He pointed to a large amp on the side of the stage forty yards away.

'That's a spare, I'll mark it as in use. It's all linked up to the others, so just jack the guitar into it and stand it in front. Do you need a sound check?'

'No, I've done it all on the sound scope in the van. It's all set to play.'

'Good man.'

'Have you seen Rob yet?'

'Yes, he's here somewhere; probably gone for a bite to eat. Got a couple of minders with him.'

The floor manager's walkie-talkie crackled into life and he switched his attention away from Brown who walked slowly across to the amp, looking around as he did so. Last thing he wanted now was for Rob Elliott to appear.

He knelt behind the amp, its size keeping him from view, and opening his box he took out a heavy duty lead plug that he'd already adapted for the job he had in mind in his garage. Taking the guitar jack plug that was supposed to go into the back of the amp, he pushed in a splitter which converted the single lead into two leads; one was a plain one with a jack plug on the end, and on the end of the other was a high voltage switch that he could throw open or closed with a remote fob button of the type used for locking car doors. The plain lead with the jack plug he pushed into the amp, then turning to look behind he saw what he knew would be there: a thick cable to the stage light show display. Industrial type electricity of four hundred and eighty volts would be switched through after the final song to offer a blinding white light from numerous high voltage bulbs at the rear of the stage, all pointing towards the audience, which would be followed by compressed air cannons shooting coloured paper snow into the air, and a massive roman candle-effect light show. Being an indoor arena, no actual flammable pyrotechnics were allowed, which meant everything had to be electric. Health and safety regulations had worked in his favour.

Working quickly out of view, he took a pair of shard pliers from his box and stripped the rubber coating off the cable, and then one by one stripped the coating off the copper leads and clipped the second lead with the switch onto them. He took out a key fob and tested the switch; the switch LED glowed red when he pressed the fob button. Good, all working as planned. He tested it once more before covering the whole lot in black insulating tape to cover his work and pushing the big amp back against the rear stage flat to hide it. There would of course be electricity put through the cable during the show for various illumination effects, but only when Rob Elliott put on the guitar and switched the lead to the amp to the on position, would it be possible for Brown to press the remote fob and close the switch, thus sending four hundred and eighty volts into Rob Elliott's metal guitar and into him.

A final look around to make sure he hadn't left any signs of anything being tampered with and he gathered his box and walked away towards the exit, with a spring in his step and a smile on his lips.

'Hey, you!'

The voice cut through him like a sharp knife. His heart leapt into his mouth and he prepared to run.

'Hang on, mate.'

He turned as a runner panted up to him.

'Are you Rob Elliott's roadie?'

'Yes.'

'He's in the Green Room and said you were to join him for a meal when you've finished.'

Brown thought fast.

'Tell him it's all done, guitar's all set up and ready to play, but I'm not feeling too good. I'm going back to the van for a lay down.'

'You do look a bit pale, mate. Anything I can get you?'

'No, but thanks for asking. I'll take a couple of aspirins – must have eaten something that doesn't agree with me. Tell Rob not to worry; just leave me alone and I'll be alright, and I'll see him after the show.'

'Okay, mate. Take care.'

The runner left as Brown made his way to the van; the roadie was still out cold in the back. There was still an hour to go before the show started, so he drove the van to the farthest car park and parked it right at the back in the dark shadows of the perimeter trees. Then, he changed the Revolution jacket for his own, put the bobble hat in his pocket and walked slowly back towards the main hall.

Showing his pass at the entrance, he was waved through and moved into the wide pedestrian area behind the seating stand, where the merchandise stalls tempted the fans with official overpriced T-shirts, jackets, flags, and just about everything else you could get a transfer printed Status Quo picture on; all made in China for pennies and sold here for pounds. He remembered in the early Revolution days when he paid two pounds each for screen printed T-shirts of the band at the local printers, which they sold at the gigs for a fiver. He got angry inside again as he thought of the money Revolution would have made from merchandise rights over the years; money that he felt he should have had a cut of.

He found a seat round the back of a burger stall and sat there, watching the excited punters come in. This was it; the big finale to his plan. Tomorrow he would be a free man, and be able to start to get his life back on track without the incessant drip, drip, drip of revenge tapping inside his head. If Elliott's appearance on stage was during the last number in the show, he could wait where he was and just go up the stairs to the back of the main stand near the end and watch from there.

Chapter 20

It was two hours later, with the show in full flow, when Palmer's car sped into the NEC and with the blues still on screeched to a halt at the back of the main hall. Security had been alerted that he was coming, and their chief opened the car door.

'I'm Jameson, head of Security. How can we help you, Superintendent?'

'Chief Superintendent.'

Palmer gave him a withering look as he got out.

'Apologies, *Chief* Superintendent.'

Palmer nodded an acceptance of the apology and straightened his coat, donned his trilby and looked around.

'We have reason to believe that Rob Elliott, who is a guest on the Quo show tonight, may have an attempt made on his life.'

'Fu…'

Jameson saw DS Singh coming around the car.

'I mean, flipping hell!'

A look of panic came over his face.

'We must cancel the rest of the show – it's well over halfway through.'

'No need to do that, Mr Jameson; don't want to alarm the public. We have our people with Mr Elliott and they are fully aware of the situation. I want to keep this very low key, so the would-be killer is unaware we are here and onto him. I take it you have a security suite with CCTV covering the arena?'

'Yes, of course.'

'Right then, the first thing to do is go there and do a visual sweep. Hopefully we can find our man with that. Lead on, if you would.'

He turned to the two plainclothes officers.

'You two mingle inside. You've got a mugshot of Brown, so keep your eyes peeled and your earpieces on. Our two chaps with Elliott are patched in, so we are all in the loop.

Your call signs are 'one' and 'two'; the officers with Elliott are 'three' and 'four'.'

They nodded they understood and made their way off into the hall.

In the security suite Palmer sat beside a CCTV operator and Gheeta beside another.

'Right,' said Palmer, pointing to an array of screens showing the audience enjoying the show. 'One camera start at the front row and take one row at a time working upwards, another at the top row and work down. My Sergeant and I know what this man looks like, so with a bit of luck we can pick him out if he's in the seats.'

'He's not, guv.'

'What?'

Gheeta pointed at the screen she was watching.

'Top of the stairs on the right, standing behind the top row of seats.'

And there he was: Peter Brown, standing behind the top row of seats and looking down at the stage fifty yards in front and below him.

'Get 'one' and 'two' up there and grab him.'

Gheeta gave the directions on her radio. Palmer turned to Jameson.

'If he sees us and runs, how many exits are there from where he is?'

'Fifteen.'

'How many?'

'He's on the top corridor, there's fifteen stairways down from there. Fire exits, we have to be able to clear this place in minutes. Twelve thousand people in here, Superin... *Chief* Superintendent. There's another fifteen exits halfway down the seat banks, and a fully open exit area at the bottom.'

On the screens the crowd suddenly erupted vocally and physically.

'What's happened?'

Palmer was worried. Jameson pointed to another screen showing the stage in close up.

'Rob Elliott's just been introduced and come on for the big finale.'

Palmer watched the screen as Elliott stood taking the fans' rapturous cheering and hugs from the Quo band members.

'Guv.'

Palmer had heard that tone in Sergeant Singh's voice before, and he didn't like it.

'Guv, Brown's doing something. I can't make it out, but he's fiddling with something in his hand.'

She turned to the CCTV operator.

'Get me a close-up.'

The camera zoomed in close on Brown.

'What's he doing?'

Palmer moved beside her and leant nearer to the screen, trying to make out what Brown was up to.

'Oh shit!'

Gheeta knew what she was looking at.

'He's got a switch, guv; a fob switch. He must have planted something on the stage.'

'Like what?'

'Explosives?'

Palmer reached over, and pulling her radio from her jacket spoke into it.

'Get Elliott off the stage – three and four, clear the stage *now*. Suspect package. One and two, keep after Brown.'

The screens showed Elliott being hustled off the stage, and the band following fast.

Brown was taken by surprise at that, and then what was happening sank in. He'd seen a roadie take Elliott's guitar off the top of the amp, switch it on and stand it ready for Elliott to pick up and play. He'd seen Elliott introduced and come on stage. He'd pulled the fob switch from his pocket and was all ready to make an explosive end to his mission of revenge – and then... and then it had all gone wrong.

They knew! They must know! Somehow that fucking Palmer had cottoned on at the last moment – he must have put

two and two together on my Facebook 'status quo' remark…
Shit! I was being too clever… Okay, smart arse copper, take
this…

The anger welled up and he pressed the fob button.

The screens they were watching in the security suite went
bright white, as the electricity pulse from Elliott's guitar that
should have hit the ground – using him as a conductor and
killing him in the process – tried to find another way to
ground through the NEC power circuit. The amps on stage
exploded with great plumes of white sparks shooting up, as
the overhead lighting rigs also exploded and showered sparks
down. The hall lights went out, and as the audience realised
this wasn't the big finale light show but something that
shouldn't be happening, the emergency lighting came on
giving them enough light to rush for the exits.

Jameson surprised Palmer with his calmness in such a
situation. He radioed his security and door staff to control the
crowds.

'Don't let them run. Keep them walking and open all
exit doors.'

The secondary tannoy system came on automatically
and Jameson used it.

'Ladies and gentlemen, we have an electrical system
malfunction. Please leave the building quietly and in an
orderly way. Walk, don't run. Do not try to collect any
belongings at any cloakrooms as they are shut for the time
being. Please go into the car parks and to your designated
assembly area, which is shown on the back of your ticket.'

He pressed a repeat key and the system automatically
kept repeating his message.

'Will the CCTV come back on?'

Jameson shook his head.

'No, the motherboards will have been melted.'

Palmer spoke into Gheeta's radio.

'Updates please, one and two. Have you got Brown in
sight, over?'

'Negative, over.'

'Okay. Three and four, what's happening with you, over?'

'Elliott's in a patrol car, sir, no injuries. Everybody seems to have got off the stage okay, over.'

'Good, well done lads. I would think that half the West Mercia force will be here pretty soon. Grab the first uniformed car and have them take over Elliott and get him off the premises; then you two join us in the hunt for Brown. Over and out.'

'Will do, sir. Over and out.'

Palmer rose and nodded to Sergeant Singh.

'Right Sergeant, let's go and find Peter Brown before he does any more damage.'

'Blowing up the NEC isn't bad for starters guv, is it?'

Outside in the dark car parks, the emergency lighting cut down through the misty darkness, giving the lines of people in their assembly places a surreal look; others who had thrown their tickets away were being directed by security staff. A host of blue flashing lights were arriving as the police, ambulance and fire departments of Birmingham responded to what they thought was a major disaster.

Palmer and Singh came out through the big stage door.

'Needle in a haystack, guv. He could be anywhere here.'

'Or he could be miles away by now.'

Officers one and two joined them.

'Anything?'

Palmer knew the answer.

'Sorry sir, not a sniff.'

Sergeant Singh's radio crackled into action.

'Officer code three, come in please.'

'Go ahead three,' Gheeta answered.

'We have the local senior officer with us and given him a quick idea of what's happened. He's got Elliott in his car, and the good news is that we've found Brown's hire car. It's locked, and Brown's not in it, over.'

Gheeta looked at Palmer for instructions.

'Tell them to move away from it; get out of sight and hopefully he'll return to it and they can grab him.'

She relayed the instructions.

'Okay, will do. Where are you? The senior officer wants to make contact, over.'

Gheeta told him, and within a minute a squad car pulled up and a uniformed officer emerged and put on his cap; Palmer noted by the three pips on his shoulder flash that he was a Chief Inspector, two ranks below himself. He held out a hand to Palmer, who shook it warmly.

'Chief Superintendent Palmer, Serial Murder Squad, Scotland Yard. This is DS Singh, my number two.'

The Chief Inspector acknowledged Singh.

'C. I. Rush, West Mercia. I got a brief update from your two chaps, but you'd better bring me up to speed.'

Palmer explained the situation as quick as he could.

'So basically,' he concluded, 'We've got a pretty devious and clever serial killer somewhere around here whose last little escapade went wrong and caused all this havoc, and who is probably still going to try and kill Mr Elliott. This is your patch Chief Inspector, so over to you.'

He noticed Rob Elliott sat in the back of the police car and gave him a smile; Elliott was as white as a sheet and trying to come to terms with the fact that he could well be a small pile of ash by now if Brown's plan had worked.

C. I. Rush thought for a while.

'Well, as you say he could still be here or he could be long gone. I think the best thing is to get the public away as quickly as we can and then do a thorough sweep search. I've sent my DS up to the security suite; I know Jameson, the Security chap here, he used to be one of my Inspectors.'

That explained Jameson's calm approach to the situation, thought Palmer.

C. I. Rush's radio interrupted their conversation. It was his DS, who told them that the concert had been officially cancelled and the hall was now empty and secured. C. I. Rush acknowledged the information and carried on talking to Palmer.

'I think the best idea is to get a controlled public exit. We'll get the barriers shut on all the vehicle exits except one, and then your chaps will be able to check every car and coach leaving to make sure this Brown chap doesn't get out that way. How does that sound?'

Palmer nodded.

'Sounds good to me. I'll get my chaps over there; they have mug shots of Brown, so they won't miss him.'

Peter Brown sat in the driver's seat of the Revolution Transit, deep in the shadows at the back of the car parks. In front of him the public panic seemed to have quietened down a lot with the arrival of the emergency services, and the police and people were getting into their vehicles and making for the exits. He had the local radio station on and heard that the police had closed the approaching M42 either side of the NEC turn off, so people could leave quickly through the main exit only.

Shit! they'll be checking the cars for me... I'd never get through in this bloody van anyway...

He moved it forward slowly and round the perimeter of the car park, the opposite way to that which the public were going towards the exit. He kept close to the edge of the tarmac in the tree shadows, no lights on. Suddenly there was a loud banging on the partition between the cab and the back; the roadie was awake and lay on his back kicking it. Brown took no notice because he'd seen something far more interesting. As he turned a corner of the car park towards the back of the hall, there was that bastard Palmer and some other officers standing talking; and there was... He couldn't believe his luck... and there was Rob Elliott in the back of a police car.

Brown laughed an insane laugh out loud and shouted at the windscreen in front of him.

'Got you! Elliott, I've got you! Prepare to join the others, you fucking bastard! Prepare to join them!'

He yanked the wheel, pointed the van at the police car and stamped the accelerator to the floor; the tyres screeched for grip as the power hit them and the van took off towards Elliott like a missile.

'Look this way Elliott, look at me! I'm the last person you'll see before you die! Remember me, do you?

Chapter 21

It was one of those autumn days that cinema films always conjure up for funerals; dim and dank, a mist hanging in the air and an eerie stillness all around. At the cemetery, Palmer knelt and laid a simple wreath on the grave; then standing up, he turned and walked the few steps back to where DS Singh and AC Bateman, both in uniform, stood with their heads bowed.

'Bloody waste of a life, eh?'

'Such a shame, guv. Such a shame.'

'Going to double the ruddy paperwork – I'll have writer's cramp by the time I finish all the reports on this one.'

'Guv! Give the dead a little respect!'

Bateman gave Palmer a sideways glance.

'Talking of reports reminds me, I haven't had the last case report updates as yet.'

'They're on my desk, sir; working on them now.'

'I'm sure I saw your nose grow a few inches just then, Chief Superintendent.'

They all smiled, then turned and walked a few paces back to where Rob Elliott, his broken legs covered in plaster and supported on crutches, stood with a private nurse beside him; he was visibly in tears. Palmer patted his shoulder.

'Could have been you, Rob. Could have been you, old son.'

They all turned and made their way back to the stretched limo.

Chapter 22

A week later, the Armitages sat in their Cornish kitchen and looked at the array of Jaijin Chinese porcelain laid out on the table.

'Does look nice, doesn't it? Pity to sell it,' Mrs Armitage said with a smile. 'You can see Maurice had taste.'

Mr Armitage was more cynical.

'All I can see is us on a world cruise, and a big bank balance to come back to, so don't get attached to any of it. The first lot is going up to a saleroom next month, then the rest will go bit by bit. It's what we deserve after all those years working for him. That house was promised to *us,* so this is our compensation – our pension. Stroke of luck Brown killing himself at the NEC; now *nobody* can point the finger at me for Maurice's murder, and we can begin selling it off and starting our life of luxury.'

He gave a little laugh.

'Turned out to be the perfect murder after all.'

Back in the Team Room at the Yard, they relaxed with a coffee. Gheeta walked slowly alongside the evidence table, looking at all the relevant personal belongings of Peter Brown that SOCA had pulled out from his bedsit and garage; they were going to be boxed up and archived, in case any distant relative emerged in the future to claim them. Claire was inputting text for the final case report as Palmer read it aloud to her from his notes. Gheeta felt very sad as she turned over the bits and bobs.

'It's not much when you think that this little lot was basically Peter Brown's total possessions.'

She picked up an old leather wallet and opened it, taking out a CD.

'Guv…'

Palmer turned in his seat as she held the CD towards him.

'According to the label on this, it's the missing CCTV from the day Jade was murdered. I'd forgotten all about that. Brown must have taken it away with him after he killed Jade. Bit irrelevant now; do we need to take a look?'

Palmer put down his papers, stretched his arms above his head, and rubbed his tired eyes.

'Better had.'

THE END

The Author

B.L.Faulkner was born into a family of petty criminals in
Herne Hill, South London and at this point we make it clear
that he did not follow in the family tradition! However his
childhood and teen years spent around many of the London
1960-70s 'faces' gave him much background material for the
Palmer books. One ex Met DI even reckons he can name who
Faulkner's characters are based on...he can't because they
aren't. They are all fictitious.
His mother had great theatrical aspirations for young Faulkner
and pushed him into auditioning for the Morley Academy of
Dramatic Art at the Elephant and Castle where he was
accepted but sadly only lasted 3 months before being asked to
leave as no visible talent had surfaced. Mind you, during his
time at the Academy he was called to audition for the
National Youth Theatre by Trevor Nunn...50 years later he's
still waiting for the call back!

His early writing career was as a copy writer with the
advertising agency Erwin Wasey Ruthrauff & Ryan in
Paddington during which time he got lucky with some light
entertainment scripts sent to the BBC and Independent
Television and became a script editor and writer on a
freelance basis working on most of the LE shows of the 1980-
90s. During that period, whilst living out of a suitcase in UK
hotels for a lot of the time, he filled many notebooks with
Palmer case plots and in 2015 finally found time to start
putting them in order and into book form. Six are finished and
published so far, more to come. He hopes you enjoy reading
them as much as he enjoyed writing them.

Find out more about B.L.Faulkner and the *real* UK major
heists and robberies including the Brinks Mat robbery and the
Hatton Garden Heist plus the gangs and criminals that carried
them out including the Krays and the Richardsons on his
crime blog at   *geezers2016@wordpress.com*

Take care and thank you for buying this book. An honest review on Amazon or any other online retailer would be very much appreciated.

B.L.

Printed in Poland
by Amazon Fulfillment
Poland Sp. z o.o., Wrocław

50225762R00172